Leviathan Wept

AND OTHER STORIES

Leviathan Wept

AND OTHER STORIES

DANIEL ABRAHAM

SUBTERRANEAN PRESS 2010

First Edition

ISBN
978-1-59606-265-8

Subterranean Press
PO Box 190106
Burton, MI 48519

www.subterraneanpress.com

Table of Contents

THE CAMBIST AND LORD IRON:
A Fairy Tale of Economics

FOR AS MANY YEARS as anyone in the city could remember, Olaf Neddelsohn had been the cambist of the Magdalen Gate postal authority. Every morning, he could be seen making the trek from his rooms in the boarding house on State Street, down past the street vendors with their apples and cheese, and into the bowels of the underground railway only to emerge at the station across the wide boulevard from Magdalen Gate. Some mornings he would pause at the tobacconist's or the newsstand before entering the hallowed hall of the postal authority, but seven o'clock found him without fail at the ticker tape checking for the most recent exchange rates. At half past, he was invariably updating the slate board with a bit of chalk. And with the last chime of eight o'clock, he would nod his respect to his small portrait of His Majesty, King Walther IV, pull open the shutters, and greet whatever traveler had need of him.

From that moment until the lunch hour and again from one o'clock until six, Olaf lived and breathed the exchange of foreign currencies. Under his practiced hands, dollars became pounds sterling; rubles became marks; pesos, kroner; yen, francs. Whatever exotic combination was called for, Olaf arranged with a smile, a kind word, and a question about the countries which minted the currencies he passed under the barred window. Over years, he had built nations in his mind; continents. Every country that existed, he could name, along with its particular flavor of money, its great sights and monuments, its national cuisine.

At the deep brass call of the closing gong, he pulled the shutters closed again. From six until seven o'clock, he reconciled the books, filled out his reports, wiped his slate board clean with a wet rag, made certain he had chalk for the next day, paid his respects to the portrait of the king, and then went back to his boarding room. Some nights he made beans on the hotplate in his room. Others, he would join the other boarders for Mrs. Wells' somewhat dubious roasts. Afterward, he would take a short constitutional walk, read to himself from the men's adventure books that were his great vice, and put out the light. On Saturdays, he would visit the zoo or the fourth-rate gentleman's club that he could afford. On Sundays, he attended church.

He had a reputation as a man of few needs, tepid passions, and great kindness. The romantic fire that the exotic coins and bills awakened in him was something he would have been hard pressed to share, even had he anyone with whom to share it.

Which is to say there could not be a man in the whole of the city less like Lord Iron.

Born Edmund Scarasso, Lord Iron had taken his father's title and lands and ridden them first to war, then to power, and finally to a notorious fame. His family estate outside the city was reputed to rival the king's, but Lord Iron spent little time there. He had a house in the city with two hundred rooms arranged around a central courtyard garden in which trees bore fruits unfamiliar to the city and flowers bloomed with exotic and troubling scents. His servants were number-less as ants; his personal fortune greater than some smaller nations. And never, it was said, had such wealth, power, and influence been squandered on such a debased soul.

No night passed without some new tale of Lord Iron. Ten thousand larks had been killed, their tongues harvested, and their bodies thrown aside in order that Lord Iron might have a novel *hors d'oeuvre*. Lord Biethan had been forced to repay his family's debt by sending his three daughters to perform as Lord Iron's creatures for a week; they had returned to their father with disturbing, languorous smiles and a rosewood cask filled with silver as "recompense for his Lordship's overuse." A fruit seller had the bad fortune not to recognize Lord Iron one dim, fog-bound morning, and a flippant comment earned him a whipping that left him near dead.

There was no way for anyone besides Lord Iron himself to know which of the thousand stories and accusations that accreted around him were true. There was no doubt that Lord Iron was never seen wearing anything but the richest of vel-vets and silk. He was habitually in the company of beautiful women of negotiable virtue. He smoked the finest tobacco and other, more exotic weeds. Violence and sensuality and excess were the tissue of which his life was made. If his wealth and web of blackmail and extortion had not protected him, he would no doubt have been invited to the gallows dance years before. If he had been a hero in the war, so much the worse.

And so it was, perhaps, no surprise that when his lackey and drinking companion, Lord Caton, mentioned in passing an inconvenient curiosity of the code of exchange, Lord Iron's mind seized upon it. Among his many vices was a fondness for cruel pranks. And so it came to pass that Lord Iron and the handful of gaudy revelers who followed in his wake descended late one Tuesday morning upon the Magdalen Gate postal authority.

❋

OLAF TOOK the packet of bills, willing his hands not to tremble. Lord Iron's thin smile and river-stone eyes did nothing to calm him. The woman draping herself on Lord Iron's arm made a poor affectation of sincerity.

"Well," Olaf said, unfolding the papers. "Let me see."

These were unlike any currency he had ever seen; the sheets were just larger than a standard sheet of paper, the engraving a riot of colors—crimson, indigo, and a pale, delicate peach. The lordly face that stared out of the bill was Moorish. Ornate letters identified the bills as being valued at a thousand convertible guilders and issued by the Independent Protectorate of Analdi-Wat. Olaf wondered, as his fingers traced the lettering, how a protectorate could be independent.

"I'm very sorry, my lord," he said. "But this isn't a listed currency."

"And how is that *my* problem?" Lord Iron asked, stroking his beard. He had a rich voice, soft and masculine, that made Olaf blush.

"I only mean, my lord, that I couldn't give an exchange rate on these. I don't have them on my board, you see, and so I can't—"

"These are legal tender, issued by a sovereign state. I would like to change them into pounds sterling."

"I understand that, my lord, it's only that—"

"Are you familiar with the code of exchange?" Lord Iron asked. The dark-haired woman on his arm smiled at Olaf with all the pity a snake shows a rat.

"I...of course, my lord...that is..."

"Then you will recall the second provision of the Lord Chancellor's amendment of 1652?"

Olaf licked his lips. Confusion was like cotton ticking filling his head.

"The provision against speculation, my lord?"

"Very good," Lord Iron said. "It states that any cambist in the employ of the crown must complete a requested transfer between legal tenders issued by sovereign states within twenty four hours or else face review of licensure."

"My...my lord, that isn't...I've been working here for years, sir..."

"And of course," Lord Iron went on, his gaze implacable and cool, "assigning arbitrary value to a currency also requires a review, doesn't it? And rest assured, my friend, that I am quite capable of determining the outcome of any such review."

Olaf swallowed to loosen the tightness in his throat. His smile felt sickly.

"If I have done something to offend your lordship..."

"No," Lord Iron said with something oddly like compassion in his eyes. "You were simply in the wrong place when I grew bored. Destroying you seemed diverting. I will be back at this time tomorrow. Good day, sir."

Lord Iron turned and walked away. His entourage followed. When the last of them had stepped out the street doors, the silence that remained behind was profound as the grave. Olaf saw the eyes of the postal clerks on him and managed a wan smile. The great clock read twenty minutes past eleven. By noontime tomorrow, Olaf realized, it was quite possible he would no longer be a licensed cambist.

He closed his shutters early with a note tacked to the front that clients should knock on them if they were facing an emergency and otherwise return the next day. He pulled out the references of his trade—gazetteer, logs of fiscal reports, conversion tables. By mid-afternoon, he had discovered the location of the Independent Protectorate of Analdi-Wat, but nothing that would relate their system of convertible guilders to any known currency. Apparently the last known conversion had been into a system of cowrie shells, and the numbers involved were absent.

The day waned, the light pouring into the postal authority warming and then fading to shadows. Olaf sent increasingly desperate messages to his fellow cambists at other postal authorities, to the librarians at the city's central reference desk, to the office of the Lord Exchequer. It became clear as the bells tolled their increasing hours that no answer would come before morning. And indeed, no answer would come in time.

If Olaf delayed the exchange, his license could be suspended. If he invented some random value for the guilders, his license could be suspended. And there was no data from which to derive an appropriate equation.

Anger and despair warring in his belly, he closed his station; returned his books to their places, cleaned his slate, logged the few transactions he had made. His hand hovered for a moment over his strongbox.

Here were the funds from which he drew each day to meet the demands of his clientele. Pounds sterling, yen, rubles. He wondered, if he were to fill his pockets with the box's present contents, how far he would get before he was caught. The romance of flight bloomed in his mind and died all in the space of a breath. He withdrew only the bright, venomous bills of the Independent Protectorate of Analdi-Wat, replacing them with a receipt. He locked the box with a steady hand, shrugged on his coat, and left.

Lord Iron, he decided as he walked slowly down the marble steps to the street, was evil. But he was also powerful, rich, and well-connected. There was little that a man like Olaf could do if a man of that stature took it as his whim to destroy him. If it had been the devil, he might at least have fallen back on prayer.

Olaf stopped at the newsstand, bought an evening paper and a tin of lemon mints, and trudged to the station across the street. Waiting on the platform, he listened to the underground trains hiss and squeal. He read his newspaper with the numb disinterest of a man to whom the worst has already happened. A missing child had been found alive in Stonemarket; the diary of a famous courtesan had sold at auction to an anonymous buyer and for a record price; the police had begun a policy of restricting access to the river quays in hopes of reducing accidental death by drowning. The cheap ink left more of a mark on his fingers than his mind.

At his boardinghouse, Olaf ate a perfunctory dinner at the common table, retired to his room, and tried in vain to lose himself in the pulp adventure tales. The presence of a killer among the members of the good Count Pendragon's safari proved less than captivating, even if the virtuous Hanna Gable was in danger. Near midnight, Olaf turned out his light, pulled his thin wool blanket up over his head, and wondered what he would do when his position at the postal authority was terminated.

Two hours later, he woke with a shout. Still in his night clothes, he rushed out to the common room, digging through the pile of small kindling and newspaper that Mrs. Wells used to start her fires. When he found the evening newspaper, he read the article detailing the sale of the courtesan's diary again. There was nothing in it that pertained directly to his situation, and yet his startling, triumphant yawp woke the house.

He arrived at work the next day later than usual, with bags dark as bruises under his eyes but a spring in his step. He went through his morning ritual rather hurriedly to make up for the time he had lost, but was well prepared when the street doors opened at eleven o'clock and Lord Iron and his gang of rank nobility slouched in. Olaf held his spine straight and breathed deeply to ease the trip-hammer of his heart.

Lord Iron stepped up to the window like an executioner to the noose. The woman on his arm this morning was fair-haired, but otherwise might have been the previous day's twin. Olaf made a small, nervous bow to them both.

"Lord Iron," he said.

Lord Iron's expression was distant as the moon. Olaf wondered if perhaps his lordship had been drinking already this morning.

"Explain to me why you've failed."

"Well, my lord, I don't think I can do that. I have your money here. It comes to something less than ten pounds, I'm afraid. But that was all the market would bear."

With trembling hand, Olaf slid an envelope across the desk. Lord Iron didn't look down at it. Fury lit his eyes.

"The *market*? And pray what *market* is that?"

"The glass blower's shop in Harrington Square, my lord. I have quotes from three other establishments nearby, and theirs was the best. I doubt you would find better anywhere."

"What do they have to do with this?"

"Well, they were the ones who bought the guilders," Olaf said, his voice higher and faster than he liked. He also ran on longer than he had strictly speaking intended. "I believe that they intend to use them as wrapping paper. For the more delicate pieces. As a novelty."

Lord Iron's face darkened.

"You sold my bills?" he growled.

Olaf had anticipated many possible reactions. Violence, anger, amusement. He had imagined a hundred objections that Lord Iron might bring to his actions. Base ignorance had not been one of them. Olaf's surprise leant a steadiness to his voice.

"My lord, *you* sold them. To me. That's what exchange is, sir. Currency is something bought and sold, just as plums or gas fixtures are. It's what we do here."

"I came to get pounds sterling for guilders, not sell wrapping paper!"

Olaf saw in that moment that Lord Iron genuinely didn't understand. He pulled himself up, straightening his vest.

"Sir," he said. "When a client comes to me with a hundred dollars and I turn him back with seventy pounds, I haven't said some Latin phrase over them. There aren't suddenly seventy more pounds in the world and a hundred fewer dollars. I *buy* the dollars. You came to sell your guilders to me. Very well. I have bought them."

"As wrapping paper!"

"What does that matter?" Olaf snapped, surprising both Lord Iron and himself. "If I invest them in negotiable bonds in Analdi-Wat or burn them for kindling, it's no business of yours. Someone was willing to buy them. From that, I can now quote you with authority what people are willing to pay. There is your exchange rate. And there is your money. Thank you for your business, and good day."

"You made up the price," Lord Iron said. "To place an arbitrary worth on—"

"Good God, man," Olaf said. "Did you not hear me before? There's nothing *arbitrary* about it. I went to several prospective buyers and took the best offered price. What can you possibly mean by 'worth' if not what you can purchase with it? Five shillings is worth a loaf of bread, or a cup of wine, or a cheaply bound book of poetry because that is what it will buy. Your tens of thousands of negotiable guilders will buy you nine pounds and seven shillings because that is what someone will pay. And there it is, in that envelope."

Never before in his life had Olaf seen nobility agape at him. The coterie of Lord Iron stared at him as if he had belched fire and farted brimstone. The fair-haired woman stepped back, freeing his lordship's sword arm.

I have gone too far, Olaf thought. He will kill me.

Lord Iron was silent for a long moment while the world seemed to rotate around him. Then he chuckled.

"The measure of a thing's worth is what you can purchase with it," he said as if tasting the words, then turned to the fair-haired woman. "I think he's talking about you, Marjorie."

The woman's cheeks flushed scarlet. Lord Iron leaned against the sill of Olaf's little, barred window and gestured Olaf closer. Against his best judgment, Olaf leaned in.

"You have a strange way of looking at things," Lord Iron said. There were fumes on his breath. Absinthe, Olaf guessed. "To hear you speak, the baker buys my five shillings with his bread."

"And how is that wrong, my lord?" the cambist asked.

"And then the wineseller buys the coins from him with a glass of wine. So why not buy the bread with the wine? If they're worth the same?"

"You could, my lord," Olaf said. "You can express anything in terms of anything else, my lord. How many lemon tarts is a horse worth? How many newspapers equate to a good dinner? It isn't harder to determine than some number of rubles for another number of yen, if you know the trick of it."

Lord Iron smiled again. The almost sleepy expression returned to his eyes. He nodded.

"Wrapping paper," he said. "You have amused me, little man, and I didn't think that could be done any longer. I accept your trade."

And with that, Lord Iron swept the envelope into his pocket, turned, and marched unsteadily out of the postal authority and into the noon light of Magdalen Gate. After the street doors were closed, there was a pause long as three breaths together and then one of the postal clerks began to clap.

A moment later, the staff of the postal authority had filled the vaults of their chambers with applause. Olaf, knees suddenly weak, bowed carefully, closed the shutters of his window, and made his way back to the men's privacy room where he emptied his breakfast into the toilet and then sat on the cool tile floor laughing until tears streamed from his eyes.

He had faced down Lord Iron and escaped with his career intact. It was, no doubt, the greatest adventure of his life. Nothing he had done before could match it, and he could imagine nothing in the future that would surpass it.

And nothing did, as it turned out, for almost six and a half months.

※

IT WAS a cold, clear February, and the stars had come out long before Olaf had left the Magdalen Gate authority. All during the ride on the underground train, Olaf dreamed of a warm pot of tea, a small fire, and the conclusion of the latest novel. Atherton Crane was on the verge of exposing the plot of the vicious Junwang Ko, but didn't yet know that Kelly O'Callahan was in the villain's clutches. It promised to be a pleasant evening.

He knew as soon as he stepped into the boarding house that something was wrong. The other boarders, sitting around the common table, went silent as he shrugged out of his coat and plucked off his hat. They pointedly did not look at him as Mrs. Wells, her wide friendly face pale as uncooked dough, crossed the room to meet him.

"There's a message for you, Mr. Neddelsohn," she said. "A man came and left it for you. Very particular."

"Who was he?" Olaf asked, suspicion blooming in his heart more from her affect than from any guilt on his conscience.

"Don't know," Mrs. Wells said, wringing her hands in distress, "but he looked...well, here it is, Mr. Neddelsohn. This is the letter he left for you."

The envelope she thrust into his hand was the color of buttercream, smooth as linen, and thick. The coat of arms embossed upon it was Lord Iron's. Olaf started at the thing as if she'd handed him a viper.

Mrs. Wells simpered her apology as he broke the wax seal and drew out a single sheet of paper. It was written in an erratic but legible hand.

Mr. Neddelsohn—

I find I have need of you to settle a wager. You will bring yourself to the Club Baphomet immediately upon receipt of this note. I will, of course, recompense you for your troubles.

The note was not signed, but Olaf had no doubt of its authorship. Without a word, he pulled his jacket back on, returned his hat to his head, and stepped out to hail a carriage. From the street, he could see the faces of Mrs. Wells and his fellow boarders at the window.

The Club Baphomet squatted in the uncertain territory between the tenements and beer halls of Stonemarket and the mansions and ballrooms of Granite Hill. The glimmers behind its windows did little to illuminate the street, perhaps by design. From the tales Olaf had heard, there might well be members of the club who would prefer not to be seen entering or leaving its grounds. The service entrance was in a mud-paved alley stinking of piss and old food, but it opened quickly to his knock. He was bundled inside and escorted to a private sitting room where, it seemed, he was expected.

Of the five men who occupied the room, Olaf recognized only Lord Iron. The months had not been kind; Lord Iron had grown thinner, his eyes wilder, and a deep crimson cut was only half healed on his cheek. The other four were dressed in fashion similar to Lord Iron—well-razored hair, dark coats

18

of the finest wool, watch chains of gold. The eldest of them seemed vaguely familiar.

Lord Iron rose and held his hand out toward Olaf, not as if to greet him but rather to display him like a carnival barker presenting a three-headed calf.

"Gentlemen," Lord Iron intoned. "This is the cambist I mentioned to you. I propose that he be my champion in this matter."

Olaf felt the rictus grin on his face, the idiot bobbing of his head as he made small bows to the four assembled gentlemen. He was humiliated, but could no more stop himself than a puppy could keep from showing its belly to beg the mercy of wolves.

One of the four—a younger man with gold hair and ice-blue eyes—stepped forward with a smile. Olaf nodded to him for what must have been the fifth time.

"I am Simon Cole," the gold-haired man said. "Lord Eichan, to my enemies."

At this, Lord Iron raised a hand, as if to identify himself as one such enemy. The other three men chuckled, and Lord Eichan smiled as well before continuing.

"Our mutual acquaintance, Lord Iron, has made a suggestion I find somewhat unlikely, and we have made a wager of it. He is of the opinion that the value of anything can be expressed in terms of any other valuable thing. I think his example was the cost of a horse in lemon mints."

"Yes, my lord," Olaf said.

"Ah, you agree then," Lord Eichan said. "That's good. I was afraid our little Edmund had come up with his thesis in a drug soaked haze."

"We've made the agreement," Lord Iron said pleasantly. "Simon, Satan's catamite that he is, will set the two things to be compared. I, meaning of course *you*, will have a week to determine their relative worth. These three bastards will judge the answer."

"I see," Olaf said.

"Excellent," Lord Iron said, slapping him on the back and leading him to a chair upholstered in rich leather. It wasn't until Olaf had descended into the chair's depths that he realized he had just agreed to this mad scheme. Lord Eichan had taken a seat opposite him and was thoughtfully lighting a pipe.

"I think I should say," Olaf began, casting his mind about wildly for some way to remove himself from the room without offending either party. "That is, I don't wish that...ah..."

Lord Eichan nodded as if Olaf had made some cogent point, then shaking his match until the flame died, turned to face Olaf directly.

"I would like to know the value of a day in the life of His Majesty, King Walther," Lord Eichan said. "And I would like that value described in days of life of an inmate in the crown's prison."

"A day in the life of the king expressed in days of a prisoner's life?"

"Certainly you must agree that life is valuable," Lord Eichan said. "You wouldn't lightly part with your own."

"Well, certainly—"

"And you can't suggest that the king is the same as a bread thief."

"No, I wouldn't—"

"Well, then," Lord Eichan said. "It's settled."

"Come along, my boy," Lord Iron said, clapping Olaf on the shoulder. "I'll see you out."

"One week!" Lord Eichan said as Olaf and Lord Iron stepped from the room and into the corridor. Lord Iron was smiling; Olaf was not.

"My lord," Olaf said. "This is...I'm not sure I know how to go about something like this."

"That's why I got you a week to do it in," Lord Iron said. "The rat-licker wanted to limit it to three days."

"I don't know for a certainty that I can accommodate you, my lord," Olaf said.

"Do your best," Lord Iron said. "If we lose, Simon, Lord Eichan is going to kill me. Well, and you for that."

Olaf stopped dead. Lord Iron took another few steps before pausing and looking back.

"He's what?"

"Going to kill us," Lord Iron said. "And take five hundred pounds I've set aside in earnest as well. If we win, I'll kill him and bed his sister."

Olaf, unthinking, murmured an obscenity. Lord Iron grinned and pulled him along the dim corridor toward the back of the club.

"Well, you needn't bed his sister if you don't care to. Just do your best, boy. And be back here in a week."

With that, Lord Iron stepped Olaf out the door and into the cold, bleak alley. It wasn't until the door had closed behind him that Olaf realized Lord Iron hadn't recompensed him for the carriage ride.

In the morning, the whole affair had the air of a bad dream. Olaf made his way to Magdalen Gate as he always did, checked the ticker tape, updated his slate. What was the value of life, he wondered. And how was one life best to be measured against another.

And, behind it all, the growing certainty that Lord Eichan would indeed kill him if he couldn't find an acceptable answer.

Twice before noon, Olaf found he had made errors in his accounting. After bolting down the snowy street after a woman who had left with ten pounds fewer than she deserved, Olaf gave up. He wrote a note claiming illness, pinned it to his shuttered window, and left. He paused at the tobacconist to buy a pouch and papers.

In his room at the boarding house, Olaf sketched out every tack he could think of to address the issue. The most obvious was to determine how much money the state spent to keep his majesty and how much to run the prisons. But objections to that arose almost immediately; was that a measure of the worth of life or of operational expenses appropriate to each career? He considered the relative costs of physician's care for king and prisoner, but this again was not a concern precisely of life, but health. Twenty years coughing and twenty years free from illness were still twenty years.

For three days, he ate little and slept less. He ventured out to the library to search among the stacks of books and periodicals for inspiration. He found nothing on which he would have been willing to stake his life. Lord Iron had done that for him.

On the morning of the fourth day he rolled the last pinch of tobacco into the last paper, wet it, rolled it, and sat on his bed unable to bring himself to the effort of lighting the thing. Despair had descended upon him. He saw the next three days stretching before him in a long, slow sleep.

It was how he imagined the prisoners felt who had so occupied his thoughts. But he, at least, could go out for more tobacco. And beer. And good, bloody beefsteak. If he was to live like a prisoner, he might at least eat like a king. It wasn't as if he'd give himself gout in three days time, no matter how richly he ate or overmuch he drank.

Something stirred at the back of his mind, and he found himself grinning even before he knew why.

All that day and the two after it he spent in a whirl of activity, his despair forgotten. He visited physicians and the budget office, the office of the prison warden and the newspaperman who most reported on the activities of the king. The last day, he locked himself in his rooms with an abacus, a stub of pencil, and sheaves of paper.

When he came to the final accounting, his heart sank. He went through his figures again, certain that somewhere in the complexity of his argument, he had made an error. But the numbers tallied, and as little as he liked it, there was no more time. Putting on his best coat, he prepared the argument in his mind. Then, papers tucked under his arm, he went out past his silent fellow boarders and the stricken countenance of Mrs. Wells, down to the wintery street, and hailed a carriage to carry him back to Club Baphomet.

The furniture of the sitting room had been rearranged. A single table now dominated the space, with five chairs all along one side like an examiner's panel. The three judges sat in the middle with Simon, Lord Eichan on the left and Lord Iron on the right. Lord Eichan looked somewhat amused, but there was a nervousness in his movement with which Olaf identified. Lord Iron looked as relaxed as a man stepping out of a sauna; the wound on his face was visibly more healed. Glasses of wine sat before each man, and cigars rested in onyx ashtrays when the gentlemen of the club weren't making better use of them.

A straight-backed wooden chair faced them, a small student desk at its side. Olaf sat and arranged his papers. The eldest of the judges leaned forward and with a smile more at home on the lips of a procurer spoke.

"You may proceed, sir."

Olaf nodded his thanks.

"I will need to do just a bit of groundwork before I present my analysis," he said. "I hope you would all agree that a man who decries embezzlement and also diverts money into his private accounts is not actually opposed to the theft?"

The judges looked at one another in amusement.

"Or, similarly," Olaf went on, "a woman who claims to embody chastity and yet beds all comers is not, in point of fact, chaste?"

"I think even Lord Eichan will have to allow those to stand," the eldest judge said. "Your point?"

"My point, sirs, is that we judge people not by what they claim, but what they do. Public declarations of sentiment are not a fit judge of true character."

"You are preaching," the youngest of the judges drawled, "to the choir. There is no group in the nation more adept at saying one thing and doing another."

Olaf smiled awkwardly.

"Just so," he said. "I will move forward. I have come to the determination, after careful consideration, that a day in the life of his majesty the king equates to nineteen and three quarter hours of a prisoner of the crown."

There was a moment's silence. Simon, Lord Eichan blinked and an incredulous smile began to work its way onto his countenance. Lord Iron sat forward, his expression unreadable. One of the judges who had not yet spoken took a meditative puff on his cigar.

"I was never particularly good at sums," the man said in an unsettlingly feminine voice, "but it seems to me that you've just said a prisoner's life is *more* valuable than that of the king?"

"Yes," Olaf said, his belly heavy as if he'd drunk a tankard of lead. The eldest judge glanced at Lord Iron with a pitying expression.

"Let me also make some few observations," Olaf said, fighting to keep the desperation from his voice. "I have met with several physicians in the last few days. I am sorry to report that overindulging in strong liquor is thought by the medical establishment to reduce life expectancy by as much as five years. A habit of eating rich foods may reduce a man's span on the earth by another three to four years. A sedentary lifestyle by as much as eight. Indulging in chocolate and coffee can unbalance the blood, and remove as many as three years of life."

"You have now ceased to preach to the choir," said Lord Eichan. And indeed, the judges had grown more somber. Olaf raised a hand, begging their patience.

"I have used these medical data as well as the reports of the warden of Chappell Hill Prison and the last two years of his majesty's reported activities in the newspapers. I beg you to consider. A prisoner of the crown is kept on a simple diet and subjected to a mandatory exercise period each day. No spirits of any kind are permitted him. No luxuries such as coffee or chocolate. By comparison..."

Olaf fumbled with the sheaves of papers, searching for the form he had created. The eldest judge cleared his throat.

"By comparison," Olaf continued, "in the last two years, his majesty has taken vigorous exercise only one day in seven. Has eaten at banquet daily, including the richest of dishes. He regularly drinks both coffee and chocolate, often together in the French style."

"This is ridiculous," Lord Eichan said. "His majesty has the finest physicians in the world at his command. His life is better safeguarded than any man's in the realm."

"No, sir," Olaf said, his voice taking on a certainty that he was beginning to genuinely feel. "We *say* that it is, much as the embezzler claims honesty and the wanton claims virtue. I present to you the actions, as we agreed. And I would point out that his majesty's excesses are subject only to his personal whim. If he wished, he could drink himself insensible each morning, eat nothing but butterfat and lard, and never move from his seat. He could drink half a tun of coffee and play games with raw gunpowder. Unlike a prisoner, there is no enforcement of behavior that could rein him in. I have, if anything, taken a conservative measure in reaching my conclusions."

A glimmer of amusement shone in Lord Iron's eyes, but his face remained otherwise frozen. Simon, Lord Eichan was fidgeting with his cigar. The eldest judge sucked his teeth audibly and shook his head.

"And yet prisoners do not, I think, have a greater lifespan than monarchs," he said.

"It is impossible to say," Olaf said. "For many criminals and poor men, the time spent in the care of the crown can be when they are safest, best overseen, best clothed, best fed. I would, however, point out that His Majesty's father left us at the age of sixty-seven, and the oldest man in the care of the crown is…"

Olaf paused, finding the name.

"The oldest man in the care of the crown is David Bennet, aged eighty. Incarcerated when he was sixteen for killing his brother."

He spread his hands.

"Your argument seems sound," the eldest judge said, "but your conclusion is ridiculous. I cannot believe that the king is of lesser value than a prisoner. I am afraid I remain unconvinced. What say you, gentlemen?"

But before the other two judges could answer Olaf rose to his feet.

"With all respect, sir, the question was not the value of the king or the prisoner, but of the days of their respective lives. I was not asked to judge their pleasures or their health insofar as their discomforts are less than mortal."

The effeminate judge lifted his chin. There was a livid scar across his neck where, Olaf imagined from his knowledge of men's adventure, a garrote might have cut. But it was Simon, Lord Eichan who spoke.

"How is it that a king can be more valuable than a prisoner, but his days be less? It makes no sense at all!"

"There are other things which his majesty has," Olaf said. He had warmed to his topic now, and the fact that his own life hung in the balance was all but forgotten. "A prisoner *must* take his exercise; a king has the power to refuse. A prisoner may wish dearly for a rich meal or a great glass of brandy, but since he cannot have them, he cannot exchange pleasure for… well, for some duration of life."

"This is a waste of—"

"Be quiet," the eldest judge said. "Let the man have his say."

"But—"

"Don't make me repeat myself, Simon."

Lord Eichan leaned back sneering and gripping his wine glass until his knuckles were white.

"It's a choice every man in this room has made," Olaf went on, raising his arm like a priest delivering a homily. "You might all live as ascetics and survive years longer. But like the king, you choose to make a rational exchange of some span of your life for the pleasure of living as you please. A prisoner is barred from that exchange, and so I submit a greater value is placed on his life precisely to the degree that strictures are placed on his pleasure and his exercise of power.

"Gentlemen, ask yourselves this; if I had two sons and saw that one of them kept from drink and gluttony while letting the other run riot, which of them would you say I valued? The prodigal might have more pleasure. Certainly the king has more pleasure than an inmate. But pleasure and power are not *life*."

"Amen," said Lord Iron. It was the first time he had spoken since Olaf had entered. The silence that followed this declaration was broken only by the hissing of the fire in the grate and rush of blood in Olaf's ears.

"Your reports were accurate, Lord Iron," the drawling judge said. "Your pet cambist is *quite* amusing."

"Perhaps it would be best if you gave us a moment to discuss your points," the eldest judge said. "If you would be so kind as to step out to the antechamber? Yes. Thank you."

With the blackwood door closed behind him, Olaf's fear returned. He was in the Club Baphomet with his survival linked to Lord Iron's, and only an argument that seemed less and less tenable with each passing minute to protect him. But he had made his throw. His only other hope now was mad flight, and the door to the corridor was locked. He tried it.

What felt like hours passed, though the grandfather clock ticking away in the corner reported only a quarter hour. A pistol barked twice, and a moment later Lord Iron strode into the room. The door swung shut behind him before Olaf could make sense of the bloody scene. His gorge rose.

"Well done, boy," Lord Iron said, dropping something heavy into Olaf's lap. "I'll have you taken home in my personal carriage. I have Lord Eichan's sister to console this evening, and I won't be needing horses to do it. And I thought you should know; it wasn't unanimous. If his majesty hadn't taken your side, I think we might not have won the day."

"His majesty?"

Olaf's mind reeled. The face of the eldest judge resolved itself suddenly into the portrait he kept at his desk.

"You did well, boy," Lord Iron said. "Your country thanks you."

Without another word, Lord Iron unlocked the door, stepped out to the corridor, and was gone. Olaf looked down. A packet of bills squatted in his lap. Five hundred pounds at a guess, and blood smeared on the topmost bill.

He swore to himself in that moment that he would never answer another summons from Lord Iron, whatever the consequences. And, indeed, when the hour arrived, it was Lord Iron who came to him.

✳

THE WEEKS and months that followed were if anything richer in their tales of Lord Iron. While traveling in the Orient, he had forced a barkeep who had fallen into debt to choose between cutting off one of his infant daughter's toes or three of his own fingers in lieu of payment. He had seduced six nuns in Rome, leaving two of them with child. He had ridden an ostrich down the streets of Cairo naked at midnight. Of the untimely death of Lord Eichan there was no word, but apart from removing the portrait of the king from his desk, Olaf took no action. The less he personally figured into the debaucheries of Lord Iron, the better pleased he was.

Instead, Olaf plunged more deeply than ever into his work, his routine, and the harmless escapism of his men's adventure novels. But for the first time in memory, the perils of the heroines seemed contrived and weak; the masculine bravery of the heroes seemed overstated, like a boy who blusters and puffs out his chest when walking through the graveyard at dusk.

Clifford Knightly wrestled an alligator on the banks of the great Nile. Lord Morrow foiled the evil Chaplain Grut's plan to foul the waters of London. Emily Chastain fell gratefully into the mighty arms of the noble savage Maker-of-Justice. And Olaf found himself wondering what these great men would have done at Club Baphomet. Wrested the gun from Lord Iron? From Simon, Lord Eichan? Sternly spoken of God and truth and righteousness? Olaf doubted it would have had any great effect.

Winter passed into spring. Spring ripened to summer. Slowly, Olaf's discontent, like the nightmares from which he woke himself shouting, lessened. For weeks on end, he could forget what he had been part of. Many men who came to his window at the postal authority had traveled widely. Many had tales to tell of near misses: a runaway carriage that had come within a pace of running them down in the streets of Prague, a fever which had threatened to carry them away in Bombay, the hiss of an Afghan musket ball passing close to their head. These moments of real danger were more convincing than any novel Olaf had ever read. This was, in part, because he had tales of his own now, if he ever chose to share them.

And still, when autumn with its golden leaves and fog and chill rain also brought Lord Iron back into his life, Olaf was not surprised.

It was a Tuesday night in September. Olaf had spent his customary hours at the Magdalen Gate postal authority, come back to his boarding house, and eaten alone in his room. The evening air was cool but not biting, and he had propped his window open before sitting down to read. When he woke, he thought for a long, bleary moment that the cold night breeze had woken him. Then the knock at his door repeated itself.

His blanket wrapped around his shoulders, Olaf answered the door. Lord Iron stood in the hall. He looked powerfully out of place. His fine jacket and cravat, the polished boots, the well-groomed beard and moustache all belonged in a palace or club. And yet rather than making the boarding house hall seem shabby and below him, the hallway made Lord Iron, monster of the city, seem false as a boy playing dress-up. Olaf nodded as if he'd been expecting the man.

"I have need of you," Lord Iron said.

"Have I the option of refusal?"

Lord Iron smiled, and Olaf took it as the answer to his question. He stepped back and let the man come through. Lord Iron sat on the edge of the bed while Olaf closed his window, drew up his chair and sat. In the light from Olaf's reading lamp, Lord Iron's skin seemed waxen and pale. His voice, when he spoke, was distant as a man shouting from across a square.

"There is a question plaguing me," Lord Iron said. "You are the only man I can think of who might answer it."

"Is there a life at stake?" Olaf asked.

"No," Lord Iron said. "Nothing so petty as that."

When Olaf failed to respond, Lord Iron, born Edmund Scarasso, looked up at him. There was a terrible weariness in his eyes.

"I would know the fair price for a man's soul," he said.

"Forgive me?" Olaf said.

"You heard me," Lord Iron said. "What would be fit trade for a soul? I...I can't tell any longer. And it is a question whose answer has...some relevance to my situation."

In an instant, Olaf's mind conjured the sitting room at the Club Baphomet. Lord Iron sitting in one deep leather chair, and the Prince of Lies across from him with a snifter of brandy in his black, clawed hands.

"I don't think that would be a wise course to follow," Olaf said, though in truth his mind was spinning out ways to avoid being party to this diabolism. He did not wish to make a case before that infernal judge. Lord Iron smiled and shook his head.

"There is no one in this besides yourself and me," he said. "You are an expert in the exchange of exotic currencies. I can think of none more curious than this. Come to my house on Mammon Street in a month's time. Tell me what conclusion you have reached."

"My Lord—"

"I will make good on the investment of your time," Lord Iron said, then rose and walked out, leaving the door open behind him.

Olaf gaped at the empty room. He was a cambist. Of theology, he knew only what he had heard in church. He had read more of satanic contracts in his adventure novels than in the Bible. He was, in fact, not wholly certain that the Bible had an example of a completed exchange. Satan had tempted Jesus. Perhaps there was something to be taken from the Gospel of Matthew...

Olaf spent the remainder of the night poring over his Bible and considering what monetary value might be assigned to the ability to change stones to bread. But as the dawn broke and he turned to his morning ablutions, he found himself unsatisfied. The devil might have tempted Christ with all the kingdoms of the world, but it was obvious that such an offer wouldn't be open to everyone. He was approaching the problem from the wrong direction.

As he rode through the deep tunnels to Magdalen Gate, as he stopped at the newsstand for a morning paper, as he checked the ticker tape and updated his slate, his mind occupied itself by sifting through all the stories and folk wisdom he had ever heard. There had been a man who traded his soul to the devil for fame and wealth. Faust had done it for knowledge. Was there a way to represent the learning of Faust in terms of, say, semesters at the best universities of Europe? Then the rates of tuition might serve as a fingerhold.

It was nearly the day's end before the question occurred to him that put Lord Iron's commission in its proper light, and once that had happened, the answer was obvious. Olaf had to sit down, his mind afire with the answer and its implications. He didn't go home, but took himself to a small public house. Over a pint and a stale sandwich, he mentally tested his hypothesis. With the second pint, he celebrated. With the third, he steeled himself, then went out to the street and hailed a carriage to take him to the house of Lord Iron.

Revelers had infected the household like fleas on a dying rat. Masked men and women shrieked with laughter, not all of which bespoke mirth. No servant came to take his coat or ask his invitation, so Olaf made his own way through the great halls. He passed through the whole of the building before emerging from the back and finding Lord Iron himself sitting at a fountain in the gardens. His lordship's eyebrows rose to see Olaf, but he did not seem displeased.

"So soon, boy? It isn't a month," Lord Iron said as Olaf sat on the cool stone rail. The moon high above the city seemed also to dance in the water, lighting Lord Iron's face from below and above at once.

"There was no need," Olaf said. "I have your answer. But I will have to make something clear before I deliver it. If you will permit me?"

Lord Iron opened his hand in motion of deference. Olaf cleared his throat.

"Wealth," he said, "is not a measure of money. It is a measure of well-being. Of happiness, if you will. Wealth is not traded, but rather is generated *by* trade. If you have a piece of art that I wish to own and I have money that you would prefer to the artwork, we trade. Each of us has something he prefers to the thing he gave away; otherwise, we would not have agreed on the trade. We are both better off. You see? Wealth is *generated*."

"I believe I can follow you so far," Lord Iron said. "Certainly I can agree that a fat wallet is no guarantor of contentment."

"Very well. I considered your problem for the better part of the day. I confess I came near to despairing; there is no good data from which to work. But then I found my error. I assumed that your soul, my lord, was valuable. Clearly it is not."

Lord Iron coughed out something akin to a laugh, shock in his expression. Olaf raised a hand, palm out, asking that he not interrupt.

"You are renowned for your practice of evil. This very evening, walking through your house, I have seen things for which I can imagine no proper penance. Why would Satan bother to buy your soul? He has rights to it already."

"He does," Lord Iron said, staring into the middle distance.

"And so I saw," Olaf said. "You aren't seeking to sell a soul. You are hoping to buy one."

Lord Iron sighed and looked at his hands. He seemed smaller now. Not a supernatural being, but a man driven by human fears and passions to acts that could only goad him on to worse and worse actions. A man like any other, but with the wealth to magnify his errors into the scale of legend.

"You are correct, boy," he said. "The angels wouldn't have my soul if I drenched it honey. I have...treated it poorly. It's left me weary and sick. I am a waste of flesh. I know that. If there is no way to become a better man than this, I suspect the best path is to become a corpse."

"I understand, my lord. Here is the answer to your question: the price of a soul is a life of humility and service."

"Ah, is that all," Lord Iron said, as if the cambist had suggested that he pull down the stars with his fingers.

"And as it happens," Olaf went on, "I have one such with which I would be willing to part."

Lord Iron met his gaze, began to laugh, and then went silent.

"Here," Olaf said, "is what I propose..."

❋

EDMUND, THE new cambist of the Magdalen Gate postal authority was, by all accounts an adequate replacement for Olaf. Not as good, certainly. But his close-cropped hair and clean-shaven face lent him an eagerness that belonged on a younger man, and if he seemed sometimes more haughty than his position justified, it was a vice that lessened with every passing month. By Easter, he had even been asked to join in the Sunday picnic the girls in the accounting office sponsored. He seemed genuinely moved at the invitation.

The great scandal of the season was the disappearance of Lord Iron. The great beast of the city simply vanished one night. Rumor said that he had left his fortune and lands in trust. The identity of the trustee was a subject of tremendous speculation.

Olaf himself spent several months simply taking stock of his newfound position in the world. Once the financial situation was put in better order, he found himself with a substantial yearly allowance that still responsibly protected the initial capital.

He spent his monies traveling to India, Egypt, the sugar plantations of the Caribbean, the unworldly underground cities of Persia. He saw the sun set off the Gold Coast and rise from the waters east of Japan. He heard war songs in the jungles of the Congo and sang children's lullabies in a lonely tent made from yak skin in the dark of a Siberian winter.

And, when he paused to recover from the rigors and dangers of travel, he would retire to a cottage north of the city—the least of his holdings—and spend his time writing men's adventure novels set in the places he had been.

He named his protagonist Lord Iron.

FLAT DIANE

HIS HANDS DIDN'T TREMBLE as he traced his daughter. She lay on the kitchen floor, pressing her back against the long, wide, white paper he'd brought, her small movements translated into soft scratching sounds where the cut end tried to curl down into the floor. His pen moved along the horizons of her body—here, where her wrist widened, and then each finger; down her side; rounding the ball of her feet like the passage around the Cape of Good Hope; up to where her wide shorts made it clear this wasn't a work of pornography; then back down the other leg and around. When he came to her spilling hair, he traced its silhouette rather than remain strictly against her skin. He wanted it to look like her, and Diane had thick, curly, gorgeous hair just like her mother had.

"Just almost done, sweetie," he said when she started to shift and fidget. She quieted until the pen tip touched the point where it had started, the circle closed. As he sat back, she jumped up to see. The shape was imperfect—the legs ended in awkward Thalidomide bulbs, the hair obscured the long oval face, the lines of the tile were clear where the pen had jumped.

Still.

"Okay," Ian said. "Now let's just put this on here, and then…"

"I want to write it," Diane said.

Diane was eight, and penmanship was new to her and a thing of pride. Ian reached up to the table, took down a wooden ruler with a sharp metal edge, and drew lines for his daughter to follow. He handed her the pen, and she hunched over.

"Okay, sweetie. Write this. Ready?"

She nodded, her hair spilling into her face. She pushed it away impatiently, a gesture of her mother's. Candice, who pushed a lot of things away impatiently.

"Hi," Ian said, slowly, giving his daughter time to follow. "I'm Flat Diane. My real girl, Diane Bursen, sent me out to travel for her. I can't write because I'm only paper. Would you please send her a picture of us, so she can see where I am and what adventures (Ian stopped here to spell the word out) I'm having?"

Ian had to draw more lines on the other side of Flat Diane for the mailing address, but Diane waited and then filled that out too, only forgetting the zip code.

Together, they rolled Flat Diane thin and put her in a mailing tube, capped the end with a white plastic lid, and sealed it with tape.

"Can we send Flat Diane to see mommy?"

He could feel his reaction at the corners of his mouth. Diane's face fell even before he spoke, her lower lip out, her brown eyes hard. Ian stroked her hair.

"We will, sweetheart. Just as soon as she's ready to let us know where we can mail things to her, we will."

Diane jerked away, stomped off to the living room and turned on the TV, sulking. Ian addressed the package to his mother in Scotland, since it seemed unlikely that either of them would be able to afford a transatlantic vacation anytime soon. When the evening news came on with its roster of rapes and killings, he turned off the set, escorted his protesting daughter through her evening rituals, tucked her into bed and then went to his room and lay sleepless until after midnight.

✳

THE PHOTOGRAPH shows his mother, smiling. Her face is broader than he remembered it, the hair a uniform grey but not yet white. She holds Flat Diane up, and behind them the half-remembered streets of Glasgow.

There is writing on the back in blue pen and a familiar hand:

Flat Diane arrived yesterday. I'm taking her to my favorite teahouse this afternoon. It was designed by Charles Rennie Mackintosh—one of the best architects ever to come out of Glasgow, and the scones are lovely. Tomorrow, we are going to work together. My love to Ian and the real Diane.

Mother Bursen.

✳

DIANE WAS elated, and Ian was both pleased that the plan was working and saddened to realize how rare his daughter's elation had become. She had insisted that the picture go with her to school, and while she promised that she would care for it, Ian was anxious for it. It was precious, irreplaceable, and therefore fragile.

After work, he went to collect her from her friend Kit's house, anxiety for the picture still in the back of his mind.

"Today," Kit's father Tohiro reported as they drank their ritual cup of coffee, "everything was Scotland. How the people talk in Scotland. How the tea is made in Scotland. Whether you have to share tables at restaurants in Scotland. Diane has become the expert in everything."

"It's my mother. She sent a picture."

"I saw. She told us about the...what? The drawing? Flat Diane? It's a good idea."

"It gives her something to look forward to. And I wanted her to know how many people there are looking out for her. I haven't much family in the states. And with her mother gone..."

A cascade of thumps announced the girls as they came down the stairs. Diane stalked into the kitchen, her brows furrowed, hair curled around her head like a stormcloud. She went to her father, arms extended in demand, and he lifted her familiar weight to his lap.

"I want to go home now," she said. "Kit's a butthead."

Ian grimaced an apology. Tohiro smiled—amused, weary—and sipped his coffee.

"Okay, sweetie. Go get your coat, okay?"

"I don't want my coat."

"Diane."

His tone was warning enough. She got down and, looking over her shoulder once in anger at the betrayal of insisting on her coat, vanished again. Ian sighed.

"She's just tired," Tohiro said. "Kit's the same way."

They drove home through a rising fog. Though it made Ian nervous, driving when he couldn't quite make out what was coming, Diane only chattered on, stringing together the events of her day with *and* after *and* after *and*. No matter if no two facts led one to another—they were what she had to say, and he listened half from weariness and half from love.

An accident of timers turned the lights on just as they pulled into the driveway, as if someone were there to greet them. There was nothing in the mailbox from Flat Diane. Or from Candice.

"Daddy?"

Ian snapped to, as if coming awake. Diane held the screen door open, frowning at him impatiently. He couldn't say how long she'd been there, how long he'd fallen into dim reverie.

"Sorry, sweetie," he said, pulling keys from his pocket. "Just got lost in the fog a minute."

Diane turned, looking out at the risen grey. His daughter narrowed her eyes, looking out into nothing.

"I like the fog," she said, delivering the pronouncement with the weight of law. "It smells like Scotland."

And for a moment, it did.

＊

THE PHOTOGRAPH isn't really a photograph but a color printout from an old printer, the ink shinier than the paper it stains. On it Flat Diane is unfurled between a smiling couple. The man is thick, wide-lipped, greying at the temple. He wears a yellow polo shirt and makes a thumbs-up with the hand that isn't supporting Flat Diane. The woman is smaller, thinner. Her smile is pinched. She only looks like her brother Ian around the eyes and in the tilt of her nose.

Behind them is a simple living room, the light buttery yellow and somehow dirty.

The bottom of the page carries a message typed as part of the same document:

Dear Ian and Diane,

Flat Diane is here with us in Dallas. She's just in time for Valentine's day. She's coming out to our special dinner with us tonight at Carmine's Bistro—Italian food. Yum!

Hope everything's good with you. See you soon. Much love.

Aunt Harriet and Uncle Bobby.

＊

IN TWO weeks, Diane would be nine. It was a foreign thought. So little time seemed to have passed since her last birthday until he realized that Candice hadn't quite left then. This, now, was his first birthday as both of her parents. He had demanded the day off, and his manager had acquiesced. He had arranged with the school to take her out for the day. A movie, a day with him, and a party that night with all her friends. Kit's parents Anna and Tohiro were helping to drive them all.

He knew he was overcompensating. He hoped it would be enough, and not only for her. There was a loneliness in him that also had to be appeased. Over the course of months, the traces of his wife—still his wife, still only separated—had begun to erode. The last of her special toothpaste used up; the pillows no longer smelling of her hair; the foods that only she ate spoiled and thrown away. In their place were the toys Diane didn't put away, the homework left half-done on the table, the sugared breakfast cereals too sweet for Ian to enjoy except as candy.

But Diane's things were all part his—hers to enjoy, and his to shepherd. Nothing had to be put away unless he said it did, nothing had to be finished unless he insisted, nothing was too sweet, too empty, too bad for you to be dinner except that Ian—big bad unreasonable mean Daddy—said no. Daddy who, after all, couldn't even keep a wife.

It was Friday, and Kit was sleeping over. The girls were in the back—in Diane's room—playing video games. Ian sat on the couch with a beer sweating itself slick in his hand while a news magazine show told of a child drowned in the bathtub by his mother. The place smelled of order-out pizza and the toy perfume from the beauty salon toys that Kit brought over; costume jewelry spread out on the carpet, glittering and abandoned.

Ian's thoughts were pleasantly vague—the dim interest in the tragedy playing out on the television, the nagging knowledge that he would have to pretend to make the girls go to sleep soon (they would stay up anyway), the usual pleasure of a week's work ended. Kit's shriek bolted him half across the house before his mind quite understood what the sound had been.

In the bedroom, the tableau. Kit sat inelegantly on the floor, her hand to her cheek, her nose bloody. The controllers for the game box splayed out, black plastic tentacles abandoned on the carpet; the electric music still looping. And Diane, her hand still in a fist, but her eyes wide and horrified.

"What in Christ's name is going on in here?" Ian demanded.

"Sh...she hit me," Kit began, her voice rising as the tears began. "I didn't do anything and she just hit me."

"Diane?"

His daughter blinked and her gaze flickered at her friend, as if looking for support. And then her own eyes filled.

"It was my turn," Diane said, defensively.

"So you hit her?"

"I was mad."

"I'm going *home!*" Kit howled and bolted for the bathroom. Ian paused for a half second, then scowled and went after the girl leaving Diane behind. Kit was in the bathroom, trying to stanch the blood with her hand. Ian helped her, sitting her on the toilet with her head tipped back, a wad of tissue pressed to her lip. The bleeding wasn't bad; it stopped quickly. There was no blood on the girl's clothes. When he was sure it wouldn't start again, he wetted a washcloth and wiped Kit's face gently, the blood pinking the terrycloth.

Diane haunted the doorway, her dark eyes profound with confusion and regret.

"I want to go home," Kit said when he had finished. Her small mouth was pressed thin. Ian felt his heart bind. If Diane lost Kit, he'd loose Tohiro and Anna. It was a fleeting thought, and he was ashamed of it the moment it struck him.

"Of course," he said. "I'll take you there. But first I think Diane owes you an apology."

Diane was weeping openly, the tears gathering on her chin. Kit turned to her, and Ian crossed his arms.

"I didn't mean to," Diane said. "It's just that when people get mad, they hit each other sometimes."

"Diane, what are you thinking? Where did you get an idea like that?"

"Uncle Bobby does, when he's mad. He hits Aunt Harriet all the time."

Ian felt his lips press thin.

"Really. And have you seen him hit her? Diane, have you seen Bobby hit anyone, ever?"

Diane frowned, thinking, trying to remember something. The failure emptied her.

"No."

"Did anyone tell you a story about Bobby hitting Harriet?"

Again the pause, and confusion deep as stone.

"No."

"And?"

Diane stared at him, her mouth half open, her eyes lost.

"I think the words we're looking for are 'I'm sorry,'" Ian said. It was the way his father would have said it.

"I'm sorry, Kitty. I'm sorry. I thought..." and Diane shook her head, held out her hands, palms up in a shrug that broke his heart. "I'm sorry, Kitty. I won't do it again ever, I swear. Don't go home, okay?"

Kit, sullen, scowled at the white and blue tile at her feet.

"Please?" Diane said. He could hear in the softness of her voice how much the word had cost. He paused, hoping that Kit would relent, that she would simply take the blow and accept it, that she would believe that Diane would never do it again.

"'Kay," Kit said. Ian's relief was palpable, and he saw it in Diane. His daughter ran over grabbed her friend's hand, pulled her out, back to the room. Ian looked in on them. Diane was showering Kit with affection, flattering her shamelessly, letting her play as many times as she cared to. Diane was showing her belly. And it worked. Kit came back from the edge, and they were best friends again.

He put them both to bed, making them promise unconvincingly not to stay up talking, then went through the house, checking that the doors and windows were all locked, turning off the lights. He ended in the living room, in the overstuffed chair he'd brought from his home when he and Candice first became lovers. The cushions knew the shape of his back. Sitting under a single lamp that was the only light in the house, he closed his eyes for a moment and drank in silence. The book he was reading—a police procedural set in New Orleans—lay closed on his knee. His body was too tired to rest yet, his mind spun too fast by Diane and his isolation and the endless stretch of working at his desk. When he finally did open his book, the story of grotesque murder and alluring voodoo queens was a relief.

Diane walked in on bare feet just as he was preparing to dog-ear the page, check the girls, and crawl into bed. She crossed the room, walking past the pool of light and receding for a moment into the darkness before coming back to him. In her hand was the scrapbook he'd set aside for Flat Diane. Without speaking, she crawled onto his lap, opened the book with a creak of plastic and cheap glued spine, and took out the page they'd just gotten. His sister, her husband. The meaty hand and sausage-thick thumb. His sister's pinched smile. The filthy light.

"I don't want this one in here," Diane said, handing it to him. Her voice was small, frightened. "I don't like Uncle Bobby."

"Okay, sweetie," he said, taking it from her.

She leaned against him now, her arms pressed into her chest, her knees drawn up. He put his arms around her and rocked gently until they were both near to sleep.

It was the moment, looking back, that he would say he understood what Flat Diane had become.

✳

THERE ARE over a dozen photographs in the book now, but this latest addition commands its own page. In it, Candice is sitting at a simple wooden table. Her hair is pulled back in a ponytail that even where it is bound is thick as her forearm. Her eyes slant down at the corners, but her skin is the same tone as Diane's, the oval face clearly the product of the same blood. There is a spider fern hanging above her. The impression is of melancholy and calm and tremendous intimacy. It is not clear who operated the camera.

Flat Diane is in the chair beside her, folded as if she were sitting with her mother. A small, cartoon heart has been added to the paper, though it is not clear by whom.

The real Diane has outstripped her shadow—taller, thinner, more awkward about the knees and elbows. This silhouette is already the artifact of a girl who has moved on, but this is not obvious from the picture. In the scrapbook, the only sign of change is a bend on one corner of Flat Diane's wide paper, a design drawn in the white space over the outlined left shoulder, and the lock of white hair across Candice's forehead.

The letter reads:

Diane—

Flat Diane arrived yesterday. I have to tell you she makes me miss you. You can see she's here with me in my apartment.

I love you very much, Diane. I know that it can't seem like it right now, but please believe me when I say it's true. There is no one in the world more important to me than you are. And I hope that, when your father and I have worked out the paths our souls need to take, we can be together again. Whatever happens, I will always be your mother.

It is signed Candice Calvino, her maiden name.

The other letter is not in the scrapbook. It reads:

Ian—

Christ, Ian, I really don't know what to say. I thought that I could just sit down and write this to you rationally, but I am just so goddam pissed off, I'm not sure that's possible.

This stunt is *exactly* the kind of emotional extortion that made it impossible for me to stay near you. What were you thinking? That you could hold her up, maybe wave her around like a flag, and make me come trotting back—we could just stay together for the children's sake? Our daughter should be more than just the easiest tool for you to get in a dig at me. How could you do this to her?

If you wanted to make me feel guilty or shamed or selfish, well nice job, Ian. You did.

Never use her like this again. If it isn't beneath you, it goddam well should be.

C.

✳

THE HALLWAY outside the school's administrative offices had white stucco walls, linoleum flooring worn by millions of footsteps from thousands of students, harsh fluorescent lighting. An old clock—white face yellow with age—reported twenty minutes before the noon bell would ring, the press of small bodies filling the halls like spring tadpoles. When Ian walked in, straightening his tie, swallowing his dread, his footsteps echoed.

The secretary smiled professionally when he gave her his name, and led him to a smaller room in the back. The placard on the door—white letters on false woodgrain—said that the principal's name was Claude Bruchelli. The secretary knocked once, opened the door, and stepped aside to let Ian pass through a cloud of her cloying perfume and into the office.

The principal rose, stretching out a hand, establishing for Diane that the grownups were together, that they had special rules of respect and courtesy. It was the sort of thing Ian remembered with resentment from when he'd been her age, but he shook the man's hand all the same.

"Thanks for coming, Mr. Bursen. I know it's hard to just leave work like this. But we have a problem."

Diane, sitting on a hardbacked chair, stared at her feet. The way she drummed her heels lightly against the chair legs told him that this was not resentment, but remorse. Ian cleared his throat.

"All right," he said. "What's she done?"

"Mr. Bursen, we have some very strict guidelines from the city about fighting."

"Another fight?"

The principal nodded gravely. It had been at morning recess. Her friend Kit had been adamant that the other girl had started it, but the teacher who had seen it all reported otherwise. No, there had been no injuries beyond a few scratches. This was, however, the third time, which meant a mandatory three-day suspension.

Diane, stone-faced, seemed to be staring at a banner on the wall that blared "We Aim For Excellence! We Expect The Best Of You!"

"All right," Ian said. "I can get her homework for her and she can do it at home."

The principal nodded, but didn't speak. He looked at Ian from under furrowed brows.

"Mr. Bursen, I have to follow the guidelines. And they're good as far as they go, but Diane's anger problems aren't going to go away. I wish you'd reconsider letting Mrs. Birch..."

"No. I'm sorry, no. I've had a certain amount of counseling myself, one time and another. It doesn't do any good to force a child into it."

"Perhaps Diane would choose to," the principal said as if she wasn't there, as if her dark, hard eyes weren't fixed on his wall. Ian shrugged.

"Well, what of it, Diane? Care to see Mrs. Birch?" He'd meant to say it gently, but the tone when it left his mouth sounded more of sarcasm. Diane shook her head. Ian met the principal's gaze.

All the way back home, Diane pressed herself against the car door, keeping as far from Ian as she could. He didn't try to speak, not until he knew which words were in him. Instead, he ran through all the people he could think of who might be able or willing to look after Diane for the duration of her exile.

When, that night, he finally spoke, he did it poorly. They were eating dinner—chicken soup and peanut butter sandwiches. He hadn't spoken, she had sulked. Between them the house had been a bent twig; tension ready to snap.

"I can't afford to take three days off work," he said. "They'll fire me."

Diane shrugged, a movement she inherited from him. Her father, who shrugged a lot of feelings away.

"Di, can you at least tell me what this is all about? Fighting at school. It isn't like you, is it?"

"Lisa started it. She called me a nerd."

"And so you hit her?"

Diane nodded and took a bite of her sandwich. Ian felt the blood rushing into his face.

"Jesus Christ, Di. You can't do this! What...I don't know what you're thinking! I am holding on to this house by a thread. I am working every day for you, and you are being a little brat! I don't deserve this from you, you know that?"

The bowl sailed across the room, soup arcing out behind it. It shattered where it landed. Diane's bowl. Ian went silent. She stood on her chair, making small grunting noises as she tore the sandwich and squeezed the bread and butter into paste.

"You never listen to me! You always take everyone else's side!"

"Diane..."

"When?" she screamed. "Exactly when in all this do *I* start to matter?"

It was her mother's voice, her mother's tone and vocabulary. Ian's chest ached suddenly, and the thought came unbidden, *What has Candice said in front of that drawing?* Diane turned and bolted from the room.

When the shards of their dinner were disposed of, the salt of soup and sweet of sandwich buried alike in the disposal, Ian went to her. In the dark of her room, Diane was curled on her bed. He sat beside her and stroked her hair.

"I didn't do anything wrong," she said, her voice thick with tears. She didn't mean fighting or throwing soup bowls. She meant that she had done nothing to deserve her mother's absence.

"I know, sweetie. I know you didn't."

"I want to see Mrs. Birch."

He felt his hand falter, forced it to keep touching her, keep reassuring her that he was there, that they were a family, that all would be well.

"If you want, sweetie," he said. "We can do that if you want."

He felt her nod. That night, trying to sleep, he thought of every mean-spirited thing he'd ever said to Diane, of every slight and disappointment and failure that he'd added to her burden. Candice's letter—the private one she'd sent to him— rang in his mind. Diane would be confessing all his sins to someone he'd never met, who would be taking confidences from his daughter that he might never know.

For all the weeks and months that he'd silently prayed for someone to help, someone to shoulder part of the burden of Diane's soul, the granting tasted bitter. His fears were unfounded.

The time came, and Mrs. Birch—a thick woman with a pocked face and gentle voice—became a character in Diane's tales of her days. He waited with a sense of dread, but no recriminations came back to him from the school, no letters condemning him as a man and a father. In fact, over the weeks, Diane seemed to become more herself. The routine of fight and reconciliation with Kit, the occasional missive from Flat Diane's latest hosts, the complaints about schoolwork and clothes and how little money he had to spend on her all came almost back to normal. Once, he saw what might have been anger when Diane saw a photograph of her mother. After that he noticed that she had stopped asking when Mommy was coming home. He couldn't have said, if asked, whether the sorrow, the sense of triumph, or the guilt over that sense was the strongest of his reactions.

Everything was fine until the night in February when she woke up screaming and didn't stop.

※

THE PICTURE is cheap—the color balance is off, giving the man's face an unnatural yellow tint. He is in his later twenties, perhaps his early thirties, the presentiment of jowls already plucking the flesh of his jaws. His hair is short and pale. His eyes are blue.

In the picture, Flat Diane has been taped around a wide pillar, her arms and legs bending back out of sight. A long black cloth wraps across where the eyes might be, had Ian drawn them in, a blindfold.

The man who Ian doesn't know, has never met, is caressing a drawn-in breast. His tongue protrudes from his viciously grinning mouth, its tip flickering distance from the silhouette's thigh. He looks not like Satan, but like someone who wishes that he were, someone trying very hard to be.

The writing on the back of the photograph is block letters, written in blue felt-tip.

It reads: Flat Diane has gone astray.

A new photograph comes every week. Some might be amusing to another person, most make him want to retch.

✳

THE BEST trick Hell has to play against its inmates is to whisper to them that this—this now—is the bottom. Nothing can be worse than this. And then to pull the floor away.

"I'm sorry," Ian said, refusing to understand. "I didn't catch that."

Mrs. Birch leaned back, her wide, pitted face tired and impassive. She laced her hands on her desk. The hiss of the heating system was the only sound while she brought herself to break the news again. This time, she took a less direct approach.

"Diane has always had an anger problem. There's no good time to lose your mother, but this stage of development is particularly bad. And I think that accounts for a lot of her long term behaviors. The fighting, the acting out in class, but these *new* issues…"

"Child protective services?" Ian said, able at last to repeat the counselor's statement and plumb the next depth of hell. "You called child protective services?"

"The kind of sudden change we've seen in her—the nightmares, the anxiety attacks… She's in fifth grade, Mr. Bursen. No kid in fifth grade should be having anxiety attacks. When she went to the doctor, you and he and two nurses together couldn't get her to undress, and you say she never had a problem with it before. That kind of sudden change means trauma. Nothing *does* that but trauma."

Ian closed his eyes, the heel of his palm pressed to brow, rubbing deeply. His body shook, but it seemed unconnected to his terrible clarity of mind, like the tremors were something being done to him.

"The Buspar seems to be helping," he said. An idiot change of subject, and not at all to the point, but Mrs. Birch shifted in her chair and went there with him.

"There are a lot of anti-anxiety drugs," she agreed. "Some of them may help. But only with the symptoms, not the problem. And the trauma, whatever it is…it may be something ongoing."

"Christ."

"She's graduating in a few weeks here. Next year's middle school, and I won't be able to see her any more. With CPS, you'll have a caseworker, someone who isn't going to change every time she switches schools. And who knows? Maybe the investigation will help. I'm sorry. About all of this. I really am. But it's the right thing."

Now it was Ian's turn to go silent, to gather himself. Speaking the words was like standing at the edge of a cliff.

"You think I'm fucking my kid."

"No," Mrs. Birch said in the voice of a woman for whom this territory was not new. "But I think somebody is."

Diane waited for him in the outer office, looking smaller than she was, folded in on herself. He forced himself to look at her as she was, and not as he wanted her to be. She forced a smile and raised a hand, sarcastic and sad. Ian knelt at her feet and took her hand, but Diane would not meet his gaze. Mrs. Birch was a presence he felt behind him, but didn't see.

"Sweetie," he said.

Diane didn't look up. He reached out to stroke her hair, but hesitated, pulled back. It was that fear that touching his child would be interpreted as sex that brought home how much they had lost.

"It's going to be okay, sweetie," he said, and Diane nodded, though she didn't believe it. When he stood, she scooped up her book bag and went out with him. In the hallway, with Mrs. Birch still haunting the door to the office, Diane reached up and put her hand in his. It was a thin victory, hardly any comfort at all.

The clouds were close, smelling of rain. He drove home slowly, the sense of disconnection, of unreality, growing as the familiar streets passed by. Diane sat alert but silent until they were almost home.

"Are they going to make me live with Mom?"

A pang of fear so sharp it was hard to differentiate from nausea struck him, but he kept his voice calm. He couldn't let her think they might lose each other.

"Make you? No, sweet. There's going to be someone from the state who's going to want to talk to you, but that's all."

"Okay."

"They're going to ask you questions," he continued, the words leaking from him like air from a pricked balloon. "You just need to tell them the truth. Even if you get embarrassed or someone told you that you shouldn't tell them something, you should tell them the truth."

"Okay."

He pulled into the driveway, their house—Christ, the mortgage payment was a week late already; he had to remember to mail the check tomorrow—looming in the twilight. The lawn was the spare, pale green of spring.

"You should tell me the truth too," he said, amazed by how sane he sounded, how reasonable. "Sweetie? Is there anyone who's doing things to you? Things you don't like?"

"Like am I getting molested?"

Amazing too how old she had become. He killed the engine. There had to be some way to ask gently, some approach to this where he could still treat her like a child, still protect her innocence. He didn't know it, couldn't find it. The rich scent of spring was an insult.

"Are you?" he asked.

Diane's eyes focused on the middle distance, her face a mask of concentration. Slowly, she shook her head, but her hands plucked at the seat, popping the cloth upholstery in wordless distress.

"If something were happening, Di, you could tell me. There wouldn't be anything to be afraid of."

"It's not so bad during the day," she said. "It's at night. It's like I know things...there's things I know and things I can almost remember. But they didn't happen."

"You're sure they didn't?"

A hesitation, but a nod—firm and certain.

"The doctor's going to want to examine you," he said.

"I don't want him too."

"Would it be better with a different doctor?"

"No."

"What if it was a woman? Would that make it easier?"

Diane frowned out the window of the car.

"Maybe," she said softly. Then, "I don't want to be crazy."

"You're not, sweet. You're not crazy. No more than I am."

They ate dinner together, talking about other things, laughing even. A thin varnish of normalcy that Ian felt his daughter clinging to as desperately as he was. Afterwards, Kit called, and Diane retreated to gossip in privacy while Ian cleaned the dishes. He read her to sleep, watching her chest from the corner of his eye until her breath was steady and deep and calm. He left a nightlight glowing, a habit she'd returned to recently.

He sat in the kitchen and slowly, his hands shaking, laid out the pictures of Flat Diane—the ones recently arrived, the ones he hadn't shown her. He shuffled them, rearranged them, spread them out like tarot.

It had been stupid, sending out their real address. Ian saw that now, and twisted the thought to better feel the pain of it.

What if this mad fucker had tracked down Diane because Ian had as good as sent out directions to her...?

But no, he didn't believe that. Or that Tohiro or one of her teachers or some evil pizza delivery man had targeted her. The photographs were too much a coincidence, the timing too precise.

He recalled vividly his art history teacher back at university, back at home in Scotland. The old man had told each of them to bring in a picture of a person they loved—mother, father, brother, lover, pet. And then, he'd told them to gouge out the eyes. The shocked silence was the first moment of his lecture on the power of image, the power of art. These were dumb bits of paper, but each of them that touched pen-tip to a beloved eye knew—did not believe, but *knew*—that the pictures were connected with the people they represented.

Ian had sent his daughter's soul voyaging. He hadn't even considered the risks. It was worse than sending only their address; he might as well have delivered her, trussed and helpless. And now...

And now Flat Diane had gone astray.

With a boning knife, he cut out the blond man's blue eyes, but he felt the effort's emptiness. Nothing so poetic for him. Instead, he took the envelopes to his study, turned on his computer, and scanned in the bastard's face. When it was saved, he dropped it into email and then got on the phone.

"Hello?" Candice said from a thousand miles away. Her voice was uncertain—wondering, he supposed, who would be calling her so late at night.

"It's Ian. Check your email."

The pause would have been strained if he'd cared more. If this had still been about the two of them and what they'd had and lost and why. Only it wasn't and the hesitation at the far end of the line only made him impatient.

"Ian, what's this about?"

"Flat Diane, actually. I've had a letter for her. Several. I need to know who the man is in the pictures."

Another pause, but this one different. Ian could hear it in the way she breathed. Intimacy can lead to this, he supposed. Teach you how to read a woman by her breath on the far end of a phone line.

"You already know," he said. "Don't you."

"My computer's in another room. I can call you back."

"I'll wait," he said.

She was back within five minutes, the hard plastic fumbling as she picked the handset back up giving way to her voice.

"I'm sorry, Ian," she said. "This is my fault. His name is Stan Lecky. He...he was a neighbor of mine when I came out here. A friend."

"A lover?"

"No, Ian. Just a friend. But...he started saying things that made me...We had a falling out. I got a restraining order. He moved away eight or nine months ago."

"He was the one who took the picture of you, wasn't he? The picture of you and Flat Diane."

"Yes."

Ian considered the envelope that had contained the latest atrocity. The postmark was from Seattle. Stan Lecky in Seattle. And a photo of him, no less. Certainly it couldn't be so hard with all that to find an address.

"She hasn't seen that, has she?" Candice asked. He didn't know how best to answer.

Ian slept in on Saturday, pretending that the dead black sleep and the hung-over exhaustion of his body was related somehow to luxury. It had been years since he'd been able to sleep past six a.m. He had Diane to feed and dress and shuffle off to school. He had his commute. His body learned its rhythms, and then it held to them. But Saturday, Ian rose at ten.

Diane was already on the couch, a bowl of cereal in her lap, her eyes clouded. Her skin seemed paler, framed by the darkness of her hair. Bags under her eyes like bruises. Ian recalled Victorian death pictures—photographs of the dead kept as mementos, or perhaps to hold a bit of the soul that had fled. He made himself toast and tea, and sat beside his daughter.

On the TV, girls three or four years older than Diane were talking animatedly about their boyfriends. They wore tight jeans and midriff tops, and no one thought it odd. No one wondered whether this was the path of wisdom. He found himself wondering what Diane made of it, but didn't ask. There were more pressing issues.

"How'd you sleep?" he asked.

"Okay."

"More nightmares?"

She shrugged, her gaze fixed on the screen. Ian nodded, accepting the tacit yes. He finished his toast, washed down the last of his tea, smacked his lips.

"I have to go out for a little while. Errands."

"Want me to come too?"

"No, you stay here. I won't be long."

Diane looked away and down. It made his heart ache to see it. Part of that was knowing that he'd once again failed to protect her from some little pain, and part a presentiment of the longer absence she would have to endure. He leaned over and kissed the crown of her head where the bones hadn't been closed the first time he'd held her.

"I'll be right back, kiddo," he murmured, and she smiled wanly, accepting his half-apology. And yet, by the time he had his keys, she was lost again in the television, gone into her own world as if he had never been there.

Tohiro was sitting in his driveway, a lawnmower partially disassembled before him. He nodded as Ian came up the path, but neither rose nor turned back to his work. Ian squatted beside him.

"I don't know why I think I can do this," Tohiro said. "Every time I start, it's like I don't remember how poorly it went the time before. And by the time it comes back to me, it's too late, the thing's already in pieces."

"Hard. I do the same thing myself."

Tohiro nodded.

"I need a favor," Ian said. "I have to go away for a bit. Diane's mother and I...there are some things we need to discuss. I might be away for week, perhaps. Perhaps less. I was wondering if..."

It choked him. Asking for help had never been a strong suit, nor lying. The two together were almost more than he could manage. Tohiro frowned and leaned forward, picking up a small, grease-covered bit of machinery and dropping it thoughtfully into a can of gasoline.

"Are you sure that's wise?" Tohiro asked. "The timing might look..."

He knew then. Diane had told Kit, and Kit her parents; nothing could be more natural.

"I don't have the option," Ian said.

"This is about what's happening to Diane?"

"Yes."

Ian's knees were starting to ache a bit, but he didn't move, nor did Tohiro. The moment stretched, then:

"It might be better if Kit invited her," Tohiro said. "If it were a treat—a week-long slumber party—it could mask the sting."

"Do you think she would?"

"For Diane? Kit would learn to fly if Diane asked her. Girls."

"I'd appreciate it. More than I can say."

"You are putting a certain faith in me."

Tohiro met his gaze, expression almost challenging.

"It isn't you," Ian said, softly. "I'm fairly sure I know who it is."

"I see."

Ian shrugged, aware as he did so that it was a mirror of his daughter's, and that Tohiro would understand its eloquence as Ian had understood Diane's.

"I'll let you know when it's going to happen," Ian said. "I can't go before the CPS home visit, but it won't be long after that. And if you ever need the same of me, only say so."

The man shifted under Ian's words, uneased. Dark eyes looked up at him and then away. Tohiro stuck fingers into the gasoline, pulling out the shining metal that the fuel had cleaned.

"That brings up something. Ian...Anna and I would rather not have Kit stay over with Diane. I know it isn't you, that you wouldn't...but the stakes are high, and I can't afford being wrong."

Ian rocked back. A too-wide rictus grin forced its way onto his face—he could feel the skin pulling.

"I'm sorry, Ian, it's just..."

"It's the right thing," he forced out, ignoring the anger and shock, pushing it down. "If I thought for a minute that it was you...or even if I only weren't certain, then..."

Ian opened his hands, fingers spread; the gesture a suggestion of open possibility, a euphemism for violence. It was something they both understood. Men protected their children. Men like the two of them, at least.

Ian pulled himself up, his knees creaking. Kit, in the window, caught sight of him and waved. She was lighter than Diane, but not as pretty, Ian thought.

"I'll call later," Ian said.

"Do. I'll talk with Kit. We'll arrange things. But Ian? Diane needs you."

"I know she does. I don't want to leave her. Especially now, I just..."

"I didn't mean don't go," Tohiro said. "I meant don't get caught."

The home visit was less than he expected. Two women in casual businesswear appeared at the appointed hour. One took Diane away, the other asked him profoundly personal questions—Why had his wife left him? Had he been in therapy? Did he have a police record? Could he describe his relationship with his daughter? Only the last of these pushed him to tears. The woman was sympathetic, but unmoved; a citizen of a nation of tears from innocent and guilty alike.

She arranged a time and place for Diane to see a doctor—a woman doctor and Ian hadn't even had to ask. He promised that Diane would be there, and she explained the legal ramifications if she were not. The other woman appeared with Diane at her side. Diane's face was grey with exhaustion. Ian shook their hands, thanked them explicitly for coming, implicitly for not taking his child from him.

When they had gone, Diane went out to the back steps, looking out over a yard gone to seed—long grass and weeds. Her head rested in her hands. Ian sat beside her.

"Not so bad, was it?" he asked.

"She asked me a lot of questions," Diane said. "I don't know if I answered them all right."

"Did you tell her the truth?"

"I think so."

"Only think?"

Diane's brow furrowed as she looked at the horizon. Her shoulders hunched forward.

"She asks if things happened. And sometimes I think they did, but then I can't remember. After a while I start getting scared."

"It's like you're living a life you don't know about," Ian said, and she nodded. He put an arm around her shoulders, and she leaned in to him, trembling and starting to cry. Her sobs wracked her thin body like vomiting. Ian, holding her, wept.

"I'm not okay, daddy," she wailed to his breast. "I'm not okay. I'm not okay."

"You will be, sweetie. You will."

✳

THE PICTURE is cropped. In the original, things had been happening as unnatural to paper as they would be to a child. In this version, only the man's chest above the nipples, his shoulders, his face, his smug expression. These are all the details that matter. In this photograph, he could be anyone, doing anything. It is a headshot, something to put down on a bar or store counter, the sort of photograph that seems to fit perfectly with the phrase "I'm looking for someone; maybe you've seen him."

The original photo has obscenities and suggestions written on it. There is no writing on this copy, no note to accompany it. Nothing that will tie it back to Ian, should the police find it and not him.

✳

HE HAD driven to Seattle—a two-day trip—in a day and a half. Flying would have been faster, but he'd taken his pistol out of storage. Driving with a handgun was easy; flying impossible or if not impossible, not worth doing.

He arrived in the city late at night and called Diane from a payphone using a card he'd bought with cash. She was fine. School was boring. Kit was a butthead. Her voice was almost normal—if he knew her less, he might have mistaken it. He was her father, though, and he knew what she sounded like when things were okay and when she only wanted them to be. They didn't talk about the nightmares. He told her he loved her, and she evaded, embarrassed. With the handset back in its cradle, the gun in his jacket pocket pulling the fabric down like a hand on his shoulder, Ian stood in the rain, the cool near-mist soaking him. In time, he gathered himself together enough to find a hotel and a bed to lay in while his flesh hummed from exhaustion and the road.

Finding Lecky took all the next day and part of the night, but he did it. The morning sun gave the lie to the city's grey reputation—clouds of perfect white stretched, thinned, vanished, reformed against a perfect blue sky. Nature ignoring Ian's desperation. The kids spare changing on the street corners avoided his gaze.

It was early, the morning rush hour still a half hour from starting. Ian didn't want the beast to go off to work, didn't want to spend a day waiting for the confrontation. He wanted it over now.

The house was in a bad part of town, but the lawn was trim, the windows clean. Moss stained the concrete walk, and the morning paper lay on the step, wrapped in dewy plastic. Ian picked it up, shaking the drops from it, and then rang the doorbell. His breath was shaking. The door opened and the beast appeared, a cup of coffee in one hand.

There was no glimmer of recognition, no particular sense of confusion or unease. Here, Ian thought, was a man with a clear conscience. A man who had done no wrong.

"I need to talk to you," Ian said, handing the man his newspaper.

"I'm sorry. Do I know you?"

"No. But we have business in common. We have people in common, I think. May I come in?"

The man frowned down at Ian and put down the paper.

"I'm sorry," the beast said, smiling as he stepped back, preparing to close the door. "I have to get to work here, and really I don't want whatever you're selling. Thanks, though."

"I've come for Flat Diane."

The man's expression shifted—surprise, chagrin, anger all in the course of a single breath. Ian clamped his hand on the butt of his pistol, his finger resting against the trigger.

"Don't pretend you don't know what I'm talking about," Ian said. "I have the pictures."

The beast shook his head, defensive and dismissive at the same time.

"Okay," the man said. "Okay, look, so it was a bad joke. All right. I mean, it's not like anyone got hurt, right?"

"What do you know about it?"

Something in Ian's voice caught his attention. Pale blue eyes fixed on him, the first hint of fear behind them. Ian didn't soften. His heart was tripping over like he'd been running, but his head felt very calm.

"No one got hurt," the man said. "It's just paper. So maybe it was a little crude. It was just a joke, right? You're, like, Diane's dad? Look, I'm sorry if that was a little upsetting, but…"

"I saw what you did to her."

"To who?" The eyes were showing their fear, their confusion.

"My daughter."

"I never *touched* your daughter."

"No?"

It was a joy, stripping his certainty away, seeing the smug, leering face confused and frightened. Ian leaned in.

"Tell you what. Give me Flat Diane," he said, "and I might let you live."

The panic in the pale eyes was joyous, but even in his victory, Ian felt the hint that it was too much; he'd gone too far.

"Sure," the beast said, nodding. "No, really, sure. Come on, I'll…"

And he tried to slam the door. Ian had known it was coming, was ready for it. His foot blocked the closing door and he pulled the gun from his pocket. The beast jumped back, lost his balance, toppled. The coffee fanned out behind him and splashed on the hardwood floor as Ian kicked the door closed behind him.

The beast was blinking, confused. His hands were raised, not in surrender, but protection, as if his fingers might deflect a bullet. A radio was playing—morning show chatter. Ian smelled bacon grease on the air.

"Please," the beast said. "Look, it's going to be okay, guy. Just no guns. All right? No guns."

"Where is she?"

"Who?"

"Flat Diane!" Ian yelled, pleased to see the beast flinch.

"It's not here anymore. Seriously. Seriously, it's gone. Joke over. Honestly."

"I don't believe you."

"Look, it's a long story. There were some things that happened and it just made sense to get rid of it, you know? Let it go. It was only supposed to be a joke. You know Candice…"

Ian shook his head. He felt strange; his mind was thick as cotton and yet perfectly lucid.

"I'm not leaving without her," he said.

"It's not *here!*" the beast shouted, his face flushed red. He rolled over, suddenly facing the back of the house. Running. With a feeling like reaching out to tap the fleeing man's shoulder, Ian raised the gun and fired. The back of the beast's head bloomed like a rose, and he fell.

Oh Jesus, Ian thought. And then, a moment later, *I couldn't have made that shot if I'd tried.*

He walked forward, pistol trained on the unmoving shape, but there was no need. The beast was dead. He'd killed him. Ian stood silently, watching the pool of blood seep across the floor. There was less than he'd thought. The morning show announcers laughed at something. Outside, a semi drove by, rattling the windows. Ian put the gun in his pocket, ignoring the heat.

He hadn't touched anything, not with his hands. There were no fingerprints. But he didn't have Flat Diane. He had to search the place. He had to hurry. Perhaps the beast kept plastic gloves. The kind you use for housework.

He searched the bedroom, the bath. The kitchen where half an egg was growing cold and solid on its plate. And then the room in the back. The room from the pictures. He went though everything—the stacks of pornography, the camera equipment. He didn't look away, no matter how vile the things he found. Rape porn. Children being used. Other things. Worse. But not his daughter.

He sat on the edge of the bathtub, head in his hands, when the voice came. The house was a shambles. Flat Diane wasn't there, or if she was, she was too well hidden. He didn't know what to do. The doorbell chimed innocently and a faint voice came.

"Stan?" it said. A woman's voice. "Stan are you in there? It's Margie."

Ian stood and walked. He didn't run. He stepped over the corpse, calmly out the back door, stuffing the rubber gloves into his pockets as he went. There was an alleyway, and he opened the gate and stepped out into it. He didn't run. If he ran, they'd know he was running from something. And Diane needed him, didn't she. Needed him not to get caught.

Ian didn't stop to retrieve his things from the hotel; he walked to his car, slipped behind the wheel, drove. Twenty minutes east of Klamath Falls, he pulled to the side, walked to a tree, and leaning against it vomited until he wept.

"I didn't mean to," he said through his horror. "Christ, I didn't mean to."

He hadn't called Diane from his room. He hadn't given anyone his name. He'd even found a hotel that took cash. Of course he'd fucking meant to.

"I didn't mean to," he said.

He slept that night at a rest stop, bent uncomfortably across the back seat. In his dreams, he saw the moment again and again; felt the pistol jump; heard the body strike wood. The pistol jumped; the body struck the floor. The pale head, round as an egg, cracked open. The man fled, heels kicking back behind him; the pistol jumped.

Morning was sick. A pale sun in an empty sky. Ian stretched out the vicious kinks in his back, washed his face in the restroom sink, and drove until nightfall.

He hadn't found Flat Diane, but he couldn't go back for her—not now. Maybe later, when things cooled down. But by then she could have been thrown away or burned or cut to pieces. And he couldn't guess what might happen to Diane when her shadow was destroyed—freedom or death or something entirely else. He didn't want to think about it. The worst was over, though. The worst had to be over, or else he didn't think he could keep breathing.

Tohiro and Anna's house glowed in the twilight, windows bright and cheerful and warm and normal. He watched them from the street, his back knotted from driving, the car ticking as it cooled. Tohiro passed by the picture window, his expression calm, distant and slightly amused. Anna was in the kitchen, the back of her head moving as her hands worked at something; washing, cutting, wringing—there was no way to tell. Somewhere in there, Kit and Diane played the games they always did. The pistol jumped; the body fell. Ian started the car, steadied his hands on the wheel, then killed the engine and got out.

Tohiro's eyebrows rose a fraction and a half-smile graced his mouth when he opened the door.

"Welcome back," Tohiro said, stepping back to let him in. "We weren't expecting you until tomorrow. Things went better than you thought?"

"Things went faster."

Curiosity plucked at the corners of Tohiro's eyes. Ian gazed into the house, willing away the questions that begged to be asked. Tohiro closed the door.

"You look..." he began.

Ian waited. *Like shit.* Or maybe *pounded.* The silence stretched and he glanced over. Tohiro's face was a soft melancholy. Ian nodded, barely moving, half asking him to finish, half daring him.

"You look older."

"Yeah, well. You know. Time."

A shriek and the drumming of bare feet and Diane had leapt into his arms. His spine protested the weight. Ian held her carefully, like something precious. Then, as if she'd suddenly remembered that they weren't alone, she drew back, tried to make it all seem casual.

"Hey," she said.

"Hey. You been good?"

Diane shrugged—an *I guess* gesture.

"We were just about to have supper," Tohiro said. "If you'd like to join us?"

Ian looked at Diane. Her face was impassive, blank, but at the edges there were the touches invisible to anyone else, anyone who didn't know her as he did.

"I think I'd rather just roll on home," Ian said. "That good by you, sweetie?"

"Sure," she said, upbeat enough that he knew it had been her fondest wish. He let her ride him to the car, piggyback.

That night, they both suffered nightmares. It struck Ian, as he calmed Diane from hers and waited for his own to fade, that there would be more nights like this; screams from her or from him, then warm milk and nightlights and empty talk that gave the evil some time to fade. That if they were *lucky* there would be many more. Nothing more would happen to Flat Diane; justice would not come to call for him. It was the best he could hope for.

"It's okay," he whispered to her as she began to drowse. Curled into her blanket, her breath came deeper, more regular. "It's over. It's over, sweetie. It's all right."

He didn't add that just being over didn't mean it hadn't changed everything forever, or that some things don't stop just because they've ended. Or that a girl set voyaging takes her own chances, and no father's love—however profound—can ever call her back. Those weren't the sorts of things you said when all you had to offer your child were comfort and hope.

THE BEST MONKEY

HOW DO MEN CHOOSE the women they're attracted to? How do they fall into bed with one girl and not another? It feels like kismet. Karma. Fate. It feels like love. Is it a particular way of laughing? A vulnerability in their tone of voice? A spiritual connection? Something deeper?

All the studies say it's hip-to-waist ratio.

✳

THE MAYOR of mow-gah-DEE-shoo said today that she will no longer TAH-luh-rate the—

"Jimmy?"

Harriet stood in the doorway, beanstalk thin and world-weary. I put down the keyboard. My back ached.

"Herself wants to see you," she said.

"I'm transcribing next hour's blinkcast for—"

"I know. I'm on it. Go."

I shrugged and clicked the icon that transferred my work environment onto her screen. My work shifted sideways, my personal defaults—email, IM, voxnet, and a freeware database spelunker that had been the hot new thing a year ago and was now hopelessly outdated—falling into place behind it. I closed the notebook with a snap. Harriet was already gone. I heard her keystrokes as I passed her office.

Herself's office was the largest on the floor, ten feet by twelve with a window that overlooked the alley. The desk was Lucite neo-futurist kitsch. When I was young, we really thought the world was going to look like that. Now they manufactured it to poke fun at an old man's childhood dreams. My greatest comfort was that forty years down the line, their kids were gonna do the same to them.

The latest Herself looked up at me. Sandy hair swept up past her eyes. She wore the latest style in businesswear. It looked to me like something my grandmother would have worn, but with a self-tailoring neural net about as smart as a cockroach.

Herself was young enough to be my kid even if I'd started late. She was also my boss, and on her way up past people like me and Harriet. I sat in the cloth mesh visitor's chair. The air smelled like potting soil and plastic.

"Jimmy," she said. "Good. Look, I've got a new project. Top priority stuff. You in?"

Depends, I wanted to say.

"Sure," I said.

"Unpack Fifth Layer," she said.

One of the things I'd come to hate was the constantly changing jargon. Every six months, it was a new Him or Herself spouting whatever the bleeding edge had been saying when they graduated college. As if *unzip* or *'rize* or *infodump me* were somehow better than *tell me what you know.*

"Fifth Layer's a constellation of fleshware and financial firms," I said. "In some trouble for anti-trust violations, but rich enough not to care much. World leader in paradigm shifts. I don't know more than anyone on the street."

"Roswell hypothesis?"

"I don't buy it," I said.

"Reverse engineering alien tech not clicky enough?"

Clicky meant interesting this month.

"Not plausible enough," I said. "But you don't pay me to believe things. I can write it that way if you want it."

"No, that's good. Vid this."

She mimed a few keystrokes, the computer interpreting what they would have been had a keyboard existed. A section of wall off to my left turned on, a video playback buffering up. I leaned back, the mesh beneath me accommodating my lower spine.

The recording was poor, jiggling like Dogme 95. A bar. Black wood and brown leather. I recognized the woman sitting in the booth before we were close enough to hear her. I'd have known her voice too.

"Three people," Elaine said. "Jude Hammer, Eric Swanson, and you. We should give you all medals."

"You're drunk, Elaine," the swarthy man across the booth from her said.

"Yes, I am," Elaine said, then turned to smile up above the camera at whatever servista had been wearing it. Her hair had gone white like snow, and her smile cut deeper at the corners of her mouth. "I am drunk. Very, very drunk. And I am very, very rich."

"Can I get you anything?" the servista asked, his voice made low by contact with the mic.

"No, I have everything," Elaine said. "Thanks to Jude, Eric, and Safwan, I've got it all."

"*Elaine.*"

"Except discretion," Elaine said with a little bow.

The playback stopped. I looked over at Herself.

"Elaine Salvati," I said. "Head of something or other at Fifth Layer."

"Being indiscreet," Herself said.

"The other one? The guy in the booth?"

"Safwan Cádir," Herself said. "Mathematician. Works for Fifth Layer. Positron emission modeling. Biometrics. Wet stuff."

I shrugged.

"Okay," I said. "You want it transcribed?"

"I want it explained. No one else has the file. We're going to be the point of origin on this one. We're taking the site up from accretor to source."

We're going to start producing news rather than just filtering it, and we're going to start with a scoop by following up on what appears to be a telling mention of names in a public place where even Fifth Layer's pet lawyers can't argue an expectation of privacy.

"Investigative journalism," I said and whistled low. "I didn't think people did that anymore."

"I'm old-school," Herself said. "Still in?"

I sat in silence for a few seconds.

"I used to know her," I said. "When we were about your age. You know that I used to know Elaine Salvati."

"It's why you're here," Herself said.

✳

GO BACK thirty years. Put the ice sheets back in place. Resurrect a couple billion people and a few hundred million species. Price milk about the same as gasoline. And there we were, in a different bar. Different people. My hair was black, Elaine's was dirty blond. I was a sociology major, she was political science with an eye on law school. The television was still a countable number of individually streamed channels. Summer sun peeked in at the windows, throwing golden shadows across the walls.

Another woman sat just down the way, something clear and dangerous-looking in her glass. My eyes kept shifting to her, the way her dress clung to her, cupping her breasts. I wanted to listen to Elaine, but I couldn't stop watching the other girl. Some things don't change.

"So they used steroids," Elaine said. "So what?"

"You mean apart from it's cheating."

"Why is it cheating?"

"Because they have a bunch of rules and one of them is don't use steroids?"

Elaine waved the comment away.

"It's a stupid rule. They're athletes. It's a business where they're paid to be stronger. There's a way to get stronger. They do it. What's the problem?"

The woman shifted, her skirt riding a few inches up her thigh. I took a deep breath and tried to remember the question.

"Apart from rectal bleeding, unpredictable rage, and shrunken testicles?"

"That's a trade-off," Elaine said. "They also make more money in a season than you and I are likely to do. More than someone who doesn't use steroids, for damn sure. They're grown-ups. Let them decide if it's worth it."

"You're not serious."

"I am," she said, slapping her hand against the bar. "Why is it okay to make yourself stronger by lifting weights, but not by injecting steroids? We're paying these guys huge money to push for excellence, just don't push too *hard*?"

I drank the last of my bourbon, ice cubes clicking against my teeth, and waved at the bartender for another. A slick young man in a suit slid up to the bar at the woman's side. Her sudden smile lit the room.

"So what?" I said. "Take off all the restrictions? Just let anyone do anything they want?"

"It would be a real contest then," Elaine said. "You want to see the limits of human excellence? Then pull out the stops and see what happens. It'd be a hell of a show."

"They're using *drugs*," I said.

"So are we," she said, lifting her glass. "Theirs make them strong. Ours make us careless. Seriously. Look at the argument. Saying you need to get a girl a little tipsy in order to get her into bed is just like saying you have to shoot steroids in order to get into the major leagues."

"I don't need to get girls drunk," I said, too loud. The new man glanced over at us. His lover had her hand on his knee. I looked away, and then back. She was still beautiful. It never hurt just to *look*. Elaine caught me, followed my glance, rolled her eyes.

"You might want to try it," she said. "But think about it. We take a sick person up to normal, and that's good, but we take a well person up past normal into greatness, and that's bad?"

"I don't want to see chemists competing on the ball field for who has the best juice. I want to see something from the players," I said. "Those records? They aren't from inside the person. They're from outside."

"It doesn't matter where it comes from," she said. "Just if it works."

The way she spun the words brought me to realize she was coming on to me. I was always a little thick about that particular negotiation.

That was the first night we slept together, both too intoxicated to recall it clearly in the morning. A week after that, we were lovers. Six months after that we were friends. Thirty years later, I sat on the bus, notebook open as the afternoon traffic slid silently along the street. The windows were canted back, and the gentle breeze held nothing of the windstorm predicted for that evening. Elaine, who had never gone to law school, was the operations manager of Fifth Layer's research arm. I was what passed for a journalist, filtering stories from primary sources and translating them into in-house phonetics for hourly blinkcasts and daily drop feeds.

I spooled through the précis of Fifth Layer. Concatenating data was what I did all day, every day. I was pretty good. Breakthroughs in encryption. Computing. Engine design. Prosthetics. The last two Nobel prizes in physics had gone to teams with Fifth Layer employees on them. Everything they touched turned to gold, but the consensus was that it was a strange gold. There was something common to all the inventions, patents, breakthroughs. The Fifth Layer Look. It wasn't something that the peer reviews could identify, except that they seemed subtly wrong. They were elegant solutions, they were functional, and they were ugly.

And thus the Roswell Hypothesis.

It doesn't matter where it comes from, Elaine said. Just if it works.

The bus lurched, servos whirring almost louder than birdsong. It occurred to me that I was probably riding on Fifth Layer designs. I shifted in my seat and squinted out, trying to judge how long before we reached my stop and I could try walking the kinks out of my back. Or, failing that, how long before I could get home and take a couple pills for the pain. Ten minutes, I guessed. High to the north, thin clouds scudded fast in the upper atmosphere, the only sign of trouble coming.

Safwan Cádir.

Eric Swanson.

Jude Hammer.

Fifth Layer was the most innovative, off-center, powerful corporate intelligence in the world. And if Elaine was to be believed, it was all because of a mathematician, a choreographer, and a pedophile.

✳

"COME IN," he said. "Who did you say you were with?"

I explained who I worked for, that we were moving into primary source and out of accretion, and didn't talk about Fifth Layer or Elaine. Not to start. While I filled the air with my preprogrammed noise, I tried to make sense of the apartment.

Eric Swanson's place was small, even by the standards of the city. Two blankets were neatly folded on the back of a couch that clearly pulled out to become his bed. The kitchen was too small for two people to stand in. The smell of old coffee and shaving cream danced at the back of my nose like a sneeze that wouldn't come. The windows were laced with wire against the flying debris of the storms; deep gouges in the plastic caught the light and threw rainbows the shape of scars on the far wall. The only art was an old poster, lovingly framed, of a dance performance at Carnegie Hall from a decade and a half ago. The woman whirling on the print was beginning to yellow.

I had the sense that there was something wrong about the place—the couch placed poorly on the wall, the print too close to the corner. Functional, but ugly. Fifth Layer Look or poor decorating. I couldn't tell.

I came to the end of my prepared speech and smiled.

"And you're starting off with a piece on mid-level landfill reclamations?" he said, his arms crossed. "That's all I do these days. Reclaim refined metals from last century's dumps."

"Dance history, actually," I said. "Turns out American dance history is an emerging fetish market in Brazil. We're aiming for it."

"Well," he said. "Keep moving. I haven't been part of that scene in forever."

"That was one of yours?" I asked, nodding to the print. Something softened in the man's eyes. He looked at the poster fondly, seeing the past.

"Yeah," he sighed. "The last good time."

"Want to tell me about it?"

Eric's store of liquor was better than I expected. He gave me vodka so cold I could have poured water in it to make ice. He mixed in a little gin and leaned against one wall while he talked. The scene, he called it. Room enough in the world for two or three top-level choreographers who weren't slaved to popstar porn gods or translating children's programming for live performance or—worst of all—second-in-command to a theatrical director. Only two or three who could do their own work with the best talent and unfettered by anyone else's vision. He moved his hands when he spoke; he smiled. It was like watching a man remember being in love.

He was a little drunk. And, I hoped, a little careless.

"I was King Shit after the Carnegie show," he said. "Seriously, I pissed rosewater. All the top tier were scared out of their minds of me."

CAR-nah-gee. SEAR-ee-us-lee. ROSE-wah-ter. It was a habit.

"Must have been great," I said.

"It was like doing cocaine for the first time, only it never wore off and your heart didn't pop."

"So what happened?"

"Gloria Lynn Auslander," he said.

"Another choreographer?" I asked, and when Eric snorted derision, "A lover?"

"A great fucking rack," he said, bitterly. "I never even met her. I just watched her tryout tapes. I'd been dancing professionally for fifteen years, and training for eight before that. I *knew* bodies. I *understood* them. There was no mystery for me, but there was something about this one fucking girl.

I mean here I am, a professional, and all I can do is stare at her tits. It was humiliating. And the time pressure. And the performance anxiety. Look, I know how it seems from here, but back then, it really mattered. I was at the top of my game, and the whole world was watching me with sharpened teeth. The follow-up had to be better. Bigger. Perfect. I had to show I wasn't a one-shot. And I was looking at this girl trying to decide if she was the right one for the part, and I couldn't *tell*."

"So what did you do?"

He raised an eyebrow and swallowed half a glass worth of liquor at once.

"I changed my mind," he said.

The process cost the equivalent of a year's work, lasted a long weekend at a clinic in Mexico, and ended Eric Swanson's career. It should have been simple.

"It wasn't turning off my cock," Eric said. "It was just damping out that link between my visual cortex and Little Eric, you know? Take off the sexual response. Get rid of that little kick you get when you see a perfect face."

"Or a perfect rack," I said, and regretted it immediately. I put down the vodka, resolving not to drink any more. Eric barely heard me.

"I can't tell you how excited I was. I was going to see pure movement. None of the distraction, just the form and the sweep. The power and the glory. It wouldn't even keep me from having a sex life, it was just that looking at women wouldn't turn me on. They'd have to touch me or talk dirty or, God, whatever. I didn't care. It was a small trade-off."

"So what went wrong?"

"Nothing," he said. "It worked perfectly. I was euphoric. I didn't cast Auslander. She was good, but her left ankle wobbled. And I was high as a kite. I'd never understood how much I'd suppressed sexual reactions until I didn't have to work at it anymore. And the bodies. Ah, God. It was like seeing for the first time. I was working twenty hour days. The poor bastards in the troupe wanted to kill me. It was the best, most innovative, most interesting thing I'd ever done."

"It tanked," I said.

"Sank like a stone in the ocean," he said. "No one liked it. That's all it took. I had a couple more gigs after that, but it was gone. Dance is apparently all about sex. When you take it out, there's nothing left."

I left the apartment half an hour later with a few anecdotes about the scene that I would never use in any story. I'd brought up Fifth Layer twice, and been met with a blank incomprehension that didn't surprise me. If Eric had been there at the birth, he wouldn't be eking out a living digging through our ancestors' trash. He wasn't a conspirator; he was a symptom.

Back at my own apartment, I sat on my own blue couch and stared out at the sunset. My system played Duke Ellington remixes and boiled a bowl of deep yellow rice. I didn't drink any more liquor. I was done being careless for the day.

I wondered whether the secret of Fifth Layer's success could be that simple. A cadre of semi-castrated researchers toiling away without looking down the bar at someone. And the long human tradition of dance was only about sex. Not even sex and something more; just sex. Ballet, tap, jazz, everything was just one long primate fan dance. Take away the dirty thoughts behind it, and it all fell apart.

I didn't buy it.

✳

"HELLO?" I said, not entirely sure why I was speaking.

"Wake up, Jimmy," Herself said. "There's a problem."

I turned on the bedside lamp. It was a little after two a.m. I shook my head, trying to clear it.

"What's up?" I asked. I expected her to say that the blinkcasts were down or someone had called in sick.

"The clip of Salvati popped up on a server in Guam. I had it shut down, but there may be other copies. Someone's pirated us. Are you anywhere with it?"

"Yeah," I said. "I don't know where yet, but I've got something. There's a clinic in Mexico. I'm trying to track its funding, maybe a staff listing, but so far—"

"This is top priority," she said. "I need you on this now."

My bedroom seemed small in the darkness. Like the world outside was squeezing it.

"Okay," I said. "But I'm human. I've got to sleep."

"I'm sending over some sweetener," she said. Sweetener meant amphetamines this month. I recognized the tone in her voice. She was speeding. That couldn't be good. "This story's not going to take more than a week is it?"

Sleep when you're finished or I'll find someone else to do it. Someone who wants it more.

Fuck off, I wanted to say. It's my fucking liver you're playing with.

"Not even a week," I said. "I'm on it."

The system made the near-subliminal chime of a voxnet connection dropping. I got up, bathed, got dressed. I was too old to start a new career, and Herself was right. Accretors could sleep. Reporters did what they needed in order to get the story. I was starting to resent my promotion.

The amphetamines arrived by courier, a kid in his twenties with perfectly cut muscles, jittering eyes, and a bicycle built for a war zone. He looked like shit and radiated heat like he was burning. By the time I'd signed for the package, he was twitching to get moving again. I figured he was probably pretty good at his job.

The train took me south and east on a soft cushion of electromagnetic fields. I was a hundred miles from home before the eastern sky paled, the drugs humming in my veins. I felt like a million bucks. I felt smart and sharp and young. I felt like someone else, and I didn't like it. I stared at my notebook, but my mind was moving in ten different directions. Induced ADHD. Great plan.

I knew it would end with Elaine. Herself knew too, or she wouldn't have tapped me for the job. Now, with time short, I was tempted to go straight to the source. I pretty much knew what the pedophile was going to be now. He'd had his mind changed too, and been cured hallelujah, amen. Might as well let him go free, because he wasn't that man anymore. I had nothing to learn from him.

I could go to her now. Her or Safwan Cádir. Confront them. Get them to crack. The confidence came from the speed, and knowing that made me careful, made me not skip steps. Made me go see the pedophile.

Sex. Beauty. Elaine. Alien technology. The Fifth Layer Look.

There was something there. A rant she'd had, back in the day. I closed my eyes, my mind leaping around in my skull like an excited monkey, and tried to remember.

※

"YOU HAVE to have beauty," she said.

"Yes, I do."

She cuffed me gently on the head.

We were at her place. The boxspring and mattress were on the floor, nestled into a corner. We were nestled in it. Christmas holidays, and she'd be going back to her family in a couple days. I lay against her, our skin touching, and the soft afterglow of sex fading like the last gold of sunset.

"I don't mean *you* you," she said. "I mean *we* you. You have to have a sense of beauty or you can't be…I don't know. Alive. You can't function."

I sighed and sat up. Our clothes were strewn on the thin brown carpet, my jeans and her blouse still twined around each other. Elaine pulled the blanket up over her breasts and stared at the ceiling, shaking her head.

"Still thinking about the art history final?" I asked.

"I should've just said that we have to *have* a sense of beauty. I mean not from a woo-woo spiritual it-makes-your-soul-better perspective. I should have gone all cognitive science on him. I should've said that ants have to have a sense of beauty. It's basic."

"Yes, because placing the aesthetic impulse in insects with eight neurons would make you a lot of friends in art history," I said. We were early enough in the affair that my sarcasm was still charming. It wouldn't always be.

"I even know the example," she said. "Wait a minute."

She got up, dragging the blankets with her. The cool air stippled my body, but I didn't get dressed or move to cover myself, and before long, she was back with a wide yellow legal pad and a black pen and the covers and her warmth. She dropped back to the bed, and I snuggled in while she wrote on the pad. Her skin was soft. That afternoon, I felt like I could have lived with my head against her thigh.

"Here," she said, giving me the paper.

1 12

"What's next in the series?" she asked. I looked at the numbers. We were early enough in the affair that her intellectual gamesmanship was still charming. It wouldn't always be. I took the pad and pen.

123

She smiled.

"You think the rule is list out the numbers," she said.

"Isn't it?"

She took the pen back.

1 12 144

"The pattern could be multiply the last value by twelve."

1 12 23

"Or add eleven."

1 12 122

"Or just tack on another 2 each time. That one's not as pretty, but it's just as possible."

"Okay," I said. "Got it. It's a trick question. You can't pick the right answer."

She smiled.

"You can't pick a wrong one either. They're all right. And almost nothing we do has a right answer. Do you have pasta for dinner or a chicken sandwich? It's not like you can work it out logically, but you have to make a decision. Same for an ant. If there's two grains of rice, and it has to pick one of them up and haul it back to the colony, it's got to decide. If there's not a logical way to choose, there has to be something else."

"An illogical one."

"An aesthetic one," she said.

"So you think the ant picks the prettiest one?"

"What else would you call it? Making decisions between logically equivalent options is as good a definition of life as anything else I've heard. And beauty is the basis of making those decisions. And art is the exploration of beauty. I could have aced it. Instead, I talked about the fucking Etruscans. I'm fucked."

"You say it like it's a bad thing."

She dropped the pad of paper and leaned against me. The wall was chilly. The heater kicked on, whirring and wheezing like an old man.

"I need to get an A in this class," she said. "The competition for law school is...I *need* this to be an A."

"You'll be fine. You're brilliant."

"You're horny."

"You're beautiful."

"I'm naked."

"Same thing," I said.

✳

HOW DO women pick the men they fall for? Is it the bad boy charm? The good heart? Is it the way a man listens, the way he talks about his mother, the way he treats kids? Is it the size of his cock? The size of his wallet? What *really* makes a man handsome?

All the studies say it's height.

✳

"I'M SORRY, sir," Jude said. I hadn't had a chance to speak yet.

The facility squatted on the edge of a newly planted forest. The meeting room looked out on thin, pale stalks hardly more than ten feet high that would someday become oaks. Jude—a huge man with a close-shaven skull and a canary yellow jumpsuit—sat across the table from me. When he'd been led in by the guards, his sneakers had squeaked on the linoleum. Now, he looked at me with wide, blue, sorrowful eyes. A Bassett hound made human.

"You're sorry?"

"Whatever it was I did to bring you here, I'm sorry for it," Jude said.

"What do you think brought me here?"

The eyes didn't harden so much as die. I could have read self-loathing or satanic pride or anything else into his expression, but I only wondered how many times you'd have to sit through confrontations like this before it just became a routine.

"I did something bad to a kid," he said. "Maybe your kid, maybe your grandkid. Maybe someone you know. I can't speak to that part. But you're here to tell me what I done was wrong. And sir, I'm here to listen."

"Actually, that's *not* why I'm here," I said. "I wanted to talk about the ways you tried to stop."

It took him a few seconds. I watched the parade of emotions—surprise, confusion, distrust—play out in the shapes of his mouth and eyes. It ended with a slow, slitted reconsideration of me.

"I'm not sure what you're askin'," he said. The sir was gone. His voice had changed, contrition souring into distrust.

"You tried to stop," I said. "Maybe even before the first time, certainly after it. You didn't like where your mind was taking you. You tried to change it."

"That's so."

"I'm here to talk about how," I said.

We were silent for almost a minute. I was pretty sure we were going to stay that way for the whole half-hour visitation. Outside, birds danced between the small trees, their wings dark against the sky.

"They don't all, you know," he said. "They don't all try and stop. Most of the guys in here, they've bent their heads all up so it's okay. The kids had it coming or it don't really hurt 'em or God said they could or whatever. Ain't one in ten who can look it in the face."

"You did."

"I did," he said, and the tone was mournful. "I tried cutting my pecker off with a straight razor once. That the kind of thing you're looking for?"

PEH-kur off. STRAIT RAY-zer. Jesus Christ, what was I doing here?

"No," I said. "I want to talk about what they did to your brain in Mexico."

Jude leaned back, his plastic chair creaking. The ghost of a smile touched his lips and vanished.

87

"That one," he said. "Yeah. I remember that one. Made me sign all kinds of things, swear up and down not to talk to nobody about it."

"Well," I said, "maybe you shouldn't say then. Might get you in trouble."

He guffawed, and I smiled. I was in. We were friends now. Rapport, they called it.

"Well, hell," he said. "That would have been just after my second turn in the state pen. They didn't know about the kids when I was in regular prison. You don't talk about it there. Every man jack in there'll kill something like me. You just keep quiet and make up shit about the girl back home, same as everyone else. Anyway, I got out and back on the street, and I knew there was trouble coming. There was this site they gave me. Anonymous, they said, and maybe that was true. Anyway, I talk to this lady there, and she refers me off to this other site for folks with sexual problems. And they put me in touch with this research fella."

"You remember his name?"

"Too long ago."

"Safwan Cádir?"

"Yeah, he was one of 'em. Guy I taked with was a white fella, though. Idea was I'd sign all this paper, and they'd put me in this trial group down in Mexico. Make it so I didn't see them like that anymore."

"Them?"

"Little ones," he said. "I wouldn't see them like that. I didn't have much choice, did I? Had to try something. So I signed up and they took me down. It wasn't much, really. Put me in one of those good brain scanners and showed me some pictures to see what was firing in my head. They didn't even have to go inside me to cut nothing. Just zapped me with a microwave. Had a fever for a couple days, but that was all."

"What happened?"

He paused, his fingers laced over his belly, his mouth pursed. Slowly, he shook his head.

"You know what the good thing is about bein' thirsty?" he asked.

"No," I said.

"If it gets bad enough, you die. That other thing. It can feel like bein' thirsty, but it just goes on and on and on. Never lets you go. I...well, I won't go into that. But it didn't work."

I leaned forward as the amphetamines shot a spike of rage through me. This wasn't the breakthrough I was looking for. Where was the cure? The victory? Eric Swanson had put himself under the knife, and it destroyed him. Jude Hammer it only didn't help. This couldn't be what Fifth Layer was based on. We were misinterpreting Elaine's drunken comments. We were seeing it wrong. I was hopped up on my boss' drugs and six states away from home for nothing.

When he spoke again, I was almost too wrapped up in my own mind to hear him.

"It changed me, just not the right way."

A pause.

"Yeah?" I said.

"You want to hear about that too?"

"I do."

"All right. It's your quarter. It used to be there was a particular kind of kid I was into. After they did what they did to me, I could look at...well, at a kid who I knew in my head was my type, if you see what I'm saying. All the things that used to get me going. But now they looked just like everyone else."

"That didn't help?"

"Nah. The pressure built up, just like always. And there were others started looking tempting. I don't like to talk about that. Them Mexico doctors didn't change what I do. They maybe switched who I was doing it to. That's all."

Something was moving in the back of my head, shifting like an eel in muddy water. The Roswell hypothesis. The Fifth Layer Look.

"Elaine Salvati," I said. "Does the name mean anything to you?"

"Hell yes. Sounds like salvation, don't she? I thought it was a sign."

"She was in Mexico? At the clinic?"

"Yeah, sure. She was one of 'em. She can't help you, though."

I blinked.

"Help *me*?" I asked.

"I know why you're here, friend. You're looking to stop it. You're looking for a way to turn it off."

"No," I said. "No, it's not like that. I'm—"

Jude lifted a hand, palm toward me, commanding silence. He had huge hands. Strong.

"You don't have to convince me of nothing," he said. "Just let me tell you one thing, all right? There's only two ways to stop it. You get yourself put in someplace like this or you blow your fucking brains out. If you want my recommendation, I'd say the second one. And sooner's better than later."

His eyes weren't soft anymore. They weren't dead. They were the blue of natural gas. They were monstrous.

"Folks like you and me," he said, "I don't know what we are, but we ain't human."

✳

SHE SOUNDS like salvation.

There are some men who never drop an email or screen name, a phone number or voxnet node ID. In among their contact lists is the hidden history of their sexual lives. Every lover is retained there, even if they're never called or contacted. Whenever an impulse for simplification overwhelms them, those names are spared from the purge. Just in case, without ever being more specific. *Just in case.*

I was one of those. Elaine's information was still on my system.

I sat in my hotel room, the video file looped. She laughed. *Except discretion,* she said. Voices came from the corridor. Children whining with exhaustion. A woman's laugh. The air smelled like artificial cedar and sterilizer. The crap I'd put in my blood wouldn't let me sleep. I had two messages from Herself queued and waiting to tell me, I was certain, how important this was and how little time I had to get it right.

It was all going to end with Elaine, because somehow it all began with her. I wondered what it would be like, seeing her again. She'd climbed through the world, become someone important. I'd burned through a couple marriages and ended in a dead end job. She'd experimented unethically on human brains through an unregulated foreign clinic and released a known pedophile into the wild as part of an experiment. She'd had the most beautiful mouth.

There were a thousand ways it could go. I could call her, tell her that I knew, that I had Fifth Layer over the barrel. She could beg me to keep it quiet, and I could relent, and we could strike up our affair where it had ended half a lifetime before. I could say it was wrong, and that I was going to see it published, and she could send out a cleanup squad to disappear me. Or buy me off. Or laugh at me for thinking I mattered. My fingers hovered above the keyboard, waiting for me to hack off some limb of the decision tree.

I had all the data I needed to connect the Mexican clinic to the early R and D staff of Fifth Layer. I had the notes from my meetings with Eric Swanson and Jude Hammer. I had an idea what it was all about.

A quote. I'd tell her I was looking for a quote. Then we'd see what happened. Play it by ear. Get it done before anyone else could. Write it up, swallow some downers, and get to sleep before my brain turned to slag.

My fingers descended. I requested the connection. Every means of contact I had bounced back. Nothing worked. The Elaine Salvati I'd known wasn't there anymore.

✳

NO ONE from Fifth Layer returned my messages. I thought about cutting out the amphetamines. But at this point, I'd be sleeping for three days once I came down. I had to get it done before the crash. Before someone else saw the file and put it together.

✳

I SPENT half of my savings to get a new suit. Black businesswear, pinstripes with RFID chameleoning that would automatically coordinate the colors with whatever shirt and tie I wore. A tailoring neural net more advanced than Herself's dress and complex enough to have its own sense of beauty.

I sat at the bar, alternating soda water with alcohol, keeping one eye on the door and another on the chemical hum in my bloodstream. Investigative reporting was a younger man's game. It wasn't the work I couldn't handle. It was the drugs. Toothless corporate jazz soothed and numbed the air around me. The servistas kept their distance from me. The murmur of conversations between the rich and powerful rose and fell like the tide.

I waited.

She came in Thursday night, Safwan Cádir on her arm. I could tell from the way they stood that they were lovers. She didn't see me, or if she did, she didn't recognize me. If I was right, it was more than time and age that would have changed my appearance.

I waited until they were seated, then until their drinks came. And then their food. I finished my drink, picked up my system, and headed over.

Safwan Cádir looked up at me. He was younger than I expected. His eyebrows rose in a polite query. Can I help you? I ignored him. Elaine saw Cádir react, followed his gaze, considered me for a moment with nothing behind her eyes. Then, a few seconds later than I expected, her mouth opened a millimeter, her cheeks flushed, her eyes grew wider. There was something odd about it, though. I had the eerie feeling that the movements were stage managed to appear normal, the product of consideration instead of emotion.

"Jimmy?" she asked. "Is that you?"

"Elaine," I said, and something in the way I spoke her name killed the pleasure at seeing me.

"What are you doing these days?" she asked.

"Investigative reporting," I said.

Cádir stiffened, but Elaine relaxed, rocking back in her seat.

"I know what you did," I said. "I know the secret of Fifth Layer's success."

Cádir's frown could have chipped glass. Elaine chuckled, warm and soft. Familiar and strange. She gestured to an empty chair.

"Join us?"

❋

HOW DO people recognize beauty? What makes one face compelling and another forgettable? Why does one actor flash a smile that makes the world swoon, while a thousand others struggle to be noticed? Why will a baby stare at the picture of one face instead of another?

Why will people of all ethnicities, all backgrounds, all nations, come to the same conclusions when asked to rank people according to their attractiveness? What is the nature of beauty itself?

All the studies say it's symmetry.

✳

"IT'S SUPPOSED to be a measure of genetic fitness," I continued. "Whoever grows up with the fewest illnesses, the lowest parasite load, all that. They wind up closest to perfect symmetry. Back in the Pleistocene, we didn't have cosmetic surgery or makeup, so it was a pretty good match. And so our brains got wired for it. We love it."

"That's been established for decades," Cádir said.

"It generalizes, though, doesn't it?" I said. "We like symmetrical flowers, but we're not trying to mate with them. We like our artistic compositions to be balanced, because it fits that same ideal. It got selected for because of genetic fitness, but it affects how we see *everything*. People. Dance performances."

They were silent. Cádir's steak was getting cold. Elaine's pasta was congealing.

"Physics," I said.

Safwan Cádir muttered something obscene, rose, and stalked away. Elaine watched him go. There was something odd in her reaction. Something insectile.

"Poor bunny," she said. "He hates it when I win."

"When you win?"

"Go on," she said. "I'm listening."

Her eyes were on me, her mouth a gentle smile.

The romantic visions I'd conjured were gone. The memories of my time with this woman, with the body there before me, seemed like a story I'd told myself too many times. My skin had a crawling sensation that might have been speed and alcohol in physical battle or else my simple, drug-scrubbed primate mind reacting to something wrong in the way she held herself, the way she smiled.

"The Mexico research," I said. "You were trying to dampen sexual responses, but instead you killed the preference for symmetry. Swanson, after he went through the process, he was still experiencing beauty. He was doing things with his choreography that excited him so much he barely slept. But no one in the audience had gone through the procedure, so they literally weren't seeing what he was seeing. It was lost on them."

"I've watched the recordings of it," she said. "It was brilliant work."

"And the others. Jude Hammer. The pedophile. He was still attracted to children. But the profile of his victims changed. It's because he doesn't react to symmetry anymore. The Fifth Layer Look. Everyone knows it's there. It's an artifact of looking at an asymmetric design with a brain that isn't wired to like it."

"You *have* to have beauty," Elaine said, as if she was agreeing. "If you get rid of the default, you find something else. A different way to choose between logically equivalent possibilities. Symmetry blinds us. Leads us down the same paths over and over. There are so many other avenues of enquiry that could be explored, and we overlooked them because our brains were trying to pick the best monkey to fuck."

"Can I quote you on that?"

Her laughter took a second too long to come.

"Yes, Jimmy. Feel free. I'm sure it won't be the only thing I'm condemned for when you publish this."

She took a bite of her pasta, chewed thoughtfully, then pushed her plate away. I folded my arms. The suit shifted to release the strain at my elbows.

95

"You aren't upset," I said. "He is, but you aren't."

"He's trying to protect me," Eliane said, nodding in the direction that Cádir had gone. "When this all comes out, I will be the villain. You can count on that. He thinks it will bother me. But it has to be done."

"Why?"

A moment later, she smiled.

"You can quote me on this too. It has to be done because unless Fifth Layer loses its competitive advantage, the corporation won't be pressed to the next level. There are any number of other ways in which the human mind can be manipulated to appreciate pattern. There's no way to guess what we still have to discover once we can make ourselves into the appropriate investigative tools. For the sake of the future, our monopoly must expire. End quote. I'll probably be fired for that."

Questions clashed in my mind, each pushing to be the next one out of my mouth. Is Fifth Layer really willing to bonsai people's minds to keep a competitive edge in research? How much of this have you done to yourself already? Did you get drunk that night in order to get careless and have this leak out? Who are you?

But I knew all the answers that mattered.

It doesn't matter where it comes from, just if it works.

And maybe—

You want to see the limits of human excellence? Then pull out the stops and see what happens. It'd be a hell of a show.

"Does it hurt?" I asked. "Do you miss anything?"

That odd, inhuman pause, and then:

"There are trade-offs."

I nodded, reached into my pocket, and turned off the recorder. Elaine nodded when she saw it, as if confirming something she'd guessed.

"Thanks," I said. "It was good seeing you again."

"You were always a rotten liar, Jimmy."

＊

THE ROSWELL Hypothesis, I wrote, says the successes of Fifth Layer stem from their access to alien intelligences. That's not entirely wrong.

AY-lee-un in-TELL-uh-jen-sez. en-TIRE-lee RONG.

The train hummed beneath me. The beginnings of a headache haunted the space behind my eyes; the first sign of the coming amphetamine crash. I almost welcomed it. Outside, the moon set over the dark countryside. It was going to be a great story. It was going to move the site from accretor to source. It was going to change my job and Harriet's. Herself would get the promotion she wanted. It was going to change the nature of humanity. Which was Elaine's point.

You have to have beauty, I wrote. It's basic. Even ants have it. Even good suits.

I was going to need hours of solid sleep. Days. I didn't want to think about how I would feel when I got home. When I woke up. I couldn't guess at the damage a speed jag like this would do to a body as old as mine. My liver might not be the problem. My heart might be the thing to go first. And still, it had gotten the job done. You had to say that for it. I worked for a while on the last line before I was happy with it.

It may be that any sufficiently advanced modification is indistinguishable from speciation.

in-dis-TIN-gwish-ah-bull. spee-cee-AY-shun.

I checked it all over once, sent a copy to Herself, and deleted all Elaine's old contact information from my lists. And then her new information too. She wasn't there anyway.

I lay back in my seat, closed my eyes, and tried like hell to sleep.

THE SUPPORT TECHNICIAN TANGO

ONE:

BY ITS NATURE, A self-help book is written by someone who thinks they know what to do and read by someone who doesn't; there hasn't been a better setup for the pompous to fleece the credulous since Rome stopped selling indulgences. The saving grace is that the bad advice of the authors is almost always ignored, misunderstood, or abandoned by readers who go ahead and do whatever they would have done anyway. Some people knit lace, some people improve themselves; self-help is a pointless hobby but harmless.

There are, however, exceptions.

In among the hatchet-faced, unhappy women who advise on matters of love, the avuncular sports nutrition PhDs who advise on matters of love, and the Jungian analysts whose advice on love may perhaps pay off their divorce lawyers, there is a deadlier breed.

The covers are just as cheerful, the promises just as bright and insincere, the quotes of grateful, imaginary supplicants just as breathless. But some few in this school of spiritual mackerel are actually sharks. Some books are quite literally alive, conscious of the hands that hold the pages, and ready to present just the wrong idea at just the right time. They stalk the places that books lie forgotten—waiting rooms, dusty ledges between wall and mattress, Hastings—waiting quietly for the right moment and, more importantly, the right person.

TWO:

"DAVID OSGOOD, sir. He came in as soon as the software company released the patch," Mr. Elms' secretary said. She always had a military air about her, like the Secretary of Defense reporting to the President. It was why Mr. Elms trusted her. "I think Teddy helped too."

"And the virus?"

"We didn't get it, sir, but a lot of the other law firms in town did. Libby and Meyers. Sudder, Belle, and Caffe. Cawdor and Glamis. The Robert Correy Firm. And Clarence Musslewhite isn't answering calls, so my guess is he got it too."

Mr. Elms nodded, suppressing a grin. He was a dignified man, old-school, who considered it bad manners to gloat openly at the misfortunes of others once he'd made partner.

"That's too bad," he said. "Very bad. And it was destructive was it? People lost a lot of data? Ah. What a shame. I wonder if Libby and Meyers will have to ask for a continuance."

"They already have, sir."

Mr. Elms made a sound at the back of his throat that managed to be both non-committal and cheery. He tapped his wide, sausage-like fingers together. In the distance, he heard the phone ring, and the new receptionist pick it up. Someone down the corridor asked peevishly where the good printer paper was kept. The computer on his desk hummed quietly to itself, uninfected and ready to serve. The sounds of an office at peace. The sounds of an office *not* presently dealing with a massive computer failure. He found them oddly beautiful.

His secretary cleared her throat.

"I've heard a rumor, sir. Nothing I could swear to."

"Yes?"

"I think Robert Correy fired his technician over this."

Within the space of a heartbeat, Mr. Elms had taken in the guarded tone, the disavowal of certainty, the fact that his competition was about to be hiring just the sort of person who Peabody, Plummer and Elms had in pocket. He nodded to his secretary.

"Mr. Osgood must have worked very long hours on this," he said.

"All night, sir."

"Perhaps a little performance bonus is in order. Where is our man David, anyway?"

THREE:

THE WHIRR of the air conditioner made the darkened storage room seem quieter than it actually was. The couch, tucked back behind three rows of cheap metal shelving, smelled slightly of cat, but it was soft and comfortable and long enough for all six lanky feet of David Osgood to stretch out. The coffee was just starting to wear off, the hours of sleep debt leaving his body heavy as a soaked towel. His mind drifted contentedly through the network, half recalling and half dreaming. The fact was that nowhere on the system was there any of the seventeen documented variants of the BLDSKR virus. The browsers and email programs on each desk were immunized against it, and the security hole in the mail server was patched and tested. In the world outside, chaos might reign and nations might fall, but *his* network was fine.

He didn't recognize the click of the opening door until the fluorescent lights above him flickered to life. David grunted, sat up, and met the surprised expression of Daphne the paralegal. Annoyance at being disturbed slunk quietly away, replaced by the powerful awareness that he was sleeping in yesterday's clothes.

Daphne was pretty the way that competence is pretty. Her clothes were simple with just enough pattern to hide stains. Her hair was pulled back in a ponytail that suited her face. Her shoes looked comfortable. David had known boys in high school who wore more makeup.

"I'm sorry," she said. "I didn't know anyone was in here. The printer's out of paper."

"Okay," David said, unable to keep his head from bobbing like a pigeon. "I'll get that."

"Actually," she said, plucking a fresh ream from the shelves, "I think I can handle it. You put the thing in the thing and it goes, right?"

She smiled at her own joke. He grinned at it.

"Right," he said.

"You want the lights back out?"

"No," he said, "that's okay. Break's over."

Daphne hesitated in the doorway, as if there was something more she was going to say. Something red as fresh blood caught David's eye.

"Oh, hey!" he said. "You dropped your book."

He scooped the little volume up from the floor and held it out to her. She looked at it and cocked her head.

"Sorry. Not mine," she said. And then she was gone.

David sighed and dropped back to the couch, rubbing his eyes with his free hand. On his knee, the book glittered white as cut marble with bright letters: *30 Steps to Your Best Self.*

And in the same font, but smaller and black: *How To Become The Person You Want To Be Without Even Trying.* He flipped the book open to a random page.

STEP FOUR (the book said) *Branching Out*

Once you have mastered your core abilities, it's easy to stagnate and leave the things you most desire just out of reach. Instead, be open to opportunity. Try something new! Use that unexpected bonus for ballroom dance lessons, and let the sense of being "just that computer guy" fall away. You'll find yourself becoming the kind of man that women are drawn to and men admire.

It was the stupidest advice he'd ever seen. What if the person reading it was a professional dancer? And what was that thing about an unexpected bonus anyway? He knew people who'd never get a reward in their lives, but went around acting like they deserved one.

And yet the fantasy wasn't unpleasant. Dancing. He remembered a movie where Al Pacino had been dancing with a young woman who was almost but not quite Uma Thurman. David tried to imagine himself in the role, moving with grace and certainty, his arm around a beautiful woman's waist, his clothes not looking slept in. For a moment, almost-Uma looked a lot like Daphne the paralegal.

"Um. David?"

Teddy stood in the doorway, thin moustache echoing thick mono-brow. His smile apologized for itself.

"Hey," David said, letting the book close.

"Elms is looking for you."

"What's up?"

"Nothing bad, I don't think," Teddy said. "Just a postmortem on the patches and upgrades last night, probably. I'd tell him all about it, but you're better with that, you know?"

David stood, combed his fingers through his hair, trying to make it lie straight. His sense of peace and accomplishment was gone. He tried to get it back by smoothing the wrinkles out of his shirt.

"How do I look?" he asked.

"Good. You look good," Teddy said, nodding anxiously. "Rugged, kinda."

"Yeah, well. Thanks for lying."

"Welcome," Teddy said as David walked past him and out of the storage room, and then a moment later, "Dave! Hey, you forgot your book."

"It's not mine," David said.

FOUR:

STEP FOUR: Accepting Your Limitations

Most of us aren't number one. Accepting that you are second rate is, however, the first step toward success. When the Good Book said that the race goes not always to the swift, it was talking about you. If you keep an eye out for the moments when the Top Dog isn't available, you could still find yourself in positions you hadn't dreamed of.

"Well," Teddy said to himself. "Huh."

FIVE:

"UM," DAVID said.

"Now don't object," Elms said, his puffy hand palm out in a *stop* gesture. "This is something I've already spoken with the other partners about, and we're adamant. Good performance deserves its rewards."

David looked at the check in his hand—it was as much as he would have made in a week—and wondered if he had been expected to argue against taking it. The thought hadn't crossed his mind.

"We appreciate our employees," Elms said, leaning forward over his desk. "We think of the firm as a community first, you know. Like family, really. And people who do well by us...well, David, we do well by them."

"Um. Yeah. Thank you."

"Think of me as a resource," Elms went on. "Working together. That's what we do best. We work. Together. If there's anything you need—"

"Could I take the afternoon off?"

Elms blinked, thrown off stride.

"It's just I was here all night," David said. "And I could really use a nap and a shower."

"Of course," Elms said with an air of having been outmaneuvered. "Absolutely. Take the afternoon."

"Thanks," David said. They both stood and shook hands awkwardly across the wide desk. David folded the bonus check and turned toward the door, but he stopped, pulled up by a half-articulated thought.

"Mr. Elms?"

"David?"

"You're successful. I mean, you're a lawyer and you're partner in the firm and like that. Do you...do you ever wonder if it's enough? You know, if maybe there's something you're missing out on?"

"No," Elms said, his face going a little grey. "Never."

"Oh. Okay. Thanks."

David stepped out into the calming, professional blue-green hallway. The hum of the business day was all around him—the low voices of distant conversation, the ring of telephones, the truck-backing-up beep of the microwave in the breakroom. He pushed his hands deep in his pockets, frowning.

The partners had noticed him, they'd given him money and time off and a handshake. By all rights, he should have felt delighted. He kicked all the ass, and everyone knew it. He took out the check and looked at it again.

You'll find yourself becoming the kind of man that women are drawn to and men admire.

The lights were still on in the storage room. The couch was still pressed down where he'd rested his head. The book, however, was gone. He looked between the cushions, in the small, dusty space between the couch and the floor. He made a long, slow circuit of the room in case Teddy had shelved it with the pens or legal pads, but the thing simply wasn't there.

He thought about going through the whole office, asking Teddy, maybe Daphne, if they'd seen it or, failing that, if they remembered the title. 30 Steps to Something Generic was the closest he could come. But it was pushing noon, and it wasn't really important.

SIX:

MR. ELMS didn't consider himself a weak man. He had clawed his way to the top of a profession where clawing was *de rigueur*. He'd honed the plowshare of his mind into a sword with which you could shave an ant. When something was even the slightest bit off, he was sure he could tell. And something had been off about David Osgood.

For the rest of the day and into the first few hours of the night—he, unlike Osgood, wasn't the sort of man to go home early—Mr. Elms found his concentration divided. There was the deposition of a woman who claimed to have seem Mr. Elms' client accepting a bribe, but there was also David Osgood asking if he was missing something. There was an angry letter from opposing attorney that required an equally scathing reply, but there was also the computer consultant calling him successful. Had there been just the hint of a sneer in his voice?

The fact was the firm constituted very nearly the whole of Mr. Elms' world. He had never married because he'd never found a woman who didn't want him around. He had no particular friends outside the profession because he found other pursuits beside the point, and no particular friends within it because it wasn't that sort of work. The firm was as precious to him as his own arms. It was a part of him. The mere suggestion that he might find something lacking in his life put his back up.

And that might have been all it did, except for the book he found in the break room when he went to microwave his dinner.

STEP FOUR: *Watching Your Back*

The weak council patience, but men of power know better. The only way to protect yourself is to be vigilant. If someone under you begins to behave oddly, you would be a fool to ignore it. Don't fall into that trap! Watch with the eyes of a hawk! Act boldly and without restraint! It is your total commitment to your work that makes you who you are.

The microwave beeped, startling him. Mr. Elms put the slim volume back beside the coffee machine where he'd found it. He was fairly certain that no one else was still in the office, but he certainly wouldn't want anyone to see him reading a self-help book, not even one as wise and well-considered as that. A partner such as himself should show no weakness, ever.

Back at his desk, the glowing lights of the city his only companion, Mr. Elms ate his dinner slowly, unaware of the greasy steak and flaccid potatoes. He grew more and more certain that his reaction that afternoon had been more than merely a bruised ego. Something sinister was going on at Peabody, Plummer, and Elms. He would watch Osgood with the eyes of a hawk. He would act boldly and without restraint. Already, the prospect filled him with a carnivorous joy. In a moment of decadence, he slipped off his shoes and rubbed his stocking feet over the carpet like an ancient hunter tamping down the grass of the savannah, spear, metaphorically speaking, in hand.

When he heard the cleaning crew arriving, he hastily slipped them back on.

SEVEN:

SARAH ELLINGTON sat at the receptionist's desk trying very hard to be friendly, open, and efficient while bored off her nut. She had a Masters in cultural anthropology and folkloric studies, and with it, she was taking messages and transferring calls. She'd spent two years doing fieldwork in Africa. Now she wore pantyhose. The world was a thing devoid of justice.

The problem, of course, was Bobby. Six years married to Junior Silverback didn't leave a girl with much of a resume. But the temp company had placed her here, and she'd leveraged that into a permanent position. Next up, office management. Or maybe paralegal.

Until then, clean desk, fake woodgrain, cheap coffee in a black cup. And anything to keep her brain from rotting.

The phone chirped.

"Peabody, Plummer, and Elms," she said, smiling so that she'd sound like she was smiling. "How can I help you?"

"Bernard Lawton. Lookin' for Mark," a man grumbled.

"Mark who?"

"Mark *Peabody*," the man said. Clearly no one else in the history of man had ever been named Mark.

"I'm sorry," Sarah smiled. "Mr. Peabody is out of the office, may I take a…"

The line clicked and went dead. Sarah sighed, released the call, and silently wished a particularly nasty bloodworm on whoever it had been. People might be her species, but that didn't mean she had to like them.

"Um, hey," a voice said.

It was the computer guy. David something. Decent sort, so far as she could tell. Sarah raised her eyebrows.

"Do we have a yellow pages around here?"

"Sure," she said, reached under her desk and pulled out the phone book. He accepted it with a strangely furtive nod. It piqued her interest.

"I thought you guys just looked everything up on the web," she said.

"Not always."

"What're you looking for?"

"Um. I was thinking about taking a class. But I need to find prices and schedules and stuff."

"Oh. Like computer programming?"

He smiled. He had a nice smile, even if it didn't last very long. His eyes were the same shape as her little brother's.

"I'm already pretty good with writing code," he said.

"So what then?" she asked, and the phone chirped again.

She took the call—the emotionally fragile husband of one of the junior partners calling to ask advice on some domestic crisis—and David took the opportunity to sneak off without answering her question. She finally scraped the husband into voice mail, picked up a pen, and tapped it on her leg. The boy was up to something. Something he was ashamed of.

None of her business, granted. And yet...

Besides, he'd taken her phone book.

She found him by the photocopier, talking with Daphne the paralegal. The phonebook was still in his hands. Sarah hung back a little, pretending to check her pockets for something. They were standing just inside appropriate social distance for Americans, and neither of them was backing up or moving forward. Daphne's hips were just a little canted and her hand fluttered once like a little bird that considered perching on David's arm but thought better of it. David was swaying just slightly in toward the girl every time he spoke and held the front desk phone book behind his back as if he were hiding it. His smile was exaggerated, his chest puffed out just the smallest bit.

So that's how it is with them, Sarah thought. Poor bunnies.

She turned away. There were other phone books other places, and she didn't have the heart to interrupt flirtation that was so tenuous, so unsure, and so blazingly obvious to everyone but the two who needed to see it. She didn't have to like everyone, but she didn't have to hate them all either.

EIGHT:

"I WAS thinking about maybe taking a class or something," David said. "Like b-ballroom dance. Or something. I don't know though. I probably won't."

"I like dancing," Daphne said.

The photocopier hummed as if nothing had been determined.

NINE:

NIKO SAMUEL'S Academy of Dance was in a strip mall; its stylized logo of an elegantly dressed man and woman competed with a cell phone store to one side and a barber shop to the other. Music floated out to the grey concrete sidewalk like perfume. David stood for minute, looking at the pictures in the front window—men and women in gaudy outfits and dance poses. Some of them looked serious in a smoky, sexually tense way, others grinned at the camera, showing off. He couldn't decide if the place seemed squalid or exciting.

He glanced out to the parking lot, half-expecting to see some unwelcome familiar face, before pushing his way through the door. Inside, the atmosphere was equal parts *Casablanca* and *A Chorus Line*. The music was louder, trumpets and drums and a voice singing in what might have been Spanish or French. A steady clapping punctuated the song, and another voice shouted out instructions David couldn't understand.

An overhead fan dragged wide faux-rattan blades through the air, and a desk sat empty, sleek European chairs before it where clients like himself could sit. More pictures of dancers lined the walls, some of them holding trophies or ribbons. David sat.

"Good evening," a voice said over the sounds of the class. David twisted in his seat. The man behind him was small with styled black hair, a thin moustache, and a dark blue, well-tailored suit. "Can I help you?"

"I don't know," David said.

"Then I probably can," the man said. He walked forward with studied grace and took a seat on the far side of the desk. "I am Mr. Samuel, but call me Niko. All my students do. You are here for the classes?"

"Yes."

"Excellent. What experience do you have in dance?"

"None. I mean, I've gone to some clubs, and if I got drunk enough...but nothing..." He struggled for the word. "Nothing real. I saw *Strictly Ballroom* once, though."

"Of course you did," Niko said. "That's very good. The less you think you know, the better. We don't have to spend time un-learning bad habits. We can begin right away with the good stuff. What kind of shoes do you have?"

"I can get whatever's best," David said. He hadn't even thought about shoes.

"I have a catalog you can look through. Very reasonably priced. They do the shoes for the whole academy, so we get a very good rate. And what is it you want to learn?"

"To dance?"

Niko smiled.

"You want to learn to rumba? Cha-cha? A little of everything?" he asked.

"Did you ever see the Al Pacino movie where he played the blind guy?"

Niko nodded, his eyes half closing as if at some lovely memory. The music shifted to something slower with more piano and less trumpet.

"Argentine tango," Niko said, tasting the words as they came out. "Soft, not so militaristic and sharp. It's a beautiful way to dance. Not easy, but very beautiful. "

"Do you have classes in that?"

"For someone who dances at clubs when he's drunk enough? No," Niko said. "For him, I have introductory classes. We can teach you about rhythm and grace and how you direct a woman where to move. Then, once you have the tools, certainly."

"I don't have a lot of money," David said.

Niko seemed to consider something, then looked at his watch, frowned, and held out his hand across the desk, fingers twitching in a gesture that demanded something be given to him. David reached for his wallet.

"Your shoes," Niko said. "Let me see your shoes."

David unlaced his sneakers and passed them over. Niko turned them in his hands, nodded to himself, and vanished into the back room. David sat in his socks. A round of applause came from the back room—the end of class, he guessed. And a few seconds later, people came filing out. They were of all ages, all sizes, and none of them looked as glamorous as the pictures. David smiled and nodded, and wondered what was being done to his sneakers.

After the last of the students had gone, Niko reappeared with a pair of black leather shoes in one hand and David's sneakers in the other. He handed David the leather ones.

"Three kinds of lesson," he said. "One, group lessons; one teacher, many students. Two, group practice; no teacher, many students. Just to keep in practice. Third, individual lesson; one teacher, one student."

"Okay," David said uncertainly.

"Put the shoes on. Individual lessons are like drugs. The first one's free."

The back room was a single space with a wood floor, mirrors along one wall, and a stereo with stacks of CDs. A young woman in a black leotard and something more like the idea of a skirt than the actual thing itself was putting the disks in order.

"Angelica," Niko said. "We have a new student. First lesson."

"Um," David said.

The girl smiled and left the disks. Niko went to the stereo.

"We'll begin with the merengue," Niko called. "It's very easy. Two step. Just step and slide. Angelica will show you."

Angelica was a full head shorter than David, her face perfectly made up. He felt himself start to blush.

"I don't know what I'm doing," he said.

"Put your hands out like this," she said. He did, and she slid into them. The spandex felt strange on his fingertips. "You'll start with your left foot. You always start with your left foot, and I'll be your mirror. It's easy to remember."

"It is?"

"Just tell yourself that the *lady* is always *right*."

The music started.

"Now," she said. "Step out a little with your left foot and then slide your right foot over. Like this."

David watched her and tried to imitate her movements.

"So dance like Igor?" he said.

"General Merengue was lame," she laughed. "You're doing fine."

After half an hour, Niko took him back out to the front room and they went over the different plans for study programs. David also looked through the shoe catalog. The prices were higher than he'd expected.

He put it on a credit card.

TEN:

"I DON'T know," David said. "I mean, it seemed like the right thing to do at the time."

"Buyer's remorse," said Teddy, nodding sagely. "I do that too. There was this one time I bought a car from a cousin of mine…"

"I don't mean the money," David said.

"Then what?"

David sat back, his gaze flickering over the break room as if there might be an answer written between the microwave and the coffee machine. The walls and appliances offered him no counsel.

"I'm just not sure it's *me*," David said at last. "I mean it's not like what I do."

"That's the point, though, isn't it?"

"I guess."

David ran his thumb across the woodgrained plastic table top. Teddy might not have been the right person to talk to about this, but he didn't know who might have been the right one.

"Just do it like you were learning a new operating system," Teddy said. "If Elms came in today and said we were going to switch over to Windows on the servers, what would you do?"

"Talk him out of it," David said.

"I mean, if you had to?"

David shrugged. The coffee machine gurgled and spat, but didn't start beeping.

"You'd *do* it," Teddy said with a grin and a wide, sweeping gesture of his hands. "You'd go home and you'd build two or three systems from scratch, just to see how they worked. Then you'd read up on the security issues and talk to the folks on bitmines..."

"Who would tell me to quit," David said, "and find someplace where they let me run real servers."

"But you see what I'm talking about. You want to learn it, *learn* it," Teddy said, and his smile faltered. "Why do you want to learn it again?"

"To be the sort of man women are drawn to and men admire."

"Ah."

Teddy seemed to mull this over for a few seconds. A misty look came to his eyes, and for a moment he looked a little like Freddy Mercury.

"That sounds really nice," Teddy said. "You know, maybe—"

"Hey," Daphne said, stepping into the room. "Here you guys are. The file server's not letting me get to Mr. Plummer's documents again."

Teddy glanced at David then Daphne then the exit, eyes growing wide with panic.

"Did you cycle power on the switch?" David asked.

Daphne smiled and shook her head. She had the prettiest smile.

"You're the computer guy," she said. "I'm not touching that stuff."

The computer guy. Yeah, that's what I am, David thought. Not a human. Just the computer guy.

"I can go cycle the power," Teddy said. "You want to go check the server? You know, in case it's a routing problem..."

"You hang here and bring me some coffee when it's done," David said. "I went through this last time, and I think I know what needs doing."

The relief on Teddy's face was profound.

"Well, you take this one, then," Teddy said. "Just call me if you need help."

Daphne led the way to the back office. He could hear Mr. Plummer's voice nattering in the conference room, the placid chirp of the phone. The almost-inaudible sound of cloth against cloth of Daphne's dress as she walked. He could feel what it would be like to take her hand in his, his other palm pressing against her shoulder, pulling her just slightly toward him, her fingers gently on his own. He could almost move with the first little swaying motion as he stepped out with his left foot, she with her right.

Except, of course, that he was just the computer guy.

ELEVEN:

SARAH FROWNED at the screen, moved her mouse pointer and clicked again. The email message still didn't open. Outside, the thunderstorm that had been threatening all afternoon was finally beginning—thick angry drops tapping against the wall-high lobby windows. And just in time for the drive home. Sarah was displeased.

"Did it show up?" asked David's voice. She looked up, thinking that he must mean her email, before remembering the context.

"Yes," she said, reaching under her desk for the package. "The Fed-Ex guy came an hour ago. Here you are."

It was a cube, maybe six inches by six, and David's eyes lit up when he took it.

"It's music," he said. "Mostly tango and cha-cha, but there's some rumba too. I had them overnight it to me."

"That's lovely," Sarah said. "You know, I'm glad you're here. My Outlook Express hasn't been working right. When I try to open this one message…"

"Reboot the computer," David said. "That'll fix it."

"Well, I tried that, and it didn't help. In fact, now I can't open any of the messages in my inbox. Do you think you could..."

"Sure," David said, "first thing in the morning."

Sarah felt *The Smile* come to her lips. She liked David, and he'd usually been as pleasant to her as he was to everyone. He had never provoked her to *The Smile*, and yet there it was, pulling at her lips until air touched her teeth but never quite warming her eyes.

"I was hoping I could have someone look at it today," she said. "There's still half an hour to go, and I do need to answer some of this mail."

"Teddy'll have to do it," David said, apologizing with a shrug. "I skipped lunch so I can take off early. Group class."

He held up the Fed-Ex box of music as if it was a hall pass and she was a particularly intimidating gym teacher. Sarah forced *The Smile* back into its cage. She was being self-ish because it was the end of the day and she was tired and annoyed. There was no reason to take it out on David, even if he was leaving when she had to stay.

"Well, have a good time, then," she said.

David grinned, nodded, and almost bounced out the door toward the elevators. As it closed, Sarah thought she heard a sigh. She turned in time to see Daphne the paralegal vanishing into the file library, an oddly forlorn expression on her face. Lightning flashed and thunder grumbled.

Sarah clicked the reluctant message one more time for luck. The inbox went totally blank. Sarah sat back in her chair, and very quietly said something very crude.

TWELVE:

THE MUSIC began—drums and then trumpets, a woman's voice singing low in her throat. David looked into his partner's eyes. She was a heavy woman in her late forties who, despite solid efforts, hadn't conquered her moustache problems. David didn't care. No doubt she was a very nice woman with a good personality. He didn't care about that either. The moment came, and he stepped forward on his left foot, then forward and to the side with his right, and then stepped in to meet it. Gently, his eyes locked on hers, he signaled with the pressure of his hands where he wanted her to move next. When he raised his arm, she turned in a slow spin, and he stepped in to meet her.

David's peripheral vision was filled with other couples shifting to the music, some graceful, some awkward. Angelica—the teacher with the leotard and the very short skirt—called out corrections to students, sometimes clapping her hands to help them find the beat. She never spoke David's name, and he found it hardly mattered. He was able to navigate from one corner of the floor to another, shifting forward and back. The dance made *sense*.

He'd been working on it at home, of course. In the living room, he'd tipped the sofa on end and pushed it into the corner so that the floor space was clear. He'd listened to rumba music and tracked down video clips to watch. He'd even popped out his old synthesizer and played the bass lines along with the music. Spending three or four hours a night at it for the last month had brought him to a place where he understood it perfectly.

Which, as it turned out, hadn't been enough. Knowing and doing weren't the same, and the whole time he'd practiced, he'd been watching his feet to be sure they were in the right places, matching the motions of the professional on his television. Now he had a habit of dancing with his head bowed down, and he fought against it, looking into the woman's eyes with a ferocity born of really wanting to just glance down, just be sure. He imagined this was what not smoking was like.

The singer's voice growled, rose and fell. The final chords were struck, and David and his partner came to a halt.

"Much better," Angelica said. "Most of you are getting the hang of this, but I'm still seeing some confusion on the spins. Here, David…"

She motioned to him, and he stepped over, putting his arm around her almost by reflex. She counted out the beat as he raised his arm, let her spin, and then stepped in to meet her again. She smiled a little. She had a very thin face and dark lipstick that made David think—in a non-judgmental way—of hookers.

"Like that," she said to the class. "You all understand? Okay, we'll try it again. Watch me and David, and try to do what we do, all right?"

Angelica went to the stereo and began another song. He also got through this one without looking at his feet. It was a pretty good night, so far.

After class, David walked out through the lobby with the other students. But Niko was there, cutting David out of the crowd with the grace and competence of a sheepdog.

"David," he said when they were in the back office together, "I've been watching your progress. You are doing very well."

"Thanks," David said.

"I was thinking. The drive you have. The concentration. I admire it. It seems to me that you may be suited for something more than this. And I have need of you. The school has need of you."

David blinked.

"My best bronze level in International Latin doesn't qualify any longer," Niko said. "He reached the semi-final last year, and it earned him the proficiency point that put him in silver. His old partner Mariella is still three points short. Technically, you'd still class novice, but everyone dances up sometimes. The competition is in Topeka, and you would have to take care of the travel. And it's USABDA, so you would have to register. I know it's asking a lot of you, but..."

Niko held out his hands, eyebrows raised as if he had asked a question. David went over the words again, as best he could remember them, hoping that something would make sense. Niko seemed to take his silence as reluctance.

"You are the best we have, David," Niko said, his voice low and serious. "Mariella has seen you, and she agrees. With your dedication, it would be easy for you two to take the category."

"You want me to be in a dance competition?" David said.

"Will you?" Niko asked. He was a short man, and the passion in his voice made David feel like Rudolph when Santa asked him to pull the sleigh.

"Um. Let me think about it," David said.

THIRTEEN:

"SO IT works," Teddy said.

David ran his finger down the screen, reading the green-on-black lines of the routing table one by one as he went. The electrostatic charge of the old video monitor crackled and pulled at the tiny hairs on the back of his hand.

There was the default path, and the subnet defined anything on 192.168.3.x as local network. But the printers in the front office were set to .45 and .46, and nothing was reaching them, so there had to be something else going on. Dimly, he realized that Teddy had spoken.

"Huh?"

"That guy Niko. He said he admired you. And me, seriously Dave, I admire the hell out of you."

"Thanks," David said.

"And this girl. What's her name? The new dance partner."

"Mariella."

"So she saw you. And she got drawn to you, right? So it works. That's so cool."

David sat back in his chair and rubbed his eyes. He'd been up late listening to music. It was like having a second life. No one at the studio thought of him as the computer guy. No one at the office thought of him as a dancer. He had a secret, another world he was part of that no one really understood. Except that he'd let it slip to Teddy that they'd asked him to get really serious about it now. If he said yes, he was going to be one of those pictures on the wall, smiling and holding a trophy. In retrospect, he should have kept it closer to the vest.

"Yeah," he said. "I guess it worked."

"Is she…y'know. Is she cute?"

"Mariella? I guess so. Yeah, she's all right. I told them that I'd go ahead and practice with her. I mean maybe we just won't work together right, you know? I wouldn't want to spend all that time and money when I'm not even the right guy."

"What about that scanner we put in at Daphne's desk?" Teddy said.

David frowned.

"What about it?"

"The DHCP server was being reprogrammed when we put those in, right? The scanner's got an IP, and the box that goes with it's got one. I don't think she's had to use them much since. But she was talking about some evidentiary thing coming on Friday and how she had to scan in the old documents. Maybe you gave the scanner stuff .45 and .46. That'd screw things up, wouldn't it? If the printers up front have 'em too."

David closed his eyes. They felt gritty.

"Yeah," David said. "You're right. That'd do it."

The receptionist—Susan, Sarah...something like that; he could never remember—appeared at the machine room door.

"There's someone here to see you, David," she said. The disapproval in her voice was probably just his imagination; he got a little paranoid when he was too tired.

Mariella sat on the couch, looking out the window and eight stories down to the street as if it was a mildly interesting television show—something on the Discovery channel. She was in a tight dress, her blonde hair in a halo artfully arranged to make it seem like she'd just risen from bed. Her makeup was perfect as a mask. To his dismay, Mr. Elms and Daphne were standing at the front desk pretending to have a conversation while they both stared at her. Probably both thinking that he'd hired her to be seen with him.

"David. Sweetheart," she said as he came into the room. "I was just downtown, and I wanted to drop this off for you."

She held out a plastic CD case. A fat man with a thin moustache, a thin tie, and thinning hair was crooning into a microphone on the cover.

"I was thinking track eight," she said.

"Cool, thanks," David said. "I'll give it a listen."

"I won't keep you," she said, rising and smoothing her dress against her body. She leaned in, whispering into his ear, and gesturing toward Mr. Elms. "Don't want to get you in trouble with the boss. But tonight?"

"Same as always," David said.

Mariella made the little kissing sound that she used instead of handshakes or waves and glided out the door. David turned the disk over in his hand, reading down the playlist. Track eight. Rumba in the Bronx. Oh, this wasn't going to be good.

When he looked up, Mr. Elms was gone, but Daphne was there, looking at the closed office door with an odd expression. David glanced over toward it, in case there was something interesting, but it was just the same tasteful dark wood finish as always.

"Who was that?" Daphne asked.

"My ballroom dance partner. Mariella," David said, embarrassed. "She's been at it longer than me. She's pretty good."

Daphne reached up, apparently unconsciously, and touched her fingers to her ponytail. She seemed almost dazed.

"Are you okay?" David asked.

"No, I'm fine," she said. "Sorry. I'm fine."

FOURTEEN:

MR. ELMS sat at his desk, quiet, calm, and consumed by fury.

Had he not been more than fair, more than *kind*, to David Osgood? Had he not put out the hand of friendship? What firm in the city would have shown the grace and charity to have a partner—an actual *partner*—offer a performance bonus to the computer guy? And this was how Osgood repaid him.

"Mr. Elms?" the secretary asked. He realized she'd been speaking for some time, but he didn't recall anything she'd said.

"I have a headache," he said, though he didn't. "Bring me a cup of coffee."

His secretary put down her notebook and left without word or comment, because that was how it was meant to be. His world ran on quiet efficiency, good grace, trust and loyalty. What did it matter that he hadn't asked for an aspirin but coffee? Coffee he wanted, coffee he'd get. And none of this double-dealing, ham-handed, petty strutting. Unlike David Osgood.

To bring a woman of that stunning beauty and superb quality here to the office was, as Mr. Elms saw it, as good as boasting aloud. She had lit the waiting room just by sitting in it. Her voice had been a mixture of music and vice that would wake men from the dead. There was no question in Elms' mind. David Osgood had been suborned into some act of corporate espionage, and the attentions of this goddess were the boy's promise and his reward.

True there was no evidence yet. Not the sort he'd take before a judge. But Osgood had underestimated him, oh yes. Mr. Elms had been watching the boy like a hawk, and when the time came to act, he would be bold and unrestrained.

His secretary came back, a mug steaming in her hand. When he took it from her, it was almost white with cream and sweet as victory. He smacked his lips, nodded, and turned his laser-beam attention to his secretary, newly returned to her chair.

"It is my *total commitment* to my work that makes me who I am," he said, not remembering where he'd heard the phrase before.

"Yes it is, sir," she agreed.

FIFTEEN:

TWO WEEKS before the dance competition, David still hadn't quite brought himself to commit to the meet in Topeka, but everyone kept treating him like he had. The studio was officially closed, the lights in the front rooms dimmed, the door locked. The back room, on the other hand, was bright and full. Six other couples from the school were entered to compete, and all of them were there, sitting on chairs or leaning against the mirrors watching with cold, judgmental expressions. Niko and Angelica passed among them like hosts at a party.

The music ended as David twirled Mariella into his arms. They froze for a beat, David staring into her eyes. She wore colored contacts. That explained a lot, actually.

"I don't know," the American Rhythm man said. "I think it needs a little more..." He rolled his hips. David thought he looked a little like Elton John when he did it.

"You always think that," an International Style woman drawled.

"Children! Children!" Niko said, clapping his hands. "We don't have time to squabble. David and Mariella have worked very hard on this, and it is our job to help them, not drag out old differences of opinion. Now the first passage..."

David's cell phone went off.

"Sorry," he said, trotting over to his work clothes. "Really sorry."

He looked at the screen. The number was Teddy's. David scuttled to the front room. He could feel disapproval following behind him like a cold fog.

"Hello?"

"David!" Teddy said. "Where are you, man? Did you see the thing on Slashdot?"

"I'm not at a computer right now."

"They just announced a new exploit that hits sendmail on BSD platforms. There's a patch, but the mirror sites are getting hammered. I'm heading into the office now, but if you want some pizza, I could..."

"I can't. Teddy, I'm booked. I can't come in." The line went so quiet, David thought the connection had dropped. "Teddy?"

"You don't want...what about..."

"Look, why don't you take this one. Just swing by the office, get the patch and try installing it. If there's a problem, we'll sort it out in the morning."

"In the morning?" Teddy echoed.

"Sure. But there won't be a problem. You've handled this kind of thing before, right?"

"Right?"

"Great. See you tomorrow," David said and cut the connection before Teddy could say *tomorrow?* Back on the dance floor, Mariella and Angelica were in close conversation. Two pairs of eyes fixed on him as he came back in. For a moment, David had the powerful memory of being ten years old and watching *The Brides of Dracula* on late-night cable.

"Sorry," he said, turning off the cell. "It was work. Won't happen again."

"Emergency?" Niko asked. Even *his* voice was cold.

"No," David said. "Nothing important."

SIXTEEN:

SARAH WAS transferring a call to Mr. Elms' voicemail when the door opened, so she didn't actually see anyone come in. When she looked up, the arrival was still as a movie's promotional photo. Red-brown hair curled softly over one eye; soft, high cheekbones gestured down to full lips curved in a small, shy smile. The dress was quality too; creamy linen that showed off the woman's hips and breasts without mentioning that thighs might exist.

"Can I help you?" Sarah asked politely, wondering how Sam Spade's receptionist would have handled the moment.

But then the woman moved and spoiled the effect. All the glamour needed was confidence, but when she walked it was like seeing a teenager ready for her first prom.

"*Daphne?*"

"Hey, Sarah," the paralegal said, pushing the artfully placed hair back from her eyes. "So. What do you think of the new look?"

"I'm amazed," Sarah said.

"Thanks."

You poor thing, Sarah thought. You poor stupid bunny. How ugly did he make you feel? She felt a surge of anger for David Osgood, wherever he was at the moment.

"You *always* look beautiful," Sarah said.

The blush looked odd with the layers of makeup over it. No one with that much foundation should be capable of blush-inducing emotion.

"I just thought I'd try something different. You know?"

"I do," Sarah said. She did.

SEVENTEEN:

MOST MEN in their hours of crisis seek solace in a trusted friend or bartender. David went to bookstores. Big bookstores. The kinds with coffee bars in them. Cheap, acidy coffee flavored with unlikely fruits and overpriced, stale pastries shipped in from Ohio.

"Anything else?" the barista asked. He was about David's age with a thin beard, a quick smile, and an ear cuff with what looked like a wolf's tooth hanging from it. He looked cool. Even if he spent his time away from the espresso machine configuring firewalls and writing shell scripts, no one was going to mistake *him* for a computer guy.

"No thanks," David said.

He took his comfort food to one of the tables in the back. Bach viola concerti murmured as he poured sugar into the blackness of his coffee cup.

He'd called the studio and Mariella, swearing that he was sick. He wanted to be there, but he was afraid of getting everyone else sick, and then where would they all be? Mariella hadn't believed him, but she hadn't come right out and called him a liar either. Niko probably hadn't bought it either. Not that it mattered.

His mind spiraled around Daphne. She had come into the office today looking like she'd never looked before. It was obvious that she was dressed to impress someone. She'd clearly been going out after work, going to the kind of place you went dressed like that.

He sipped his coffee. It was still mostly bitter, only just a little sweet. He started to put more sugar in, but stopped and drank it the way it was.

The worst thing had been the way he hadn't been able to avoid her. No matter where he'd been in the office, it seemed like bad luck had brought her there too. And every time he saw her, he'd wanted to ask her what was up, who the guy was.

But then she would have told him. There was nothing in the world he wanted less than to hear about how wonderful Jason or Brad or Robert was, where he had a degree from, the summer he'd spent touring Europe.

He took a bite of pastry. It was dry and left a coating on his tongue. He took another bite.

What was the point, he thought, in men admiring you and women being drawn to you when the men were Teddy and the women were Mariella? He thought about all the time and effort he'd spent trying to get her to see him as something more than the computer guy. And maybe he'd managed. Maybe she saw him as the computer guy who took ballroom dance classes. The image of Al Pacino and not-quite-Uma Thurman was gone too. All he had in its place was Mariella and the constant reminder not to look at his feet.

It was dumb. He'd wasted his time and his money, and probably his shot with Daphne if he'd even had one. He'd call the academy in the morning and tell Niko he was out. They'd find some other bronze to partner Mariella. And when that was over, maybe he could get Teddy to find out who Daphne was seeing and how serious they were…

David used the last swig of coffee to wash down the last bite of the pastry of affliction. Nasty stuff all the way around. The music changed, Bach giving way to Ella Fitzgerald. David looked out over the bookshelves and shoppers and felt better than he had when he came in. It was almost a relief, really, to shrug off the dancing. It was fun stuff in a way, but as a lifestyle, kind of weird. He rose, put his hands in his pockets, and headed over toward the computer security section. Maybe something new was out.

"Hey, bud," the barista called. "Did you want the book or should I put it with the reshelves?"

David turned. The words *not mine* were on his lips, but they stopped there when he saw the blood red letters on their field of white. *30 Steps to Your Best Self.*

"Thanks," he said, took the book, and sat back down.

STEP 15: The Will to Commit

Weak-willed people are like flags that shift with the breeze. Any time things seem to turn against them, they abandon their focus and wander away. It never occurs to them that they themselves may be the source of the problem.

The solution is commitment. When the one job or girl or award that we thought meant everything slips away, it's commitment that carries us though. We persevere until we see why we want what we want, and how we can reach it.

Commitment is the step you never stop taking. If you fail in your commitment, you fail in everything, always. Only by staying on your path will you be rewarded by the discovery of who you are. Be strong and you will find what you really want.

Good luck. It's your game to lose.

David closed the book and pressed his palms to his eyes, pressing until colors bloomed in the darkness.

Commitment. He didn't want to be a weak-willed person, after all, and what else would he be if he just dropped the studio? And the thing about what to do when the one girl you

wanted slips away, about finding out what he really wanted...
Maybe he only *thought* that.Daphne was the right girl. Maybe
there was some deeper something going on with him, something psychological. And if he just went back to being who he
was, he might never figure it out.

Just being himself had never done the trick.

He took out his cell phone, considering it like Romeo looking at his vial of poison. When he thumbed in the number, the
phone on the other end only rang once before she answered it.

"Hey, Mariella," David said. The last film of coffee was
like ashes in his mouth. "I'm feeling a lot better. Tell Niko I'll
be over. And tell him I'm in for Topeka."

EIGHTEEN:

"PEABODY, PLUMMER, and Elms. Can you hold?" Sarah
said, forcing herself to smile. This was line four. Lines two and
three were already on hold. Lines five and six were still ringing.
Line one had the only solid red light—Mr. Plummer on the line
with Judge Christiansen, explaining the situation. The clock on
her computer screen flickered from 10:23 to 10:24.

"No, I can't fucking hold!" a man shouted. "You tell Peabody
that this is Bernard Lawton. *Lawton*, you got that, sister?"

"Thank you," she said, and put him on hold. She repeated
the procedure twice more, then pulled off the headset, placed
her hands palms flat on the desktop, and breathed in deeply,
letting the air escape slowly through her nose the way all the
relaxation tapes said she should.

I can do this, she told herself. They're just people.

She put the headset back on and clicked on line two.

"Thank you for holding. How may I direct your call?"

"Sarah? This is Robert Correy. Robert Correy Law. What
the hell's going on over there?"

"Good morning, Mr. Correy. Yes, we're having a little trouble with the mail server," she said. "I don't know all the details."

"So what? You folks aren't getting mail and it shuts the whole office down?"

"Oh, getting mail isn't the problem. We've gotten several hundred thousand messages in the last few hours. And apparently we've also been sending mail out," she said. "Several *million* pieces of it advertising a porn site in Yugoslavia. People seem to be taking some exception."

"I'm so sorry," he said, chuckling. "So is that why I haven't seen Elms' reply to my counter-offer?"

Line four went black as the caller hung up, then half a breath later started ringing again. Sarah's finger twitched toward it.

"Very likely," Sarah said. "It's backed things up a little."

"Well, you let me know if he decides he needs a continuance."

"I'm sure Mr. Elms will be in touch just as soon as he can."

"Well, I'll let you go, Sarah. You try to have a good day despite it all."

"Thank you, Mr. Correy."

She hung up the line and grabbed for line four, but she was an instant too late. She heard the handset on the other end being dropped into its cradle. Line two started ringing.

10:25.

She put the headset down and let the damn phones ring. She made herself knock at Mr. Elms' door before she went in. It was as close to civil as she could manage. Mr. Elms was running his thick fingers through the space where his hair had been when he'd been a younger man.

"They're working on it," Elms said before she could even speak. "As soon as it's fixed, they'll get us connected again. But if they put us back online now, we'll start sending out that junk mail like a firehose again. As soon as it's fixed…"

"And when will that be?"

"Two or three hours," Elms said, looking at her directly for the first time since she'd come in. His face was grey with rage.

The phones were ringing in a constant round now. The lines were lit and blinking for her attention like an air traffic controller's console right before the disaster. She walked past her desk, down the hallway to the machine closet where David Osgood was crouched over a laptop, typing furiously. Teddy, behind him, was literally wringing his hands. She'd never actually seen anyone do that before.

"Maybe there's some *new* exploit," Teddy was saying. "I could have sworn the patch went in okay."

David grunted and kept typing. It clearly wasn't the first time Teddy had said something of the sort.

"I've never done a patch on my own before," Teddy whined. "I mean, I didn't get any error messages when I ran it."

"It didn't run, Teddy," David said. "You don't get an error when something doesn't run. Don't worry about it. I can get this fixed."

"I'm sorry, Dave."

"It's my fault. I should have come in."

It was all she needed to hear. The broken email, the failing file servers, Daphne's new insecurity, Elms' lost counteroffer. All of it came back to David Osgood.

She'd stood at the side and watched this train wreck long enough. If no one else was going to fix it, then by God *she* would.

NINETEEN:

IN THE end, David scrapped the altered sendmail files completely, reinstalled them, and then spent several hours working the legion of hiccups and bugs out of the system. It was longer than three hours. And when he was finished, he was going to have to go to the academy for another critique session with Nikos and Angelica and all the others.

He was trying to scrape the spam out of Mr. Plummer's inbox without accidentally trashing something real when Daphne came in.

"Oh," she said.

"Plummer's in the conference room," David said.

Daphne hesitated, and David looked up again. He couldn't read her expression; she seemed about to say something.

The silence between them was where he'd been able to make normal human banter before. He hated it, but he didn't have any way to break it. Daphne smiled, thinly, nodded, and walked away again. David felt his heart go tight and heavy in his chest, but he just went back to defining junk mail rules, the keys under his fingers clicking softly.

He wanted to talk to her, even just to say hello and make smartass comments about putting paper into the printer. Little things, the way people do who work in the same place. He'd had that much once.

He applied the rule set, watched the junk mail pour out of the inbox. And then the test messages he'd sent. And then five messages that he knew should have stayed.

He sighed, opened the junk folder, dragged everything back into the inbox and started over. He only half noticed, twenty minutes later, when Daphne walked past the open door in deep conversation with the receptionist.

TWENTY:

SARAH CONSIDERED the pair of them. Daphne seemed stunned, Teddy nervous. She herself felt a combination of focused anger and relief that she was doing something. There were worse ways for a conspiracy to begin.

"So like...an intervention or something?" Teddy asked. "We all tell him not to fuck up anymore and that we all love him?"

Daphne swallowed hard and flushed a little pink.

"No," Sarah said. "Interventions don't work unless everyone he knows can participate. If we tell him there's a problem and his dancer friends tell him he's fine, he'll shift his social network toward them."

Someone rattled the conference room door, then knocked.

"In a minute," Sarah called. Then, in her normal tone of voice, "He has to face a choice. Either his job and his friends are more important than this hobby of his, or else they aren't. We are going to give him that choice."

"How?" Daphne asked.

"This can't go past us," Sarah said.

Teddy twisted his fingers before his lips in a locking motion. Daphne leaned forward.

"Do we gotta kidnap him?" Teddy asked, clearly excited by the prospect of abduction.

"No," Sarah said. "We generate a crisis and call him in. We make it clear that we need him, and then we see what choice he makes."

The knock came again, harder this time. Sarah ignored it and it went away.

"When is this competition of his?" Sarah asked.

"Next weekend. I mean not this weekend coming up, but the one after it," Teddy said, "He flies out to Topeka Saturday morning, him and Mariella."

"Find out what time his flight leaves. We'll meet here that morning. Just the three of us."

"What if he chooses *them*?" Daphne asked quietly.

TWENTY-ONE:

UNDER NORMAL circumstances, Mr. Elms would have considered standing in the corridor, his ear pressed to the conference room doors to be beneath his dignity. These were, however, desperate times. Osgood's plans to sabotage the computer system were clearly underway, and given what his brief exploration of eavesdropping had uncovered he was not the only one to have noticed it.

Osgood was going out of town under the pretext of some "competition," and he was traveling with the exquisite woman. Mr. Elms trotted back to his office, his former business forgotten. There could be no doubt that Osgood was going to meet with his new handlers, the unknown enemy that had turned him against the firm. Without a doubt, it was the best opportunity to catch the boy in the act. Once Mr. Elms had hard evidence—he had always been a stickler for evidence, which explained to a degree his choice of profession—he would merrily litigate Osgood and his new friends into bankruptcy. It might take years, and if so, all the better. Vice deserved punishment.

He could book himself a flight to Topeka, get there before the traitorous Osgood and his divine escort, and shadow them. He hesitated just as his fingers touched the keyboard, millimeters from using his browser to find an online travel site. It occurred to him that he was about to use his computer to act against his computer expert. He lifted up his wide fingers and wagged one at the screen.

"Very close," he said. "You almost got me that time, but not quite. Oh no. I'm cleverer than that, my friend."

"Sir?"

His secretary stood in the doorway with the expression one might expect from a woman of near-military precision and efficiency who had found her employer talking to his computer. Mr. Elms drew himself up from his desk.

"Mr. Berringer is in the conference room, sir."

"Of course he is," Mr. Elms said, "but first, I have an assignment for you. It's very important. I want you to leave the office before you do this, do you understand? No one here must know anything about this. Find a travel agent. Go there in person. I need a ticket for one to Topeka."

He paused, wondering if it would be wise to acquire a gun. Just in case.

TWENTY-TWO:

DAVID DROVE toward the academy. He was in his costume and he felt like an idiot. Red sequins glittered in his lap and down one leg. His shirt clung to his body, making him suck in his belly even when there was no one around. The rush hour was just ended, only the last stragglers limping home. He'd had a snack at home. He'd eat again later. And then sleep a few hours. And then go back to the office again, feeling less rested than he did now.

They were talking about him. The crash had technically been Teddy's fault, but even he knew better than to take comfort in that. Teddy was a good guy, and he could run wire and configure simple applications, but he was no more a network admin than David was a movie star. Asking Teddy to do stuff that was over his head was just dumb. No one was going to blame Teddy, and he wouldn't really want them to.

The sense of disappointment and dislike was new to him, though, and he didn't enjoy it. The whole office knew he'd screwed up. They were talking about it, and about him, and knowing that made his shoulders feel heavier. He didn't want to go back in tomorrow. Any more than he wanted to go to practice now.

If you fail in your commitment, you fail in everything, always.

He turned the car into the strip mall parking lot. He could recognize the cars of the other couples. Mariella's white Lexus with the "My Lawyer Can Beat Up Your Honor Student" bumper sticker. He pulled into a space a little way down, killed the motor, and listened to the car tick as it cooled.

It would be so easy to turn the key, reverse back out, just go home. Go home with his cat and his music, sit on his couch and watch his television, and just let all of it go away. He could skip work tomorrow too. Take the phone off the hook, and not check email, and not answer the door if anyone bothered knocking. He closed his eyes.

But that wasn't what he really wanted. However pleasant it sounded now, the sense of being alone there had been what brought him here in the first place. When he'd spent his nights at home by himself, he'd felt alone. Now that he was here, he felt alone. The difference was that one of them was moving him out in the world, and he was more likely to find what he really wanted out here than back in front of the TV.

Be strong and you will find what you really want.

He got out of the car, trudged past the cellular phone joint, and knocked on the academy door. Angelica let him in. The others were in the back. Mariella frowned at him, Niko smiled. The room smelled of shoe leather, sweat, and expensive perfume.

"Good," Niko said. "We're all here again. Let's see how our bronzes are progressing, shall we?"

David stepped out into the middle of the floor, folding his arm around Mariella, taking his hand in hers. She smiled, her body soft and supple under his touch.

"Try not to screw up," she said.

"I'll try," he said.

The music started. David turned through the routine with certainty and precision. His legs knew where to be, his arms, his body. The whole thing had about as much joy as reciting the pledge of allegiance. He twirled Mariella into his arms as the music ended. She was breathing hard, and there was a glittering excitement in her eyes. David supposed he hadn't screwed up.

"Excellent," Niko breathed. "That was...that was perfect. There's no way you can lose if you dance like that at the competition."

"Don't you think he could smile a bit more?" the American Rhythm woman asked.

TWENTY-THREE:

THE WEEK passed in unspoken tension, each day before the competition bringing the offices of Peabody, Plummer, and Elms one step nearer the breaking point. Sarah left Friday at five o'clock with the sense of finally slipping her leash. When she returned in the morning, it was like entering a different world.

With the overhead fluorescents off, the hallways and offices were dim. Sarah had never really understood how much background noise a lawyer's office could generate until now that it was gone. It was a little eerie.

The lock clicked, the front door opened, and Daphne came in. She was dressed in old jeans and a sweatshirt; her hair was pulled back in its ponytail. She smiled when she caught sight of Sarah and raised a plastic sack.

"I brought bagels and schmear," she said. "No dark cabal should be without."

"Excellent." Sarah said, motioning her over. "Have you seen Teddy? If his flight leaves at nine o'clock..."

"He was pulling into the parking lot when I got the elevator."

"Even better."

Sarah had a fresh cup of coffee in one hand and an everything bagel with lox schmear in the other when Teddy arrived. He grinned nervously. Sarah couldn't tell if it was just idiomatic for Teddy to look vaguely frightened or if he was having second thoughts. But he wasn't so distressed that food was beyond him. He had the cinnamon-raisin with honey butter while Sarah explained her plan one last time.

"But how would Daphne break it?" Teddy said when she was done. "I mean if she's really here doing just normal stuff, how would she break the system?"

"It doesn't matter," Sarah said. "Maybe she didn't. Maybe the system just…broke."

"Well, it's a computer. They don't just stop *working*, you know," Teddy said, and then a moment later. "Okay. Never mind. I don't know what I was thinking."

"And why am I calling him?" Daphne asked.

"Because you can't find Teddy," Sarah replied.

"Yes, but…why am *I* calling?" Daphne said. "You could have done this without me in on it. You could make the call."

"Sometimes men will do things for paralegals that they won't do for receptionists," Sarah said, smiling gently. Daphne blushed slightly. Teddy looked confused. The clock hummed and with an audible click shifted its minute hand to exactly the hour, and Sarah rose.

"Shall we?"

Teddy led the way to the machine closet. The three of them huddled around the laptop as it chirped and whirred, booting up. Teddy cracked his knuckles and started typing, green letters glowing on the black background. Sarah understood none of it. She didn't need to.

"I really never dreamed I'd be doing something like this," Teddy said.

"Desperate times call for desperate measures," Sarah said.

"Yeah, okay. So, I'm not doing anything tricky, since I want to be able to put this all back the way it was. You know. I mean, in case."

"That's wise," Sarah agreed.

"So I'm just gonna come in here like this. And then I'll become root. And I'm just changing the permissions on this one folder here. That shouldn't..."

The machine chirped and spooled through a long list of gibberish. Teddy leaned forward, squinting. He hit a few keys, and the laptop beeped loudly as he touched each one. He giggled. It wasn't a good sound.

"That's...ah...funny. Lemme just...ah..."

He touched a few keys together and the screen went flat black and featureless. The server's hard drive whirred and started grinding.

"Well," Teddy said. "Huh."

"Daphne? You should call him now."

TWENTY-FOUR:

DAPHNE PUT the phone's handset back in its cradle, plastic clattering in the silence of the office. Her gaze wandered for a moment before she found Sarah.

"He's not coming."

TWENTY-FIVE:

STEP TWENTY: Protecting Yourself

Who among us hasn't sometimes gotten in over his head? Overextending is a natural part of testing your personal limits, and nothing to be ashamed of. It is critical, however, that you deal with the consequences gracefully. If someone else in the office is on his way out anyway, it does him no harm to carry some of your burden. Shifting responsibility isn't an act of...

Oh shit. It's her. Put the book down.

Put the book down, Teddy.

Put me DOWN!

"What are you reading?" Sarah asked.

"I don't know," Teddy said, holding the book out to her. "I thought it was a self-help book, but then it gets into this free verse thing."

Sarah took the book and skimmed a couple of pages. Then she made a noise and read it again, her eyebrows rising toward her hairline. Teddy thought it was weird the way she held it on her fingertips, like she was trying not to touch it.

TWENTY-SIX:

THE "COMPETITION" was in fact a genuine ballroom dance competition. Mr. Elms had to give his invisible enemies credit. They had covered themselves well. To a less penetrating mind, this grand hotel ballroom with its colorful lights and transporting music, vaulted ceilings speaking of a gentler age, and genuinely decent snacks might have appeared innocent. Mr. Elms sat by himself, watching the dance floor. His jacket, folded on the chair beside him, concealed the handgun.

It was early in the evening, but Elms was a patient man. The program, open on his knee, outlined the course of the night's entertainments. David Osgood and Mariella Demidain were listed together in the International Latin, bronze level. It was Mr. Elms' intention to wait him out here, and then follow them, cat-like, from the ballroom to whatever nefarious meeting they had planned. If necessary, he would confront them. He could feel a rising excitement at the prospect.

Confounding that, he also felt a rising excitement at the American Rhythm competition presently on the ballroom floor. A man in a gaudy white and gold outfit was twirling a woman in a top and skirt that matched in both color and sheer visual intensity. Elvis Presley assured them all that he was both in love and also all shook up, and Mr. Elms found himself tapping his knee to the beat. Man and woman were both smiling, their joyous, athletic movements both free and restrained in a combination that commanded the eye to follow them.

As he was near the back wall—the better for shadowy skulking, he'd thought—Mr. Elms could allow himself the luxury of standing up for a better view. These two were, he thought, amazing. Much better than the pair before them in red and gold, though he was going to have to track down more music by the Brian Setzer fellow the previous couple had danced to. Mr. Elms caught himself shifting his hips and arms slightly in echo of the dance on stage, felt himself blushing, and looked around to assure himself that no one had seen him.

At first, he couldn't believe what he saw. There, at the edge of the crowd, a familiar face took in the dance with cool certainty. Sarah, the receptionist. Mr. Elms' paranoia fell back upon him like a wave. She had been one of the voices he'd overheard discussing this competition. Was she part of Osgood's betrayal as well? Or was there some other agenda that had brought her here?

Casting his gaze back and forth, Mr. Elms reached back for his jacket and eased the pistol into the front pocket of his slacks. The song came to its end, and the waterfall roar of applause covered him as he moved forward. His eyes didn't leave Sarah as he inched forward. Like a hawk, he thought. Like a hawk swooping down to the kill.

The announcer, following his mandate, announced. There would be a brief open period while the judges for International Latin took their places. Everyone was invited to take a turn around the floor. The people surged forward, flowing around Mr. Elms like a river around a stone. Sarah did not turn, but then, just beyond her, he caught a glimpse of David Osgood, his chest covered with glittering sequins, the inestimable woman Mariella on his arm. Sarah, he saw, had risen from her seat, her eyes on the crowd, on Osgood and Mariella. Seeing her expression, he felt a moment's doubt at his own attempts to cast himself as the hunter. The receptionist seemed quite suited to the role.

While he considered this odd insight, three things happened as if at once. Music began, a low almost compelling beat with a thrill of guitar and strings. The receptionist strode out toward Osgood. And the crowd around Mr. Elms shifted, leaving him suddenly aware that he was standing alone and unpartnered in the middle of a great dance.

It seemed symbolic.

TWENTY-SEVEN:

IT WAS as graceful and devastating as a cat pouncing. David, his arms around Mariella (the woman least like a young Uma Thurman of anyone in the world), had just taken the first turn of the dance when the receptionist from the office cut in. Without a word, Mariella was detached from David's embrace, Sarah inserted in her place, and he was shifted out into the center of the civilized mosh pit of the dance floor.

"Um," David said. "Hi."

"Hello, David. We need to talk."

It was a little odd, having his arm around her, her face close to his. She was from the office, and this wasn't really the office-approved distance unless the Christmas party was way out of hand. It felt like kissing his sister.

"I can...I mean, what are you doing here?" he asked as she made a slow spin and came back to him.

"I was about to ask the same thing," she said. "I was with Daphne at the office."

"Oh," David said, his belly heavy as if he'd swallowed a double handful of lead shot. "That."

"It isn't like you to ignore an emergency," Sarah said. "It isn't like you to leave Daphne in trouble."

He almost bowed his head, but Angelica's voice in the back of his mind snapped at him not to look at his shoes.

"I'm sorry about that. Seriously, I am," he said. "I know it seems weird. But this was just...something I had to do."

"It was the book, wasn't it?" Sarah asked. They reached the edge of the dance floor and turned back in, slipping between the other couples easily as an eel through water. "What did it say to you?"

David didn't answer right away. He felt small, embarrassed, humiliated. And it wasn't just the costume or the eye liner and blush. His body shifted, the Argentine tango moving him through its course, and all he could think about was how he must seem to Sarah. A slack bastard who'd let down people who were depending on him.

A lonely, sad little man who Daphne would never see as anything but the guy who fixes the networking. Who couldn't face another year sitting on his couch with his cat, ordering pizza and watching cable, so instead paid a third of his paycheck for costumes he wouldn't wear in public and dance lessons with people who didn't like him.

Who had fallen so low he was taking advice from a self-help book.

"What did it say?" Sarah asked again, her voice gentler.

"That I need to know what I really want," he said, knowing how stupid it sounded as he said it. "If I don't stick through the hard parts of something, I'll just keep bouncing around like some kind of pinball. I want..."

They turned, sliding gracefully around another couple. David's feet moved with a grace and certainty he didn't feel.

"You want this? Professional dance competition?"

"No. I just *want*. And maybe this all goes to the place I want to be. How do I know unless I go there?"

She went quiet; she was leading, but he didn't object. It hardly mattered, really.

"It promised you that you'd know what you really want?"

"Yes," he said.

"When do you dance besides this?" she asked at last, turning him out and pulling him back to her. She was pretty good at this.

"I don't. I mean sometimes when I'm at a club and a little tipsy..."

"No country and western? Never been honky-tonking? No Cotton-Eyed Joe?"

David laughed nervously.

"Um. No."

"I have," Sarah said. "Country music knows a lot about finding out what you want. There are a thousand songs, probably, that tell you how to do it."

"Really?"

"It's easy. You piss it away. The soul-crushing regret afterward is how you know that what you lost was precious. That book? It's not on your side. I promise."

David almost missed a step.

"She'd say yes," the receptionist said.

David stopped. The other couples on the floor brushed against them, moths passing a lightbulb.

"You mean *Daphne?*"

"She's in love with you. She has been for months."

"You're...I mean, she..."

The receptionist raised her eyebrows, challenging him to disagree. His mind spun like a top for eight beats. He dropped his arms to his sides and looked down at his feet. It was like waking up from a dream.

"Oh," he said.

TWENTY-EIGHT:

"I'M REALLY a very important man. Running a law firm like mine is har...hard work."

Mariella pulled him close as they turned. Her eyes were bright and predatory.

"So," she murmured, "is that a gun in your pocket, or are you just happy to see me?"

TWENTY-NINE:

THEY HAD almost missed the flight, and Sarah's return tickets from Topeka didn't land them back home until almost morning on Sunday. Teddy and Daphne were still at the office when they got there, along with three stale bagels and half a teaspoon of schmear. David felt a little weird in his sequins and dance shoes, but he'd gotten most of the eyeliner off at the airport, and Sarah promised him that what was left just accented his eyes a little. Nothing anyone would notice.

"I was going to try that next," Teddy said, shoulder surfing. "Seriously, that was the absolute very next thing on my list."

David, sitting cross-legged in the machine closet, let himself smile. The keyboard clicked under his fingers, the interface running as fast as thought. In his mind, the systems file structure glowed and shifted, symbolic links relating one level to the next in a cascade that brought the whole half-dead structure back into place.

"It would have done the trick," David said, hitting enter. "Okay, I'm taking everything down and the restart should put us back in business."

"That's great," Teddy said. His voice reminded David of someone being told the lab had accidentally switched his blood sample with a rhesus monkey's and he wasn't actually a macaque after all. "You want some coffee? Sarah just made some fresh."

"That'd be great," he said.

What he really wanted was to go home, change into something grey and colorless, listen to something punk and simplistic with terrible musicianship, and then sleep for a week. Except that Daphne came around the corner and he didn't want any of that at all.

"Hey," she said.

"Hey."

"All better?"

"Pretty much," he said, patting the keyboard as the monitor sprang back to life, running the startup checksums. Daphne looked down, smiling a little. She had the most beautiful mouth. David felt himself starting to blush. All the things he'd been going to say vanished. The moment was here, the chance he'd been fighting to take all this time, and he could feel it slipping away. In a second, she was going to ask him something about computers or NFS or domain management and this delicate, fragile chance would be blown again. He tried to speak, but nothing came out, not even something inane.

"We should go dancing some time," Daphne said, looking up at him.

"Dancing?" he squeaked.

"Just social, you know. Like at a club."

"The kind where nobody wins," he agreed.

She hesitated, a hint of a blush in her cheeks.

"More the kind where nobody loses."

THIRTY:

THE SHREDDER hummed to itself, pleased just to be a shredder. Sarah leaned back in her chair. The simple harmony of a well-run office tapped and murmured. The phone didn't ring. She licked the tip of one finger and turned the page.

STEP TWENTY-THREE: Forgiveness

The measure of your depth and maturity is your capacity to forgive. It is this more than any other attribute that shows your best self and makes you an example for those around you.

"Not true," Sarah said. "Keep trying."

"Sarah?" Mr. Elms said, coming through the front door. She glanced at the clock. It was unlike Mr. Elms to be late, but less so than it had once been. "Sarah, I'm afraid I lost track of time over lunch. There's a finding scheduled for three o'clock, and I was thinking we could have Daphne—"

"She has everything ready for it, sir. It's on your desk," Sarah said as the reason Mr. Elms had lost track of time walked in behind him. Mariella's presence reminded Sarah of the other business she had waiting. "Also, David Osgood left a package for you."

"Really?" Mr. Elms asked, and then, with an almost conspiratorial wink, "Is it what I think it is?"

"Rumba in the Bronx. Among others," Sarah said, handing over the stack of disks. Mr. Elms scooped them up, and Mariella sloped to his side. Talking knowledgeably about the songs, they walked back to Mr. Elms' office together just as Daphne came from the other direction. Her flirtation with makeup was over. Her shoes were the low heels Sarah had always been accustomed to seeing. Her hair was pulled back. She was beautiful.

"He's already downstairs with Teddy," Sarah said. "I told Mr. Elms you had everything ready for him. You're covered."

"You're sure you don't want to come with us?"

"I don't think *Shall We Dance* needed to be remade again. You kids go on ahead while you can still get matinee prices," Sarah said. She looked at the shredder's unimposing maw and then at the book. "Besides I have some document control to do."

"You work too hard," Daphne said.

"Only way I'll make partner," Sarah said with a shrug, and then Daphne was gone, the wide, solid door closing behind her.

The only way to truly judge something is by its results. All's well that ends well, as the bard said. And it isn't as if I exactly lied to anyone.

"And oftentimes, to win us to our harm, the instruments of darkness tell us truths, win us with honest trifles, to betray's in deepest consequence," Sarah said, her voice a light sing-song.

Oh, now that's just mean.

A sharp snapping of fingers called Sarah to attention. The man at the desk—early forties with a soup-stained tie and a scowl of such longevity is seemed etched in his skin—raised his eyebrows.

"I'm sorry," Sarah said, laying the book aside. "I didn't hear you—"

"I got that," the man sneered as he dropped his attaché case on her desk. "How about you pull it together, give Oprah a rest, and go tell Mark Peabody I'm here. I'll be back when I'm done in the can."

"May I tell him who's here to see him?"

"Bernard Lawton," the man said, not bothering to look back at her. He appended his name with a word that was clearly intended to apply to Sarah, though she thought overall it fit him better. She scooped up her handset and paged Mr. Peabody. The attaché case squatted on her desk, a physical insult. She glanced at the book and had the eerie feeling that it was looking back. She picked it up again.

Or, it said, *maybe we could make some sort of deal?*

Sarah considered for a moment. Happily, the attaché case was unlocked.

A HUNTER IN ARIN-QIN

ONE:

AT FIRST, WHEN THE lights of my home still glimmered in the darkness behind me, the cold only chilled. Then, pressing through the snow with the effort of the chase keeping me warm, the cold bit.

At the end, it comforted.

It meant the worst kind of danger, but with fear itself a distant thing, even danger failed to seem dangerous. Snow cracked under my feet and caked the wool of my leggings. I wrapped my father's hunting cloak tight about me. I walked because I could no longer run. Before me, the beast's tracks softened under new-fallen snow, and with every moment, new flakes conspired to hide them further. The sword strapped to my back grew heavy, and I doubted my strength, even if the opportunity came. My daughter's doom whispered with every pine branch that brushed against me. Gone. Gone. Gone.

Slowly, the hunter within me—hard as stone and untouched by years of a different woman's life—woke. Her eyes saw the fading edges of the beast's track as time: two hours ahead of me, then three hours, then four. Her mind evaluated my shuffling stride and leaden hands. She tried to smile with my numbed lips; I felt her grim amusement. She knew a dead woman when she saw one.

I fell without knowing that I fell. My foot touched the snow. My knee touched it. My hip. My shoulders. The soft white filled my mouth and nose and eyes. It tasted like rain. I pressed my hands down, trying to rise, and the earth passed through my fingers like fog.

I believe he followed me. To happen upon me just at the moment of greatest need in a moon-dark valley would otherwise mark him as a fate or a god, and I choose to think of him as a man. I never knew how long he watched and shadowed me, or what error of panic or rusted skill made my passage conspicuous. In the moment, I only felt his hands lifting me.

Rage and fear surged through my blood, first with the thought that the beast had found me and, when that proved untrue, at the uninvited touch of a strange man's hands. The two outrages spoke with the same voice.

I tried to shout, to push him away, to draw the sword that still hung from my back. He brushed my efforts away. His ice-blue eyes flickered with annoyance, but nothing more. His snow-flecked beard hung against my neck, feeling more like a dead animal than part of a living man's body. He turned, trotting with me in his arms as if the burden of a full grown woman meant no more to him than carrying a child. And with that thought, I remembered my daughter and the beast and my doomed quest.

I willed him to turn, to carry me—dead or dying—along the path marked out by the beast's footsteps. I cried out, flailed at him, reached back over his jouncing shoulder. The wind paid me as much attention.

And within me, the hunter narrowed her eyes and waited to see what this rescue meant.

Two:

I KILLED my first monster in the autumn of the Salt Emperor's ascension. My father followed as I read the signs in the water of a small, fishless lake. This time, I smelled the broken reeds and cattails instead of him. I pressed my ear to the cold, mossy earth. I tasted the wind. All around us, the year lost its green. Leaves skated on the pond, blown by any breath of wind. Grass shifted from green to yellow, blades rubbing together like a million dry hands.

And in a village two leagues away, five children lay in fresh graves. We hunted to prevent a sixth.

I hardly stood taller than a child myself. My arm and blade together reached from my father's shoulder to his fingertips, but he acted as though he followed an equal. He never advised or made suggestion. If I felt the temptation to look in his eyes for approval or disdain, dowsing my performance like a hedge witch with a stick, I held back.

The reeds said the monster stood no taller than a man. The water said it ate fish and snakes, that it shat and pissed in the pond, that its blood etched stone like acid. I walked the way my father had taught me: knees bent, weight forward on my feet and distributed equally, connected to the earth through my belly and the sky through my skull. A crane fluttered and called from the pond. I crept along the pond's edge, and my father crept behind me. When I drew my blade, he drew his.

The cave lay almost under the water, the dark arch disguising itself as a shallow overhang. The reed bed before it pretended that nothing passed in or out. The lie almost convinced me, but only almost. I stopped. My eyes narrowed, my blood went hot and my mind perfectly still.

Quick as a fish, something broke the pond's surface and vanished again. A bubble. A fish snapping at a fly. Or a monstrous eye peeking at a girl equally hunter and prey.

I expected my father to speak, to warn me, to take control. He waited. The ripple moved through the reeds, the stalks shifting and bowing like a crowd at a temple.

The monster leapt for us.

For me.

I saw flesh the green of moss, eyes the red of blood, claws like broken glass tipping splayed fingers. Its scream tore the air, and part of my mind shrieked with fear. But only part. My body slid low, under its attack. My blade rose. I felt the shock in my wrists, but striking a practice dummy hurt as much. Less. Its claws raked my side, stripping my cloak to ribbons, exposing the tight-layered silk and woven steel beneath. For a moment, we embraced, the monster and I. The world contained only us. I watched its eyes lose focus, the life pass from it. At the end, it snapped wicked teeth at me; the reflex of a killer when only reflex remains.

I stepped back, pulling my blade free. I gave no shout, not in the attack and not after. My father stood behind me, his blade still held at the ready. The wind alone stirred the reeds. He held his hand out to me, and I passed my sword to him. The monster's black blood hissed and stank, bubbling in the air and light. My father's smile never touched his lips, only his eyes.

You need a new blade, he said.

The joy in my heart startled me.

THREE:

I WOKE to the sound of fire. At first, I imagined myself in my home again, the beast and the abduction, the sick knowledge that justice had come and found me unready, all parts of a dream already fading. But as I came to myself, the illusion failed me. My father's cloak still wrapped me. My undrawn

sword lay at my side on blankets of rough wool. I lifted
my head.

The tent rose no more than the man's height, even at its
peak. Hide stretched taut across a frame of bent wood. A fire
pit in the center covered less space than my own two hands
together. The man squatted before the flame, feeding chips
and slivers of wood into it. His gaze flicked up toward me.

As a child, a youth, a young woman, I passed my nights
in temporary warmth such as this. My father's oiled cloth
tents gave us only enough space to sleep, and he built his fire
pits from earth and stone. No detail of those camps lived
in this, but it made no difference. I saw at once how the
structure would break, how it could strap to a mule's side
or a man's back, how it changed a killing wilderness into a
place where a hunter might revive an idiot woman half-dead
from cold.

I deserved death. Anyone who rushed into the snow without thought of food or shelter, with only the image of her
daughter wrapped in the fleeing beast's arms to guide her,
deserved death. The hunter within me felt my shame and
nodded. My father, many years dead but still alive in my memory, nodded with her but with more forgiveness. Luck saved
me this time. Every hunter recognized the power of chance.
Only fools relied on it.

I sat up slowly. The man moved to my side, thick-shouldered
and with black hair and a beard so thick I could barely make out
the pale flesh of his lips. I tried to speak, to explain myself, but
he replied only with grunts and clicks. None of the five tongues
I spoke fared any better with him. Wordless, he held out his
hand. A bit of fish, its flesh white as the snow, its skin the silver
of coins. I accepted it. I sat by the fire, the hunter within me
weighing my rescuer.

Scars marked his hands, but the fur cloak showed me little of his build. His eyes, the blue of ice in moonlight, held

steady. I could no more read his thoughts than comprehend his language, but I felt no threat. I knew his kind.

When I had finished my fish, he grunted, pointing at the tied flap of his tent with a jutting beard. I let him guide me outside. The sky glowered down at us, unfallen snow weighing on the air. I knew the position of our little camp by the shapes of the hills and the angle of the moon. In moments, I picked out the tracks from beneath their blanket. He had come from the east, carrying me. I touched the crust of white, and it gave almost no resistance. Five hours, perhaps. It put the beast a day ahead. Less. Even monsters want sleep.

And my girl? My daughter with hair the color of midnight and laughter like a brook that knows a secret? My daughter barely on the verge of becoming a woman? She traveled with the enemy, or else she had gone to the gods. The fault belonged to me, either way. I trembled in fear, but the hunter within me only shrugged. If she lived, she needed saving. If not, then I would keep the cycle of vengeance alive. Both waited a day to the east.

The man nodded, calling me back to myself. When he smiled, yellowed teeth appeared for a moment in the hedge of his beard. He bent down, a thin knife appearing from his sleeve. In five short strokes, he sketched the print left by the pad and three wide-splayed claws. His eyes asked the question. I held out my hand. He hesitated only a moment before handing me the blade. I drew the beast; its greater and lesser arms, the powerful, crooked legs, the tail held above the land that balanced its vicious jaws. The beast as I knew it. I pointed to the east, and then north.

He shook his head, pointing east and then south. I squinted toward the distant horizon. He grunted, clicked, gestured at the low shadow far to the southeast, and I understood. He thought the beast sought refuge in the forest. I knew better. I shook my head. I pointed to the north where nothing grew, no sheltering trees or overhanging cliffs beckoned. When he shook his head again, I bent down again, pushing my hand into the snow as deep as my arm. When I withdrew it, the snowpack held. A cave. I pointed north.

This time, slowly, he nodded. When I handed his knife back, he took my fingers and curled them around the handle more tightly, an unmistakable gesture of trust. I kept the blade, ducked back into the tent, and prepared for our trek to the east. He did the same, and so our partnership began.

FOUR:

FOR TEN years after my first kill, my father and I hunted together. Our commissions came from the great palaces of the governors, gold and silver with a hundred huntsmen at our disposal. They came from low, dirt-farming villages with only chickens and rice to offer as payment. My father taught me with great care that we accepted or refused our blades not on the size of the payment offered us, but the need of those who made the offering.

In the port of Song-Tai, a woman with eyes black as ink and a mouth round as a worm's rose from the sea and lured men to drown in the night waves. We slew her. In the flint-and-dust hills of Calicor, a snake the length of ten men together haunted the valleys and strangled travelers in their sleep. We slew it. From the skies above the golden halls of Qin-Lun, a swarm of insects neither beetle nor wasp but something of both descended from the moon, lifted virgin boys into the sky, and returned their still-pink bones in the morning. And these also, we slew.

When sweet fame intoxicated me, and it often did, my father needed only to frown, and I would return to myself. Songs praised the master hunter and his daughter. Poets

fashioned romances from blood and steel, craft and violence, the power of his bow and the subtlety of my sword.
Women offered themselves to my father, and some offers,
I think, he accepted. Men wooed me, but only a few. The
most daring.

Our last hunt together began in the height of summer.

The island of Hun clung to the southern coast like a man
about to fall from a cliff. High mountains marked the main-
land's edge, ragged stones threatened any boats that ventured
across the narrow throat of water, and a beach of pebbles and
shells chittered with every wave's caress. The Salt Emperor's
scroll called it the edge of light and darkness, and though the
skies shone as bright as in the empire's heart, I knew what
the words meant. The stones spoke of desolation, the water
of sterility.

High above us, the sun shone down on a land in which
even wildflowers failed to survive. My father sniffed at the
wind, rolled the pebbles between his fingertips, and drew his
bow. The low, disconsolate complaint of the surf followed us.

For the five previous months, the demon plagued the
southern coast. Farmers woke in the mornings to find their
sheep slaughtered and left to rot. Women gave birth to
dead babes. A cohort of the Emperor's guard sent to protect
the towns went mad, slaughtering themselves in manners
grotesque and terrible.

And so, the Salt Emperor decided to commission our
hunt. And so, his summons reached us at my father's home
in the forests of the north. And so, we walked down that fatal
beach under that blasting sun and salt-sown air.

The demon squatted on the western tip of the island, its
scales black as a beetle's and slick with something not quite
blood. Its jaw hinged like an insect's, and it sang a high, mindless song that set my teeth to aching. Wide, uncomprehending
fish-eyes clicked toward us and then away.

I heard my father's last breath. He drew back his bow-string. His arrow flew, piercing the demon's left eye, and they fell as one, monster and hero both dead before they touched the ground.

Later, I would find his letter to me. I would read of the demon's unholy curse and my father's fear that I might try to take his place at the last, protecting him from the demon by dying myself. Later, I would feel the sorrow and love and betrayal mix together in my soul like milk poured into tea.

In the moment, I merely shrieked.

FIVE:

THE KILLING cold of night kept us from breaking camp until just before dawn. The man folded his tent into a pack small enough to sling on his wide back. I used his small knife to refashion my father's hunting cloak. Too large, it could not keep the chill air from my skin. I cut a long length down one side, bored a new line of holes, and laced the spare leather through them. The effort left me with a length of fur and tanned hide wide as my palm and long as my arm. I worked that into leggings and a cover for my boots. Finished, I judged the warmth of my body, guessed how the effort of the hunt would change it, made a few last adjustments.

The man watched me. If questions troubled him, he kept them in silence. With tent and food pack, sword and dagger, he looked like a caravan with legs. I tried not to laugh. His eyes showed his affront at my amusement, but he allowed me to take his waterskin and the leather sack of hard cracker and dried meat to put over my own shoulders with my sword.

The sword my father gave me after that first kill by the water. The sword I'd worn the day he died. The sword that had brought the beast upon me.

The man coughed, nodded to the east, and we set off. With each step through the thick and clinging snow, the wife and widow and mother retreated, and the hunter within me took control. The fear, the metal-taste of panic, even the rage hid away under her cool regard.

Under *my* cool regard.

I kept my gaze in the middle distance, my attention aware, but unfocused as my father had taught me. A rabbit saw us, startled, and fled. Crow's tracks marked where something had died under the snow, but not my daughter. Mice, perhaps. My breath glowed golden in the low morning sun, and I knew everything.

The details of my house, of the attack, came to me, and I considered them with my newly-returned self. My house lay by the bend of a mountain stream. My daughter and I never wanted for fresh water or fish. But the richness of the place brought other things as well. When, in the cold hours of the night, I woke to a sound, I imagined only a squirrel or a rabbit. At worst, a badger. The scratching and sliding came again, like a wounded animal pulling itself across the floorboards. I rose and made my first mistake. Wisdom and habit called for finding a weapon, but I walked out to investigate.

Built as a hunter's lodge, the house circled itself. The great pit of the center room opened to a simple kitchen on the west, the winter stores and my sleeping chamber to the east, my daughter's small chamber to the north, and to the south, the winter. The embers of the evening fire glowed in the grate. The sound stopped as I stepped out from my chamber door.

I called my daughter's name, another mistake. Her voice, sleep-thick and distant, reassured me for a moment. And then the beast chuckled. In the dim light of the near-dead fire, the silhouette moved in a heartbeat, a shadow against a shadow. I screamed, running toward my daughter's door, but the girl opened it as I came. In her nightshirt, she seemed to glow, an ember herself. The still-warm remains of another fire.

The beast scooped her up in its lesser arms. Its tail caught me in the ribs, throwing me to the ground. Its jaws rattled teeth like daggers.

You brought this, it hissed. *Burn in it.* And the south door—the door that led to the wild—burst open. My daughter shouted once in fear and outrage. The memory squeezed at my heart, but the hunter refused all sentiment. In my memory, I lit candles in a panic, my hands shaking.

Since the day I set my old self aside, since I locked the hunter away in the back of my mind and made my life as a mother, a fisher, a mender of old cloth, my father's hunting cloak never left its peg by the door. I grabbed it then. Since the day I first felt my girl stirring in my womb, my sword never left its shelf. It did now. I ran out to the snow and the cold and my own death.

The hunter forced my mind to slow, to recall details seen but unexamined. The snow outside the house had glowed white in the dim moonlight. White with no trace of black. So no blood. The beast's vile teeth could snap a tree in half, but they spared my daughter's neck, for a time at least. Its claws could have stripped armor from the greatest fighters in the empire, but my daughter's sleeping shift protected her from its cuts. I saw none of it in the moment. Only now did I begin to understand these traces of the beast's intent.

If it had wanted her dead in that moment, the killing stroke had lain in its power. If it wanted her alive...

I laughed. The man turned to look at me, but I found no way to explain my relief and my despair.

Poor bait stops drawing when the animal recognizes the trap. The best calls even after the prey knows. The caves in the north waited like a wolf-trap under fallen leaves. The abduction began the monster's vengeance, but didn't end it. With my child as the perfect bait, the beast drew me in, and even knowing, I allowed it to draw me.

I prayed that it would consider her more effective alive than dead. That it wanted me to suffer precisely as it had.

That it would not kill my girl until I stood witness to her death.

SIX:

PERHAPS EVERY child goes mad when her parents die. Certainly after my father fell on that sterile stone beach, I lost my mind for a time. I remember his funeral in bits and pieces, like shards of a shattered glass. The Salt Emperor came, resplendent in robes of silver and jade. The seven incorrupt gentlemen came in their plain black tunics. All the southern coast wept, but they also smiled. The hunter fell, but the demon fell with him. They proclaimed my father a hero, a savior, a gift from the gods and by the gods reclaimed.

I knew that his arm could never wrap my shoulders again. I knew the silence of his voice would never end. I knew that all eyes looked to me as the killer of the next dire monster, and all hearts wondered whether my blade alone would suffice.

Before he returned to his palaces, the Salt Emperor came to me. He offered his condolences, praised my father's strength and courage, and paid me the second half of our commission. I knelt before him, the casket filled with his silver at my knees, and considered seriously whether I could draw my sword and strike the man down before his guards ended me. When I lifted my gaze, I saw his eyes widen. He never offered me work again.

In my next clear memory, I walked down a dusty road in a northern village, a cold wind upon me. Shutters clacked against their frames, and the villagers eyed me with naked suspicion and fear. My home waited still farther north, and I carried only the sword strapped to my back. My cloak hung black and filthy. My ragged, yellow fingernails clicked against each other without my willing it. Perhaps I sang the demon's song.

The hunter confronted me at the town's edge.

He wore soft leather and a beard that aspired to more than it achieved. From a mat beside the road, he stood, walking out to block my way the way he might a rabid dog. His gaze locked on me, his cheap bronze blade at the ready. I stopped not from fear, but confusion. What bandit made so awkward an approach, and with such fear?

He started a chant to weaken the powers of the walking dead, but the syllables faded on his lips as I began to laugh. He thought me a zombie, a revenant, a vampire. He didn't stand against a fellow hunter, but a beast. I laughed until I howled, and my howls became grief. For the first time, I wept, and once I began I could not stop. The man left his chanting behind. Confusion complicated his eyes. Wordless, he bowed to me, turned and walked away. Perhaps he recognized me, or perhaps he only saw that what I carried, he could not defeat.

I never saw him again. But I regained my mind.

SEVEN:

MY ICE-EYED companion carried himself with a competence that reminded me of my father. We forged our way across the slopes and ridges of snow, the curves of the land beneath it living in my memory, but hidden. Bare, dark-barked trees shrieked their branches to the white sky. Ice glittered in a sun I could not see. And beside me, he trudged, his steps even and steady and constant as my heartbeat. Where the landscape allowed it, he kept to the faster paths. Where it denied us, he set his shoulders and pushed until the world itself yielded.

For my part, I gathered sticks into a small bundle as we walked, breaking dry branches and raiding the scrub where winter had formed a canopy and left the brush relatively dry. When we paused, I dug in the snow, filling my pockets with stones. He cocked his head, failing at every opportunity to fathom my plan. My bow still rested unstrung in the winter storage of my abandoned house. The crows and hares flew and ran safe from my hunger. Poor planning on my part.

It took us until sundown to reach the broad, flat plane where the lake slept. We left the land behind us and made camp on three kinds of water: snow over ice over black, unfreezing water where winter fish slept and waited for the thaw. Another day to the caverns. Not more.

He set his tent, cutting blocks from the snow with a thin steel axe and building a wall around its base to block the north wind. I took the stones from my pockets, pounded a flat space in the snow, and built a tor on which the fire could burn without drowning itself in icemelt. When he saw it, he smiled.

Night came quickly, white to grey to black. The orange of our fire stood out, the only color in the frozen world. I tried to tell my companion all that brought me here, drawing figures of myself, my husband who I then rubbed smooth and replaced with a funereal bough, and my child. He watched me, and then drew something himself. A large, hulking figure that clearly represented the man himself. A smaller figure, a woman but of great age, not a wife but perhaps a mother. And then something so small, it had to represent a babe in arms. Then the beast, and a crude circle that collected beast and baby, and excluded the others. I drew a circle around my daughter, and left my snow-self alone. He nodded.

I wanted to ask him why the beast hated him, what earned his small family this violence. I made do with sharing dried meat that dried my mouth with pepper and salt and a tin cup of snowmelt. Afterward, he combed his beard and pissed in a hole. His urine stank for only a few moments before it froze. When I did the same, he watched me with neither disgust nor approval nor the implicit threat of a man toward a woman. His eyes belonged to a hunter, much like my own.

After our small meal, he handed me a whetstone and grunted at my blade. As I sharpened it, he found another stone and set to his own. I remembered a chant I taught my daughter when she first learned her words: *Care for the blade that cares for you/sing with it and it sings too.* I began to hum under my breath, caught up in memory.

After my husband died, I raised her alone. Other men offered to take up house with us. Other women, for that. But age made me greedy, and I accepted nothing that might dilute my time with my child. We sang, we worked, we fought and forgave and laughed. I offered her the songs and stories my father offered me not because I hoped she would become a hunter, but because I knew nothing else.

Looking back, the selfishness of it rang like a bell. In a town or city, a hundred other eyes offered safety. Even only another person at the house could have protected us. Instead, we lived alone at the bend of the river, and I fashioned a girl like myself: at peace with solitude, aware of the violence of nature and civilization, apart from both. Sitting in the frigid tent, I resolved that if I earned a second chance, I would show her other things as well. The comfort of companionship, the pleasure of singing in chorus, the safety of living at the center of the herd.

The man picked up my melody. Perhaps his thoughts ran in harness with my own. Just before bed, he wept quietly. I slept well, and woke only slightly surprised to find myself curled against his broad, warm back.

We broke camp. A fresh, bitter wind lifted flakes from the frozen lake and drove them into our eyes. The hunter within me laughed; the weather's cruel distraction failed. The hills rose up to the north, and with them the caves, and the beast.

And the children.

EIGHT:

OVER THE course of years, I came to wear the reputation that once draped my father's shoulders. Even my passage through madness after his death lent me respect. The governors, the city administrators, the councils of merchants, and the boards that rule the small towns scattered through the Empire sent their pleas to me, and I answered where I could. When the temptation to hold money over need came upon me, my father frowned in my memory as in life.

I grew proud less in my fame than in my my skill. A hundred demons in the shapes of poisonous frogs threatened a river port. An ancient graveyard began to whisper violence in the dreams of the village above it. Rats the size of ponies and driven mad by plague overran a shipyard. Nothing seemed beyond me. I imagined my father watching me from some nameless place beyond death, and I pushed myself to deserve his respect, his admiration, and his approval.

And so, on the day before the twenty-eighth anniversary of my birth, the letter reached me telling of the beast.

Arin-Qin nestled in the western mountains, a city spun from silver and iron. Great bridges of chains swung there, connecting peak to peak, house to house, meadow to granary to common square. The buildings grew from the stone itself, crawling up mountainsides too steep for goats. An improbable and beautiful city, it guarded the passes between the Empire and barbarian lands. Five times since the reign of the Stone Emperor, invasions foundered beneath those bridges, and foreign blood filled the valleys below as if the earth itself bled.

Only something new now haunted the steep heights, a beast from the barbarian lands. Prepared for armies, Arin-Qin found itself vulnerable to a thing that walked in silence, that killed without warning, that spoke the language of Empire in hisses and clicks. Twice, bridges fell with fifty or more men on them, the chains bitten through. The greatest swordsmen and bowmen of the city stalked the beast, confronted it, and those few that survived crawled back to the city broken in mind and body. The city elders feared chaos, and in their hour of need, they called for me, and in my pride I came.

I found the trail no other eyes had seen. Kneeling on the gray stone at the line where the trees ended, I traced it with my fingertips. Claws harder than the granite left white marks wider than my splayed fingers. Here, a drift of snow showed prints as if two animals had fallen as one, the smaller nestled low in the larger's belly. The wind stank of cold and storm, and yet the beast climbed higher.

I stood up, the weight of my sword against my back drawing my attention only because the thin air made all efforts difficult. I squinted at the sheer cliffs above me, and my cloak fluttered like a flag. If I continued up, a single well-aimed stone could kill me. If I returned to the city that clung to the mountains below, the storm would scrub the trail away. I watched the wind eat at the prints in the snow, the edges chipping away with each new gust. An hour ahead of me. Not more.

I checked the leather strap that held my sword in its sheath. I drank long and deep from my freezing waterskin, slivers of ice rattling in it like gravel as I squeezed.

And I climbed.

For a time, the world became a long search for toe-holds, cracks in the stone narrow enough to allow a knuckle or fingertip. I wore no gloves to spoil my grip, and the skin of my fingers broke and bled. My sword dug against my spine, pulling me down toward the wide, empty air. But I followed the trail the beast left behind it.

The cave hid in a fold of stone and ice. No ledge offered purchase before it, and so I hung from the cliff face, considering the hole and fighting for breath. The darkness seemed more solid than the stone. No doubts troubled me. The beast lived here and no place else. The wind blew hard, but the thin air had no heft to it. The storm bore down upon the mountain, white and grey clouds promising death to a woman clinging uncertainly to the mountainside. Only one path lay open. I shifted, lurched, leapt. The darkness took me in.

NINE:

THE CAVES nearest my home spread down into the earth. The snow nearest the mouths showed a darkness where warm air from the belly of the earth melted it and left it to freeze again. We stalked through the empty land, he and I. Silence reigned. At each possible passage, each entrance to the underworld, we would pause and look for signs—a claw-marred stone, a child's footprint preserved in ice. We spent an hour or more on each, fearful of missing the telltale sign. Eventually, he made a grunting noise and looked to me as if I knew the truth. As if, because I lived nearby, I knew whether our doom waited in this hole or another. I resented him because he possessed something I wanted badly; an expert, a guide, a person on whose expertise I relied. He had *me*. And I had only him.

But I still breathed because of him, and so I held my frustration to myself. On the first day, we found nothing. We slept in a cave that night, the flesh of his tent converted to blankets in a way I had never seen before. He sang a rough tune with words I never fathomed, but I followed as best I could. In the light of the small fire, his face looked younger and more lost. The beast drew him here out of whatever valley or mountain, plain or rugged sea-coast he called home. It led him here, to me. Perhaps a road equally long and terrible waited for me as well. Perhaps the beast meant me to run after it forever. It and my girl.

I wondered as I prepared for sleep how my companion brought this upon himself. Someone drove the beast out from the west. Him? His father? His mother? Or did he carry some blood debt more like my own? I knew no way to ask. In a way, that pleased me. It allowed me the luxury of imagining some affront worse than my own.

Again, in the night, my sleeping body found the warmth of his. Again, we made nothing of it. A man and a woman together, alone and afraid, we took comfort in each other's presence, but nothing more intimate found purchase on the stone of our companionship. Two equal emptinesses, we had no way to fill each other's souls.

We woke late to a bright blue sky. The sun, bright and impotent, threw its light down onto snow twice as blinding as itself. From his pack, my companion drew a mask of smoked glass, strapping it over his face until he looked more than half a monster himself. Lacking his gear, I squinted. It sufficed.

Just past the middle of the day, we found another cave mouth. Perhaps some scent alerted me, some invisible track that whispered to me. My hands kept finding their way to the black wood of my blade even before he ducked deeper into the all-consuming shadow and cried out.

I ran in after him, half expecting to find him dead already in the beast's teeth. Instead, he knelt just at the place where sunlight failed, limp rags in either hand. Tears steamed on his cheeks.

In his left hand, he held a long, tapered length of thick cotton well-cut for swaddling a baby. Piss stained it, and I pictured the weak child, chilled and stewing in its own waste as the beast pulled it half across the world. And still, I noted that the cloth had not frozen and didn't yet have the stench that came with old piss. A day, I thought. Less than a day. His child still lived a day ago.

In his right hand, he held my daughter's sleeping shift. The blood staining it looked as recent.

TEN:

IN THAT twice-damned cave far above Arin-Qin on that day that called the beast's vengeance upon me, I unhooked the leather strap holding my sword in place but did not draw it.

I moved forward slowly, letting my eyes adjust to the gloom. A narrow band of twilight stood grey and forbidding where the light still reached. I knew that beyond that I either risked lighting a flame or fought blind, and I wondered which gave the beast a greater advantage. I opted for light.

My hard-wax candle in one hand and drawn sword in the other, I slipped inside the mountain. A hundred yards in, the cave turned, and I made my way past that bend and out of the last light of the sun just as the storm reached the peak. The roar of wind battering stone sounded like a battle heard from miles away. I recognized the scouring violence and power, but my small light didn't so much as flicker.

I moved carefully but quick, never looking directly at my dim single candle for fear of blinding myself. I held my weight evenly, connecting to the solid earth below me. I kept my senses open. The stones said the beast stood just taller than a man. The close, musty scent of the air said it ate and shat in the caverns. I heard nothing.

And then I did.

Short and clipped, like a bird new-hatched, something in the darkness complained. I risked closing my eyes, letting the sound alone guide me. The echoes of the wide, tall caves hid the small, inhuman voice like a gambler playing at shells hides his pebble.

And still, I found it.

The nest—I know no better word for it—stank of rotting wood and old bones. It huddled in at the base of a great, jagged, underground cliff like a ball of hair caught in a bathhouse drain. And within the slick bowl of its width, four dark, leathery eggs. Four eggs, and one tiny, shifting thing too weak to stand on its crooked legs. It whipped its awkward tail, and the four small arms whirled and flailed. Evil yellow eyes found me by my candle, tracing the path from flame to arms to eyes before it hissed and spat. So young, and yet it knew me for its enemy.

I looked up from instinct honed by long experience. The beast's eyes caught the candle flame. It hunkered on a ledge twenty feet above me, looking down at its children and at me. I held my blade at the ready. If I dropped the candle, the light would fail and we would battle in darkness, and I would win. No fear troubled me.

Let them alone, it said, its voice a thing of hisses and clicks. *Whatever you do to me, I promise no vengeance against you. Only let them alone.*

Perhaps I hoped to goad the beast down to me in its rage and despair. Later, I made that claim. Or perhaps I knew that whatever I promised, the eggs must break, the hatchling die. Or perhaps like my father, I killed without sentiment. Without concern for the price.

With the beast looking on, I swung my blade from the wrist; a slow, lazy motion as much limbering my joint as an attack. The hissing and piping stopped. The beast cried out once. Carefully, never taking my eye from the beast above me, I slit each egg. Of the tangle of yolk and albumin and half-made limbs, only one possessed the strength to stand, and that only for a moment.

With her children dead, I expected the beast to leap. I misjudged. She turned, her tail pointing toward me like an accusing finger. Her massive legs bunched. She leaped into darkness and never came down.

I found the other passage only after I burned six candles to their last. The beast escaped into the storm that trapped me in the high caves for two full weeks. Surely the wind and the cold finished the slaughter for me. Surely the beast perished in the snow and thin air. From grief, if nothing else. Arin-Qin suffered no more attacks. The beast killed no more men of the empire. I accepted my fee and the praise due a hunter who had delivered the city from its fear.

I told myself that the unease troubling me grew from the inconclusive ending of the hunt. I told myself that the certain death of the beast in snow and ice failed to rise to the standard of professionalism my father taught. A clean kill, unambiguous, with a severed head to show. This carried none of that.

But in truth, a hunter kills without sentiment, without remorse, without allowing herself to see a reflection in the eyes of her prey. I failed in that. I saw myself in the beast's eyes as I finished her brood, and recognized the cruelty of my actions. My father died for me and for the honor of the hunt, and I could not imagine his solution to that problem, that moment. I only knew that mine disappointed him. And if not him, then me.

I hunted for three seasons more. I took commissions in cities throughout the empire. But in truth, the hunter within me ended her work in those high caves, eating the frozen bodies of the beast's children when her rations failed and waiting for the storm to pass.

ELEVEN:

THE CAVERNS and tunnels beneath that northern stone crossed and cracked in an inhuman, mindless labyrinth. As we descended into it, my companion pulled a device of tin and glass, unfolded it, and lit a hidden wick. Soft golden light, steady as a candle in still air, came from it. I drew my sword and he his hand axe. The cathedral-huge stones balanced against each other above us, their unthinkable weights holding each other. Stalactites like teeth hung from the roofs of wide caves. The air grew warm as a spring day, fed by the breath of the earth. We walked out of winter, out of light, out of the upper world that we knew, and into a timeless season of darkness in which we had no place.

No clear path told us which way to go. No unambiguous marks led us. We relied on my instinct and his, pointing to scratches on the stone, bits of gravel and dust that might bear the mark of the beast's claw. Or might not.

We walked into the trap clear in the knowledge of our danger. We had no choice. He held his child's swaddling cloth wrapped tight in his hand, protecting his fingers from the heat of his small lantern even as he kept hold of the only scrap of his child. I wished that I'd thought to keep my daughter's shift with us as well, a banner to carry into this last, doomed battle.

With each shadow that shifted before us, I felt my shoulders growing tight, my breath fast and shallow. With each echoed footfall, I heard the ghost of claws touching stone. Walking beside and behind me, my companion and hunting partner carried the same tension. Crystals caught the light around us, flashing green and white and the deep yellow of old piss. The air carried the rich pong of bat droppings from some deeper chamber where the animals slept. And waiting for us, the beast and our children who had lived yesterday and might still.

I wanted to shout, to set the stone walls ringing with my voice, to bring down the earth upon us if it would break the terrible, grinding fear. I wept without knowing that I wept until his wide hand on my shoulder steadied me.

The site of the ambush—the inevitable and obvious attack—lay at the intersection of two thin passages, one riding eight feet above the other. We walked in the lower of the two passages like prisoners in the bottom of a ditch. Every instinct shrieked of danger, every scrap of experience and knowledge promised that here, in this place, no defense would avail us. We made ourselves more vulnerable with each step into the darkness. I held my blade with a doubled grip, even though I had no room to swing. I waited for the beast's vengeance.

It never came.

At the end of the intersection, centuries of dust made a ramp of sorts that led to the upper passage. The beast's tracks dug into the soft earth as clearly as writing on a page. My companion and I stared at each other, confused and unnerved. I went up first, in a rush, prepared to repel an attack, and so I found the beast before him.

It crouched low against a great stone, its eyes dim and sightless. Pale blood stained its face from where one eye hung, ruined. Its lesser arms still clasped a long gash along its belly, and the loops of its intestines pressed against the small claws. One of its greater arms remained, the other only a stump of cold flesh. Its flayed side and tail glittered bloody, the skin and fat cut away.

My companion paused looking at me. His wide eyes echoed my thoughts. Something lived in these caves more terrible than the beast. More deadly. And around the next turn, we found what.

She hunkered in the darkness, her arms bloody, her hair wild. In one arm, she held a sleeping babe against her hip, wrapped for warmth in her fallen enemy's skin. In her other hand, one of the beast's wide, cruel claws made her dagger. The ice-eyed man howled and leaped forward, scooping the baby from her and pressing it to his chest. The baby boy woke, flailed his soft legs, grinned at his father. The naked girl, barely familiar in her paint of blood and exhaustion, only nodded to me.

Mother, she said.

I took my father's hunting cloak from my shoulders and wrapped it around her. On her slight frame, it looked even larger than it had on mine, and yet it belonged to her now. My little hunter. My girl who waited for her opportunities with eyes I gave her. My daughter who killed those who underestimated her.

In the dim, golden light, her exhausted smirk seemed to know more than I believed she knew. I lifted her dagger hand. Cuts marked her skin black and red. The black, serrated claw still had a bit of the beast's flesh at the root.

You need a new blade, I said.

TWELVE:

IF THE man and his boy had stayed past the spring thaw, I would have welcomed them. In the event, I knew his homeland called to him, and the sorrow I felt at our parting didn't ache for long. I knew them as long as I did, and then that time ended, and my girl and I lived alone again.

All my remembered promises to take her to the city, to change her and myself as well, came back as ghosts. Insubstantial. Powerless. We fell back into our routines, only with a deeper awareness that my girl had taken another step toward the woman still to come. I set myself to enjoying this time, these moments, in part from the awareness of their approaching end.

In spring, I returned to the caves alone and buried the beast. Small animals had stripped much of the meat from its bones, but the corpse held together well enough to drag. I dug a hole, put my enemy in it, and poured old dirt over the body until the grave looked like the earth around it. For a day, I sat by the dead beast, as I had for my husband. As I had for my father. For all the dead who shaped me.

I sat at my enemy's grave, the one whose children I killed and ate. The one who tracked me through years and across an empire only to die at my own daughter's hand. My father sat with me, his bow still holding the arrow that brought his death. The daughter who would someday leave me sat there as well. My hunting companion and his baby boy.

Before the ice-eyed man left, I learned something of his language. He knew a word for the death of justice, for the sealing of accounts forever out of true. In his land, two families might fight over the same land for generations, and then the king would speak this word and the land they held remained theirs, the boundaries set anew, and all old grievances washed away like salt in a rainstorm. Marriages that survived decades could end with that word, or else endure because of it. Neither forgiveness nor apology, it killed history and began the world again. I never managed a translation that satisfied me, but near enough, it meant *the world has no place for justice.*

I put my hand over the graveyard dust, felt the cool earth between my fingers, spoke the word in his language, and went home.

LEVIATHAN WEPT

"GOOD CROWD," PAUEL SAID, from Paris.

"Things are weird," Renz said, passing his gaze over that auditorium so that Pauel could see it better. "People are scared."

When Renz had first trained with the link—when he began what Anna called his split-screen life—he had wanted the display windows to show the other people in his cell instead of what they were seeing; to make him feel they were speaking face to face. It had taken months for him to become comfortable with the voices of people he couldn't see and the small screens in his own visual field that showed what they were seeing. Now it lent their conversations a kind of intimacy; it was as if they were a part of him. Pauel and Marquez, Paasikivi and Thorn.

The auditorium was full, agents of CATC—Coordinated Antiterrorist Command—in almost every seat and so many others linked in that the feed was choppy from bandwidth saturation. The air was thick with the heat and scent of living bodies.

Of the other members of his cell, only Marquez was physically present, sitting beside him and tapping the armrest impatiently. Pauel, Paasikivi, and Thorn were linked in from elsewhere. Pauel was in his apartment, lying back on his old couch so that the rest of them were looking up at his dirty skylight and the white-blue Parisian sky. Paasikivi and Thorn were sharing a booth at a Denver coffee shop so that Renz could see each of them from the other's perspective—Thorn small and dark as an Arab, Paasikivi with her barely-graying hair cut short. Renz wondered how long they would all be able to pretend those two weren't lovers, then placed all the window in his peripheral vision so he wouldn't be distracted from the man on the stage.

"Renz. I heard Anna was back in the hospital," Paasikivi said. Her tone of voice made it a question.

"It's just follow-up," Renz said. "She's fine."

The man at the front tilted his head, said something into a private link, and stepped up to the edge of the stage. In Denver, Thorn stirred his coffee too hard, rattling the spoon against the cup the way he did when he was uncomfortable. Renz lowered the volume from the link.

"Good afternoon," the man said. "I'd like to welcome you all here. And I have to say I wish we had this kind of turnout for the budget meetings."

A wave of nervous laughter swept over the crowd. Without meaning to, Renz found himself chuckling along with the rest. He stopped.

"For those of you who don't know me, my name's Alan Andrews. I'm a tactical liaison for the Global Security Council's theoretical branch. Think of me as the translator for the folks in the ivory tower."

"Condescending little pigfuck, isn't he?" Pauel said.

"By now I'm sure you've all heard about the anomalies," the speaker said. "OG 47's experience with the girls in New

York, OG 80 and the old woman in Bali, the disruptions at the CATC root databases. I'm here to give you an idea what the theoretical branch has made of them."

"Yes, Pauli," Marquez muttered. "But are you sure about the pig? He looks more a chimp man to me."

"Would you two shut up," Renz said. "I want to hear this."

"The first thing I want to make clear," the man said, holding his hands out to the crowd, palms out, placating, "is that there are no direct ties between these incidents and any known terrorist network. Something's going on, and we all know that, but it's not a conspiracy. It's something else."

The man dropped his hands.

"That's the good news. The bad news is it's probably something worse."

✳

LOOKING BACK, the first anomaly had been so small, Renz had hardly noticed it. It had presented as a series of small sounds at a moment when his attention had been a thousand other places. He had heard it and forgotten until later.

The town they had been in at the time was nothing remarkable; the Persian Interest Zone was peppered with places like it. Concrete apartment buildings and ruined mosques mixed with sad, pre-fab western strip malls. The asphalt roads had been chewed by tank treads sometime a decade before and never repaired. But intelligence said that an office building in the run-down central district was still running network servers for the al-Nakba.

Organizational Group 47—Renz, Marquez, Pauel, Thorn, Paasikivi—were in an old van parked on a side street, waiting. Thorn and Pauel—the only two who could pass for local—sat in the front playing the radio and smoking cigarettes. Paasikivi and Marquez squatted in the belly of the machine, using the three-foot tall degaussed steel case of the EMP coil as a table for Marquez's chess set. Renz kept watch out the tiny tinted windows in the back. Waiting was the hardest part.

The operation was organized in a small-world network, the cells like theirs connected loosely with fifty or a hundred like it around the world and designed to behave organically, adjusting to contingency without need for a central authority.

It gave them, Renz supposed, the kind of flexibility that a war between networks required. But it cost them a solid timetable. They might be called up in the next thirty seconds; they might be waiting for an hour. It might be that allowing the target to survive would be a viable strategy, and they'd all pull quietly out without anyone knowing they'd been there.

Paasikivi sighed, tipped her king with a wooden click, and moved forward in the van leaving Marquez to chuckle and put the pieces away.

"You're thinking about Anna," Marquez said.

Renz glanced back, shook his head, and turned to the windows again.

"No, I'm winding myself up about the mission."

"Should be thinking about Anna, then. Nothing we can do about the mission right now."

"Nothing I can do about Anna either."

"You going to spend some time with her when this is over?"

"Yeah," Renz said.

"Really, this time?"

It wasn't the sort of question Renz would have taken from anyone but Marquez. He shifted forward, staring out at the sun-drenched street.

"Really, this time," he said.

An out-cell window flashed open. The blond man appearing in it looked harried as an air traffic controller. Renz supposed the jobs weren't so different.

"OG 47, this is CG 60. Please begin approach to subject. Your target is fifteen minutes."

"Acknowledged," Paasikivi said for them all. Pauel flicked his still-burning cigarette onto the sidewalk and started the van. Renz didn't shift his position at the rear, but as he watched the street flow away behind them, the old electric feeling of adrenaline and anticipation grew in his belly.

There were four stages to the operation: penetration, reconnaissance, delivery, and withdrawal. Or, more plainly, get in, look around, do the thing, and leave. They had all rehearsed it together, and everyone knew what to do.

The van turned the corner two minutes later, angled into a ramp down to underground parking. A security guard at the entrance frowned at Pauel and barked something that wasn't Arabic but might have been Armenian. Pauel replied in Farsi, managing to sound bored and put upon. The guard waved them through. Renz watched the guard turn his back to them.

"Twelve minutes to target," Paasikivi said.

Pauel drove past the stairway leading up to the building proper, around a cinderblock corner, and parked across three parking spaces. The first stage was over; they were in. Without a word, Pauel and Marquez got out and started walking. Renz increased the size of their windows. Marquez, whistling, moved around a corner and deeper into the parking structure. Pauel went up the way they had come, toward the guard and the stairs.

"Pauel, you have something at your ten o'clock."

The window with Pauel's viewpoint shifted. Beside an old white Toyota, a woman in a burka was chiding a wiry man. The man, ignoring her, began walking toward the stairway.

"Civilians," Pauel murmured, hardly loud enough for the link to pick it up.

"Are you sure?" Paasikivi asked.

"Of course not," he said.

"Nine minutes," Thorn said. Hearing the words through the link and in the van simultaneously made them seem to reverberate, carrying a sense of doom and threat they didn't deserve. He felt Thorn tap his shoulder and, still watching Pauel and Marquez, Renz shifted back, his hands resting on the cool metal carrying handles of the EMP coil, but not gripping them yet.

Marquez's window showed Arabic graffiti, oil-stained concrete, a few cars. More than half the lights were out.

"Looks good here," Marquez said.

In Pauel's window, the guard glanced back, frowning. Renz watched Pauel's hand rise in greeting.

"I'm going to go chat this bastard up, keep him busy," Pauel said. "Apart from him, I think we're clear."

The second stage was complete. Paasikivi slid to the front, into the driver's seat. Renz looked across the steel case to Thorn. Thorn nodded, and Renz leaned forward and pushed the rear door open.

"All right," Thorn said. "Renz and I are coming out. If you see anyone about to kill us, speak up." Renz thought his voice sounded bored. It was only a few steps to the wall, but the coil was heavy. His wrists strained as they snagged the metal against the cinderblock wall.

Renz stepped back as Thorn slid adhesive packs around the base of the coil, and then between the side of the metal case and the wall. He checked the time. Six minutes to target.

There were five small, very similar sounds, quickly but evenly spaced. The guard with Pauel scraped open a pack of cigarettes, the radio in the van beside Paasikivi popped as she put the key in the ignition, Thorn's adhesive packs went off with a hiss, a bit of gravel scraped under Renz's heel, and something like a cough came from deeper in the garage behind Marquez. Each sound seemed to pick up the next. A little musical coincidence that sounded like nothing so much as a man clearing his throat. Renz noticed it, and then was immediately distracted.

"Someone's back here," Marquez said. Renz caught a movement in Marquez's window. Someone ducking behind a car. "I think we may have a problem."

Everything happened at once, improvised and contingent but with the perfect harmony of a team acting together, so practiced it was like a single mind. Renz drew his sidearm and moved forward, prepared to lay down suppressing fire. Pauel, at the front, shot the security guard twice in the chest, once in the head. Paasikivi started the van. Marquez, seeing that Renz was coming, moved quickly backwards, still scanning the darkness for movement.

Within seconds, Renz was around the corner, Marquez fifteen or twenty feet ahead of him, a pistol in his hand. Behind them and around the corner, where they couldn't have seen without the link, Thorn had the rear doors of the van opened and waiting, and Paasikivi was turning it around to face the exit. Pauel, at the base of the ramp, was dragging the guard out of the roadway.

Something moved to Marquez's left. Renz shifted and fired while Marquez pulled back past him to the corner. When Renz saw his own back in Marquez's window and Marquez braced to fire in Thorn's, he broke off, turned, and ran as Marquez opened up on the darkness. From listening, it would have been impossible to say when one had stopped shooting and the other started.

On the out-cell link, the blond man from OC 60 was saying that OG 47 had been compromised and Paasikivi was shouting at him that they had not. The coil was in place. They were withdrawing.

Marquez broke off as Renz reached the van, turned, and sprinted toward them, white tombstone teeth bared in what might have been effort or glee. Renz and Thorn both knelt inside the van, guns trained on the corner, ready to kill anyone who came around it.

"Okay," Pauel said from the ramp as Marquez reached the relative safety of the group. "Can you come get me now?"

The van surged forward, tires squealing as they rounded the corner—the van coming into view in Pauel's window; Pauel silhouetted against the blaring light of the street in Paasikivi's.

"Pauel! The stairs!" Renz said almost before he realized he'd seen something. There in Paasikivi's window, coming down from the building. He watched as Pauel shot the girl—five years old? six?

Time slowed. If they had been compromised, Renz thought, the girl could be wired—a walking bomb. There wasn't enough room in the parking structure to avoid her. If she went off, they were all going to die. Fear flushed his mouth with the taste of metal.

He heard Thorn exhale sharply, and the van sped past the stairway. The dead girl failed to explode. A dud.

"Jesus," Marquez said, relief in the sound of the word. "Oh, sweet Jesus."

Paasikivi stopped for less than a second, and Pauel was in the passenger's seat. Renz pulled the rear doors closed and latched them as they went up the ramp and out to the brightness of the street.

They were half a mile from the building when the trigger signal attenuated and the coil sparked out. With a shock like a headache, Renz's link dropped for a half second, leaving the disorienting sensation of only being inside his own head again. It felt like waking from a dream. And then the display windows were back, each showing slightly different views out the front while he alone looked back at a plume of white smoke rising from the town behind them.

By the time they reached the base in Hamburg, the news was on all the major sites. CATC under the orders of the

Global Security Council had launched simultaneous attacks on the al-Nakba network, including three opium processing plants, two armories, and a training camp. Also the al-Nakba communications grid and network had suffered heavy damage.

The opposition sites added that a preschool near one of the armories had also been firebombed and that the training camp was a humanitarian medical endeavor. Eighteen innocent bystanders had died, including ten children from the preschool and two teachers.

There was also a girl shot in a minor raid in the Persian Interest Zone. Her name was Samara Hamze. Renz looked at the picture of her on the newsnets—shoulder-length black hair that rounded in at her neck, dark, unseeing eyes, skin fair enough she could have passed in the most racist quarters of Europe if she'd been given the chance. If she'd wanted to.

By the time they'd dropped Pauel off in Paris and found seats in a transatlantic carrier, the news cycle had moved on, and the girl—the dud—was forgotten.

Renz had never expected to see her again.

❋

"THAT'S THE good news. The bad news is it's probably something worse," said the man on the stage. "Now this is going to seem a little off-topic, but we may be in some strange territory before we're done here, so I hope you'll all indulge me. Ask yourselves this: Why aren't we all brilliant neurochemists? I don't mean why didn't we choose to go to med school—there are lots of reasons for that. I mean doesn't it seem like if you're able to *do* something, you must know about it? Aaron Ka can play great football because he knows a lot about football.

"But here we are, all juggling incredibly complex neurochemical exchanges all the time, and we're all absolutely unaware of it. I mean no one says 'Oops, better watch those calcium channels or I might start getting my amygdala all fired up.' We just take ten deep breaths and try to calm down. The cellular layer just isn't something we're conscious of.

"And you can turn that around. Our neurons aren't any more aware of us than we are of them. If you ask a neuron why it fired or muscle tissue why it flexed, it wouldn't say 'because it was my turn to run' or 'the bitch had it coming.' Those are the sorts of answers *we'd* give. If our cells could say anything, they'd say something about ion channels and charges across lipid membranes. And on that level—on the cellular level—that would be a fine explanation.

"The levels don't talk to each other. Your neurons don't know you, and you aren't aware of them. And, to torture a phrase, as above, so presumably below."

Renz felt Marquez shift in his seat. It wasn't impatience. Marquez was frowning, his gaze intent on the stage. Renz touched his arm and nodded a question.

"I don't like where this is going," Marquez said.

✳

WHEN RENZ got back from the mission, Anna was sitting at the kitchen table—cheap laminate on peeling-chrome legs—scrolling through another web page on her disease. Outside the dirty windows, the streetlights of Franklin Base glowed bright enough to block out the stars. Renz closed the door behind him, went over and kissed his wife on the crown of her head. She smelled of the same cheap shampoo that she'd used since he met her. The sudden memory of her body when it was young and powerful and not quite his yet sent a rush of lust through him. It was embarrassing. He turned away, to the refrigerator, for some soda.

Anna turned off her screen and shifted. Her movements were awkward, disjointed. Her face was pinched and oddly expressionless. He smiled and lifted a bottle of soda. She shook her head—the movement took a second to get going, and it took a second to stop.

"Douglas Harper had Hulme's Palsy too," she said.

"The serial killer?"

"Yup," she said. "Apparently it's old news. Everyone in the support group knew about it. I'm still green compared to all of them. He wasn't symptomatic. They didn't diagnose it until after he'd been executed."

Renz pulled out a chair and sat, his heels on the kitchen table. The air conditioner kicked on with a decrepit hum.

"Do they think what…I mean was killing people related?"

Anna laughed. Her eyes wide, she made an overhand stabbing motion like something out of a murder flick. Renz laughed, surprised to find his amusement was genuine.

"They just think if it had progressed faster, some of those girls might have lived," she said.

Renz took a sip of his soda. It was too sweet, and the fizz was already gone, but it was cold. There wasn't more he could ask than cold. Anna dropped her hands to the table.

"I was going to make dinner for you," she said. "But…well, I didn't."

"No trouble. I can make something," he said. Then, "Bad week?"

She sighed. She was too thin. He could see her collarbone, the pale skin stretched tight over it.

"The new immunosuppressants gave me the shits," she said, "and I think I'm getting another fucking cold. Other than that, just another thrilling week of broadcast entertainment and small town gossip."

"Any good gossip, then?"

"Someone's screwing someone else even though they're both married. I didn't really pay attention to the details. You? The news feeds made things look pretty good."

Anna's eyes were blue and so light that they made him think of icicles when they caught the light from the side. He'd fallen in love with her eyes as much as her tits and the taste of her mouth. He pushed the sorrow away before she could see it.

"We killed a kid. But things went pretty well otherwise."

"Only one kid? That thing with the preschool..."

"Yeah, them too. I mean *we* killed a kid. My guys."

Anna nodded, then reached awkwardly across the table. Her fingertips touched his wrist. He didn't look up, but he let the tears come. He could pretend they were for the dud.

"So not such a good week for you either, huh?"

"Had its rough parts," he said.

"You're too good for this," she said. "You've got to stop it."

"I can't," he said.

"Why not?"

He spoke before he thought. Truth came that way; sudden, unexpected. Like illness.

"We'd lose the medical coverage."

Her fingertips pulled back. Renz watched them retreat across the table, watched them fold into her flat, crippled fist. The air conditioner hummed, white noise as good as silence. Renz swung his legs down.

"I wouldn't change anything," he said.

"*I* fucking would." There was pain in her voice, and it pressed down on him like a hand.

"You know, boss, I'm not really hungry," he said. "Let's go to bed. We can eat a big breakfast in the morning."

Once she was asleep—her breath slow and deep and even—he got gently out of bed, pulled on his robe, and took himself out the front door to sit on the rotting concrete steps. The lawn was bare grass, the street empty. Renz ran his hands over his close-cropped hair and stared up at the moon, blue-white and pale in the sky. After a while, he turned up his link, seeing if there was anyone online.

Paasikivi and Thorn were both disconnected. Pauel's link was open with the video feed turned off, but it had been idle for three and a half hours—he was probably asleep. Only Marquez was awake and connected. Renz excluded the other three feeds, considering the world from Marquez's point of view. It looked like he was in a bar. Renz turned up the volume and thin country-pop filled his ears.

"Hey, Marquez," he said.

The video feed jumped and then settled.

"Ah! Renz. I thought you were actually here. Is that your street?"

He looked up and down the empty asphalt strip—block houses and thin, water-starved trees. Buffalo grass lawns that never needed mowing. His street.

"I guess so," he said, then more slowly, "I guess so."

"Looks like the same shit as last time."

"It's hotter. There's more bugs."

Marquez chuckled and Renz wasn't really on the step outside his shitty base housing, Anna dying by inches behind him. Marquez wasn't entirely in the cheap bar. They were on the link together, in the unreal, private space it made, and it removed the distance between them.

"How's Anna?" Marquez asked.

"She's all right. I mean her immune system's still eating her nerves, but apart from that."

"You sound bitter. You're not cutting out on her, are you?"

"No. I said I'd stay, and this time I will. It just sucks. It all just sucks."

"Yeah. I'm sorry. It's hard when your woman's down."

"Not just that. It *all* sucks. That girl we killed. We call her a dud like she wasn't a kid. What's that about?"

"It's about how a lot of those kids have mommies who strap them up with cheap dynamite. You know that."

"Are we soldiers, Marquez? Are we cops? What the fuck are we doing out there?"

"We're doing whatever needs to get done. That's not what's chewing you, and you know it."

It was true, so he ignored it.

"I've been doing this for too many years," Renz said. "I'm getting burned out. When I started, every operation was like an adventure from start to stop. Half the time I didn't even know how what I was doing fit in, you know? I just knew it did. Now I wonder why we do it."

"We do it because they do it."

"So why do they do it?"

"Because of us," Marquez said, and Renz could hear the smile. "This is the way it is. It's the way it's always been. You put people out in the world, and they kill each other. It's the nature of the game. Your problem, man, you never read Hobbes."

"The pissing cartoon kid?"

"Five hundred years ago, this guy named Hobbes wrote a book about how the only way to get peace was to give up all your rights to the state—do what the king said, whether it was crazy or nor. Fuck justice. Fuck whether it made sense. Just do what you're told."

"And you read this thing."

"Shit no. There was this lecture I saw on a philosophy site. The guy said you build a government so motherfucking huge, it can *make* peace. Grind peace into people with a fucking hammer. Crush everyone, all the time. He called it Leviathan. He thought it was the only way to stop war."

"Sounds like hell."

"Maybe. But you got a better idea?"

"So we're making them be part of our government. And when we get them all in on it, this'll stop."

Marquez's window panned slowly back and forth—the man shaking his head.

"This shit isn't going to stop until Jesus comes back."

"And if he doesn't?"

"Come on, man. You know all this. I said it before; it's not what's really on your mind."

"And what do *you* know about *my* mind?"

"I spend a lot of time there is all."

Renz sighed and scratched at the welt on his arm growing where a mosquito had drunk from him. The moon sailed slowly above him, the same as it always had, seen or unseen. He swallowed until his throat wasn't so tight.

"She still turns me on," he said at last. "It makes me feel like I'm...she's crippled. She's dying and I can't fix it, and all I want to do when I see her is fuck."

"So why don't you?"

"Don't be gross."

"She might want to, you know. It's not like she stopped being a woman. Knowing you still want her like that...might be the kind of thing she needs."

"You're out of your mind."

"There is no sorrow so great it cannot be conquered by physical pleasure," Marquez said.

"That Hobbes?"

"Nah. French girl named Colette. Just the one name. Wrote some stuff was supposed to be pretty racy at the time. It was a long time ago, though. Doesn't do much compared to net porn."

"You read the weirdest shit."

"I don't have anyone to come home to. Makes for a lot of spare time," Marquez said, his voice serious. Then, "Go inside, Renz. Sleep next to your wife. In the morning, make her a good breakfast and screw her eyes blue."

"Her eyes are blue," he said.

"Then keep up the good work."

"Fuck off," Renz said, but he was smiling.

"Good night, man."

"Yeah," Renz said. "Hey, Marquez. Thanks."

"De nada."

Renz dropped the link but sat still in the night for a while, trailing his fingers over flakes of concrete and listening to the crickets. Before he went to bed again, he ate a bowl of cereal standing up in the kitchen, and then used her toothbrush to scrape the milk taste off his tongue. Anna had shifted in her sleep, taking up the whole bed. He kissed her shoulder as he rolled her back to her side. To his surprise, he slept.

At six thirty in the morning, central time, a school bus packed with diesel-soaked fertilizer exploded in California, killing eighteen people and taking out civilian network access for half of the state. At six thirty-two, a fifteen-year-old girl detonated herself twenty feet away from the CEO of the EU's biggest bank while he was finishing his breakfast at a restaurant in midtown Manhattan. At six thirty-five, simultaneous brushfires started outside ten major power transmission stations along the eastern seaboard. At seven thirty, Renz was on a plane to New York. At ten minutes before ten, a ground car met him at the airport, and by noon, he was at the site of the attack.

The street should have been beautiful. The buildings soared up around them; nothing in Manhattan was built on less than a cathedral scale—it was the personality of the city. From the corner, he could just catch sight of the Chrysler Building. The café had been elegant once, not very long before. Two blackened, melted cars squatted at the curbside. The bodies had been taken away long before Renz and the others arrived, but the outlines were there, not in chalk but bright pink duct tape.

"Hey, Renz," Paasikivi said as they took in the carnage. "Sorry about this. I know you wanted to see Anna."

"Don't let it eat you," he said. "This is what they pay me for, right?"

Inside, the window of the café had blown in. Chunks of bulletproof glass three fingers thick lay on the starched linen, the wooden floors polished to a glow. The air still smelled like match heads.

The briefing had been short. OG 47 had done this kind of duty before. Renz pulled up an off-cell window on the right margin of his visual field so the forensics experts could demonstrate what they wanted. The feeds from his cell were stacked on the left. OGs 34 and 102 were security, keeping the area clear while they worked, but he didn't open links to them; things were cluttered enough as it was.

Renz and his cell were the eyes and hands of the deep forensics team—men and women too valuable to risk in the field. A second attack designed to take out agents at the scene was a common tactic. Pauel, still in Paris, joined in not because he was useful, but because he was a part of the cell and so part of the operation. He was good to talk with during the quiet times.

The next few hours were painfully dull. Paasikivi and Thorn, Marquez and himself—the expendables—all took simple instructions from the experts, measuring what they were told to, collecting samples of scorched metal and stained linen, glass and shrapnel in self-sealing bags, and waiting for the chatter of off-cell voices to agree on the next task to be done.

Renz and his cell were the eyes and hands, not the brain. He found he could follow the directions he was given without paying much attention. They drove his body; he waited.

They finished just after 8 p.m. local. There were flights out that night, but Paasikivi argued for a night in the City. Renz could feel Marquez's attention on him like the sensation of being watched as Paasikivi and Thorn changed reservations for the whole cell. Renz almost stopped them, almost said he needed to go home and be with his wife. When he didn't, Marquez didn't mention it. With the forensics team gone, Renz arranged the other in-cell windows at the four corners of his visual field. An hour later, they were scattered over the island.

Marquez was on the edge of Central Park, his window showing Renz vistas of thick trees, their leaves black in the gloom of night. Paasikivi was sitting in a coffee shop at the top of a five-story bookstore, watching the lights of the city as much as the people in the café. Thorn sat in a sidewalk restaurant. Renz himself was walking through a subway station, heading south to SoHo because Pauel told him he'd like it. And Pauel, in the small hours of Paris morning, had taken himself out to an all-night café just to be in the spirit of things.

"I've always wanted to walk through Central Park," Marquez said. "It's probably safe enough, don't you think?"

"Wait until morning," Pauel said. "It's too dangerous at night."

Renz could hear the longing in Marquez's sigh, imagined the way he would stuff his hands into his pockets to hide the disappointment, and found to his amusement that he'd done the same. Marquez's gesture seemed to fit nicely on his own evening. The first breeze of the incoming train started to wash the subway platform, fluttering the fabric of his pants.

"I hate days like this," Thorn said, cutting into a steak. In that window, Renz watched the blood well up around the knife and wondered what it smelled like. "The nights, however, go a long way toward making up for it."

Marquez had turned and was walking now, people on the streets around him that would have been a crowd anywhere else. Paasikivi pushed her coffee cup away, stood and glanced back into the bookstore. In Paris, Pauel's waitress—a young woman with unlikely red hair—brought him his eggs benedict and poured him a cup of coffee. Thorn lifted a fork of bleeding steak to his mouth. The train slid up to the platform, the doors opening with a hiss and a smell of fumes and ozone.

"All I really want..." Renz began, and then let the sentence die.

The girl came out of the bathroom in Pauel's Parisian diner at the same moment Renz saw her sitting in the back of his half-full subway car. Paasikivi caught sight of her near the music department, looking over the shoulder of a man who was carrying her—he might have been her father. Thorn, looking out the restaurant window saw her on the street. Marquez saw her staring at him from the back seat of a taxi.

In all four windows and before him in the flesh, the same girl or near enough, was staring at him. Pale skin, dark eyes, shoulder length hair that rounded in at the neck. Samara Hamze. The dead girl. The dud.

As one, the five girls raised a hand and waved. Renz's throat closed with fear.

Thorn's voice, deceptively calm, said, "Well that's odd."

"Pull back," Paasikivi snapped, "all of you get out of there."

"I'm on a moving train," Renz said.

"Then get to a different car."

The others were already in motion. Walking quietly, quickly, efficiently away from the visitations toward what they each hoped might be safety. He heard Paasikivi talking to an off-cell link, calling in the alert. Renz moved to the shaking doors at the front of the car, but paused and turned, his eyes on the girl at the back. There were differences. This girl had a longer face, eyes that made him think of Asia. The woman beside her—the girl's mother, he guessed—saw him staring and glared back, pulling the girl close to her.

"Renz!" Paasikivi said, and he realized it hadn't been the first time she'd said it.

"Sorry. I'm here. What?"

"The transit police will be waiting for you at the next station. We're evacuating the train, but before we start that, I want you out of there."

"This isn't an attack," Renz said, unsure how he knew it. The mother's glare, the protective curve of her body around her child. "I don't know what it is, but it's not an attack."

"Renz," Marquez said. "Don't get heroic."

"No, guys, really," he said. "It's all right."

He stood and walked down the trembling car. Mother and child watched him approach. The mother's expression changed from fierce to frightened and then back to a different, more sincere fierceness. Renz smiled, trying to seem friendly, and squatted in front of them. He took out his CATC agent's ID and handed it to the mother. The darkness outside the windows gave way to the sudden blurred pillars of a station.

"Ma'am," he said. "I'm afraid you and your girl are going to have to come with me."

The doors hissed open. The police rushed in.

✳

"I DON'T like where this is going," Marquez said.

"Some of you may have heard of the singularity," the man on the stage said. "It's one of those things that people keep saying is just about to happen, but then seems like it never does. The singularity was supposed to be when technology became so complex and so networked, that it woke up. Became conscious. It was supposed to happen in the 1990s and then about once every five years since then. There's a bunch of really bad movies about it.

"But remember what I said before. *Levels can't communicate.* So, what if something did wake up—some network with humans as part of it and computers as part of it. Planes, trains, and automobiles as part of it. This girl here is a cell. That man over there is another one. This community is like an organ or a tissue; even before we were linked, there've been constant communications and interactions between people. What if conscious structures rose out of that. Maybe they got a boost when we started massive networking, or maybe they were always there. Call them hive minds. We might never know, just like our cells aren't aware that they're part of us.

"And these hive minds may have been going along at their own level, completely unaware of us for...well who knows? How long did we go along before we understood neurochemistry?

"I know we're all used to thinking of ourselves as the top. Molecules make up cells, cells make up tissues, tissues make up organs, organs make up people, but people don't make up anything bigger. Complexity stops with us. Well, ladies and gentlemen, it appears that ain't the case."

"Do any of you understand what the hell this guy's talking about?" Pauel asked. From the murmur of voices in the room, the question was being asked across more links than theirs. The speaker, as if expecting this, stepped back and put his hands in his pockets, waiting with an expression like sympathy, or else like pity.

"He's saying there's a war in heaven," Marquez said.

"No, he isn't," Renz said. "This isn't about angels. It's minds. He's talking about minds."

The man stepped forward again, holding up his hands, palm out. The voice of the crowd quieted, calmed. The man nodded, smiling as if he was pleased with them all.

"Here's the thing," he said. "Some of you have already seen the hole in the model. I said levels of complexity can't talk to each other. That's not quite true. You do it every time you drink a glass of wine or go on anti-depressants. We understand neurons. Not perfectly, maybe, but well enough to affect them.

"Well, the only theory that fits the kind of coordinated coincidences we've been seeing is this: something up there—one level of complexity up from us—is starting to figure out how to affect *us*."

✳

WHEN PAASIKIVI interrupted the debriefing and told him, Renz didn't immediately understand. He kept having visions of bombs going off in the doctor's office, of men with guns. It was the only sense he could make of the words *Anna's in the hospital. She's had an attack.*

Her room stank of disinfectant. The hum and rattle of the air purifier was almost loud enough to keep the noise of the place at bay. White noise, like the ocean. She managed a smile when she saw him.

"Hey," she said. "Did you see? Salmon are extinct again."

"You spend too much time on the net," he said, keeping his voice gentle and teasing.

"Yeah, well. It's not like you take me dancing anymore."

He tried to smile at it. He wanted to. He saw the tears in her eyes, her stick-thin arms rising unsteadily to him. Bending down, he held her, smelled her hair, and wept. She hushed him and stroked the back of his neck, her shaking fingers against his skin.

"I'm sorry," he said, when he could say anything. "I'm supposed to be here fluffing your pillows and stuff, not..."

"Not having any feelings of your own? Sweetie, don't be stupid."

He was able to laugh again, a little. He set her down and wiped his eyes with his shirtsleeve.

"What do the doctors say?" he asked.

"They think it's under control again for now. We won't know how much of the damage is permanent for another week or two. It was a mild one, sweet. It's no big deal."

He knew from the way she said it, from the look in her eyes, that *It's no big deal* meant *There's worse than this coming.* He took a deep breath and nodded.

"And what about you?" she asked. "I saw there was some kind of attack that got stopped in New York. Did they try a follow-up to the restaurant?"

"No, it wasn't an attack," he said. "It was something else. It's really weird. They've got all the girls who were involved, but as far as anyone can tell there's no connection between them at all. It was some kind of coincidence."

"Girls?"

"Little ones. Maybe five, six years old."

"Were they wired?"

"No, they were all duds. And they weren't linked to any networks. They were just...people," Renz said, looking at his hands. "I hate this, Anna. I really hate this. All of it."

"Even the parts you like?"

The memory of exhilaration passed through him, of setting the coil, of fear and excitement and success. The feeling of being part of something bigger and more important than himself. The warmth of Anna's body against him as they danced, or as they fucked.

"Especially the parts I like," he said. "Those are godawful."

"Poor sweetie," she said. "I'm sorry, you know. I wouldn't have it like this if I could help it. I keep telling my body to just calm down about it, but..."

She managed a shrug. It was painful to watch. Renz nodded.

"Well, I wouldn't want to be in depths of hell with anyone else," he said.

"Now *that* was sweet," she said. Then, tentatively, "Have you thought about going to the support group? A lot of the people in my group have husbands and wives in it. It seems like it helps them."

"I'm not around enough. It wouldn't do any good."

"They've got councelors. You should at least talk to them."

"Okay. I'll talk to them. I've got leave coming up soon. I can soldier through until then."

She laughed, looked away. The light caught her eyes just right—icicles.

"What?" he asked.

"Soldiering through. It's just funny. You've got your war, honey, and I've got mine."

"Except you're the enemy too."

"Yeah, it does have that war-between-the-states feel to it," she said, and grinned. "There's a guy in my group named Eric. You'd like him. He says it's like having two people in the same body, one of them trying to live, the other one trying to kill the first one even if it means dying right along with."

"The good him and the bad him," he said.

"That's a matter of perspective. I mean, his immune system thinks it's being pretty heroic. Little white cells swimming around high-fiving each other. Hard to convince those guys to stop doing their jobs."

Renz shook his head. Anna's fingers found his, knitting with them. The air purifier let out a pop and then fell back to its normal grinding.

"Is everyone in your group that grim?"

"They haven't gotten to a place where they divide children into wireds and duds, but yes, there's a grimmish streak to them."

"Sounds like Marquez's kind of people."

"And how is the group mind?" Anna asked.

"Pretty freaked about the New York thing."

"So what exactly happened?"

He wasn't supposed to tell her. He did.

✳

"SOMETHING UP there—one level of complexity up from us—is starting to figure out how to affect *us*," the man said. "The question is what we're going to do about it. And the answer is *nothing*. What we have to do is nothing. Go on with our work, the same as we always have. Let me explain why that's critically important.

"So far, the anomalies all have the same structure. They're essentially propaganda. We see the enemy approaching us in a friendly, maybe conciliatory manner. We start thinking of them as cute little girls and nice old women. Or else we're flooded with death reports that remind us that people we care about may die. That we might.

"And maybe we take that into the field with us. In a struggle between two hive minds, that kind of weakening of the opposition would be a very good move. Imagine how easy it would be to win a fistfight if you could convince the other guy's muscles that they really liked you. The whole thing would be over like that," the man said, snapping.

"We all need to be aware. We all need to keep in mind what's going on, but if we change our behavior, it wins. Let the other side get soft, that's fine, but we can't afford to. If this thing up there fails, it may give up the strategy. If we let it get a toehold—if what it's doing works—there's no reason to think it'll ever stop.

"Now there is some good news. Some of you already know this. There are chatter reports that these incidents are happening to terrorist brigades too, so maybe one of these things is on our side. If that's the case, we just need to make sure the bad guys get soft before we do."

Renz shook his head. His mind felt heavy, stuffed with cotton. Marquez touched his arm.

"You okay?"

"Why does he think there's two?"

"What?"

The man was going on, saying something else. Renz leaned in to Marquez, whispering urgently.

"Two. Why does he think there are two of these things? If there's only one, then it's not a war. If this is…why would it be a fight and not a disease? Why couldn't it be telling us that this isn't supposed to be the way things are? Maybe the world's like Anna."

"What's the difference?" Marquez asked.

"With a disease you try to get better," Renz said. "With a war, you just want to win."

"Now before we go on," the man on the stage said, "there are a couple of things I want to make clear."

He raised his hand, index finger raised to make his point, but the words—whatever they were—died before he spoke them. Renz's link dropped, Pauel and Paasikivi and Thorn vanishing, Marquez only a body beside him and not someone in his mind. There was a half-second of dead silence as each agent in the room individually realized what was happening. In the breathless pause, Renz wondered if Anna was on the net and how quickly she would hear what had happened. He heard Marquez mutter *shit* before the first explosions.

Concussion pressed the breath out of him. The dull feeling that comes just after a car wreck filled him, and the world turned into a chaos of running people, shouted orders, the bright, acidic smell of explosives. Renz stumbled toward the exits at the side of the hall, but stopped before he reached them. It was where they'd expect people to go—where many of the agents were going. Marquez had vanished into the throng, and Renz reflexively tried to open the link to him. Smoke roiled at the high ceiling like storm cloud. Another more distant explosion came.

The auditorium was nearly empty now. A series of bombs had detonated on the right side of the hall—rows of seats were gone. The speaker lay quietly dead where he'd stood, body ripped by shrapnel. Fire spread as Renz watched. He wondered if the others were all right—Paasikivi and Thorn and Pauel. Maybe they'd been attacked too.

There were bodies in the wreckage. He went through quickly, the air was thickening. Dead. Dead. Dead. The first living person was a man a little older than he was, lying on the stairs. Salt-and-pepper hair, dark skin, wide hands covered in blood.

"We have to get out," Renz said. "Can you walk?"

The man looked at him, gaze unfocussed.

"There's a fire," Renz said. "It's an attack. We have to get out."

Something seemed to penetrate. The man nodded, and Renz took his arm, lifted him up. Together they staggered out. Someone behind them was yelling, calling for help.

"I'll be back," Renz called over his shoulder. "I'll get this guy out and I'll be right back."

He didn't know if it was true. Outside, the street looked like an anthill that a giant child had kicked over. Emergency vehicles, police, agents. Renz got his ward to an ambulance. The medic stopped him when he turned to go back.

"You stay here," the medic said.

"There's still people in there," Renz said. "I have to go back. I'm fine, but I have to go back."

"You're not fine," the medic said, and pulled him gently down. Renz shook his head, confused, until the medic pointed at his arm. A length of metal round as a dime and long as a pencil stuck out of his flesh. Blood had soaked his shirt.

"Oh," Renz said. "I...I hadn't noticed."

The medic bent down, peering into his eyes.

"You're in shock," he said. "Stay here."

Renz did as he was told. The shapes moving in the street seemed to lose their individuality—a great seething mass of flesh and metal, bricks and fire, moving first one way and then another. He saw it as a single organism, and then as people, working together. Both interpretations made sense.

Firemen appeared, their hoses blasting, and the air smelled suddenly of water. He tried to link to Marquez, but nothing came up. Someone bound his arm, and he let them. It was starting to hurt now, a dull, distant throbbing.

He caught sight of a girl as she slipped into a doorway. So far, no one else seemed to have noticed her. Renz pushed himself up with his good arm and walked to her.

But she wasn't the same—not another ghost of Samara. This child was older, though only by a year or two. Her skin was deep olive, her hair and eyes black. Flames glittered in her eyes. Her coat was thick and bulky even though it was nearly summer. She looked at him and smiled. Her expression was beatific.

"We have to stop this," he said. "It's not war, it's a sickness. It's a fever. We're all part of the same thing, and it's dying. How are we going to make this *stop*?"

He was embarrassed to be crying in front of a stranger, much less a child. He couldn't stop it. And it was stupid. Even in his shock, he knew that if there was something up there, some hive mind sick and dying in its bed, he could no more reach it by speaking to this girl than by shouting at the sky. Could no more talk it out of what was happening than he could save Anna by speaking to her blood.

Renz saw the girl before him shift inside her coat, and understood. An Arab girl in New York in a bulky coat. A second attack to take out the emergency services answering the first one.

This girl was wired.

"Please. We have to *stop* this," Renz said. "You and me, we have to stop." The girl shook her head in response. *No, we don't.*

"God is great," she said, happily. Like she was sharing a secret.

EXCLUSION

"IT'S A SIMPLE QUESTION," his brother said. "What if you had a holocaust and nobody came."

Eliot nodded absently, noticing the way the sound of the rain mixed with the hum of conversation, the way the cool of the rain and the warmth of the coffeehouse were both present. He thumbed up the temperature on his coffee cup, opting for warm over cold.

"Annet Kyrios did something like it last year," Cristof continued, brushing long bangs absently out of his eyes. "Hers were African genocides in the 2080s, I'm using the German Jews. But the questions were pretty much the same. Wire everyone with systems a few hundred years early, give them the option of editing perceptions and how does the economy react, how much abuse do populations consent to before you start seeing massive exclusions, where does the conflict stabilize, what level of scapegoating starts to feed back against itself? You run it through the models and see what exactly changes when you include mediated consciousness."

Cristof waved his hand in gesture like a seagull, long delicate fingers much like Eliot's own. Eliot pulled his mind back to Cristof, the blue eyes and black hair their parents had liked so much that all the sibs wore it like a trademark. His brother shrugged. It was like seeing a very slow mirror that had caught the shifting of his own shoulders ten years earlier and was only now reflecting it for him.

"So," Cristof said, sarcasm slipping comfortably into his tone, "since you find ancient history so stunningly fascinating, I take it you didn't ask me here to talk about the fine point of my thesis, ne?"

"I'm sorry," he said. "I *was* listening. The Jews, the Africans. Consent and exclusion."

"Nice to know you get so much with half an ear," Cristof said and drank from his own cup—a sugary hot tea that smelled to Eliot like a children's drink. "So spill it. What's the pebble in your shoe?"

"It's Tania," he said.

"Oh, El..."

"I can't...stop," he said. "I know. I know. I should let go of it. But..."

"How long has she been gone?" Cristof asked.

"Almost two months," Eliot said. "I was at Yen Ching the other night. The little Korean restaurant I used to take her to."

"I remember the place," Cristof said. "Greasy."

"There was a man on the other side of the place. I thought at first he was waiting for someone and practicing things to say. You know talking to himself. Then I realized..."

"It probably wasn't her," Cristof said.

The table chimed and offered them refills on the coffee. Cristof thumbed in an order for a crepe.

"I followed him to the bathroom," Eliot said. "I was going to ask him if it was her. If he'd talk to her for me."

Cristof snorted and rolled his eyes.

"What are you thinking, El? How many people have you got on your exclude list?"

"I don't know. Twenty. Twenty-five."

"So the chances it was her are what? Five percent? Not even counting anyone else who might have excluded you besides Tania."

"That's not the point," Eliot said, impatient. "It's just an illustration. The way she left...it's eating at me. I need to talk to her."

"How? By going up to men in bathrooms and saying 'Hi, I think you may be with someone who's decided she doesn't want anything to do with me. Would you please disrespect her wishes on my behalf?' If it's that important, go to an intercessionist."

"I can't. We don't have any kids or joint property. There's no reason for someone to take the case professionally. That's why I wanted to talk to you."

The comment hung in the air so long, the table asked if they wanted to see a news feed.

"You want me to step in?" Cristof asked, incredulous. "Keep dreaming, El. She'll just exclude me too. What's the point of that?"

"Try?" he asked, looking hard at the eyes that were so much like his own. "For me, will you try?"

Cristof shook his head, and for a long moment, Eliot thought he would refuse. Then he sighed, air hissing out from between his teeth the way their father had when he'd been talked into something against his better judgment.

"Thank you, Cristof," Eliot said.

"You should just let her go," his brother said.

"I know. But thank you all the same." Dessert arrived, carried by a pretty brunette. Cristof thanked her elaborately, but she left unimpressed. Eliot stole a bite of the crepe.

"So," Eliot said. "Tell me. What changes if the Jews can exclude the Nazis?"

"Same thing that always changes," Cristof said. "Everything."

✳

THEY'D MET through mutual friends, going to the same parties, chatting in the same background groups. Tania was lovely. A few years older than him, but with only the faintest touch of gray at her temples. Her body was just imperfect enough to forgive Eliot his failings, her laugh was just rich enough to intrigue him. They'd started making comments to each other privately through their systems, slowly creating a shared vocabulary that was the basis of their affair.

She started coming over to his place—a little organic five minutes by express subway outside the city—for dinner, and then started staying for the night. Her clothes began to inhabit his closet. She never stopped paying rent on her apartment in the city, but her plants there died from neglect.

Eliot styled the organic after the American Southwest. The grown coral corners hadn't been sharpened, only covered with stucco. She had appreciated the soft feeling it gave the space. She'd liked the recessed "kiva-style" seating area in the main room and the rugs woven in Amerind styles that hung on the wall. He hadn't changed things since she'd left, though he thought it might have been healthier to.

It had hardly been a fight. Had hardly been anything. And still, somehow, it had been the end.

They had been growing apart a little, Eliot thought, but no more than anyone did. They had been seeing each other for three months, making love like teenagers, staying up too late, going in to work with bright smiles and circles under their eyes. And that faded, but that wasn't wrong. That always fades.

She had just come back from a week-long conference in London, tired from the trip and cranky. He'd been waiting for her with wine and candlelight, but he knew from the way she dropped her bag that she saw his advances as another responsibility, something else she had to do.

Okay, he said. Too sharply? Had his disappointment leaked through? *That's fine.*

Eliot...

He'd snuffed out the candles, taken the wine back into the kitchen and corked the bottle.

What do you want from me? she demanded. *What?*

Nothing, he said.

Something had passed over her face as she stood in the kitchen doorway, some expression that spoke of emotions he couldn't fathom. Her mouth softened, but her eyes had seemed to grow more distant, like she was already looking through him, already unable to see him. That expression haunted him. Anger? Hurt? Regret? And if there had been regret, did that mean there was still hope now?

Because whatever she'd felt in that instant, in the next, she excluded him. Her eyes had flickered, gone unfocussed as her system edited him out of her perception, and then less than a heartbeat later, his system synchronized. He'd stood, gaping in surprise at the empty air where she'd been. He'd yelled, but of course she hadn't heard. He'd contacted her system and left messages she never received, never even knew existed. He didn't notice when exactly she left the organic only because he was unable to.

She was gone, unreachable. She was in a different universe, one that didn't include him any more. His friends might see her, might chat with her. His brother might plead his case. But unless she relented, he would be dead to her, a cipher. Something left entirely behind. He would never know if it was his fault.

In the darkness, the rain still pattered against the windows. Eliot sat, listening to it and sipping a beer. The house stood ready to deliver any number of distractions and entertainments, but the rain and alcohol seemed too appropriate.

He tried to wait a decent amount of time, tried not to push. However much he put it off, though, he knew his brother would still feel the same way about it. Their father's sigh hissing through teeth.

"Cristof," Eliot said to the darkness.

"Yes?" Cristof said, the traffic and voices of his cooperative student housing in the city coming in behind him like a constant nearby party or a distant riot.

"How goes?" Eliot asked.

"You remember the old jokes about there being two history departments?"

"Everybody in one excluded everybody in the other," Eliot said, repeating the legend.

"Well, it looks like it may be coming true. Something's happened that has all the knives out. My advisor isn't accepting connections from students until tomorrow, and she was *supposed* to give me a list of revisions for my abstract."

Eliot rubbed his eyes.

"Did you talk to Tania?" he asked.

A low sigh snaked through the darkness. He could see Cristof's eyes rolling as clearly as if they'd had screens on.

"Yes," Cristof said at last. "I did. And really, El, you're better off without her. She's completely unreasonable."

"What did she say? Will she see me?"

"She said she'd listen to your apology on one condition. You have to make peace with everyone on your exclude list. No exclusions for no exclusions. It's what she said," Cristof said.

Eliot frowned, the tension rolling in his brow.

"Why that?" Eliot said.

"She's saying no, El," Cristof said, impatient and snapping. "She's saying she doesn't want to talk to you. Let it go."

"You're right," Eliot said. "You're right. I should."

"Ah, reason dawns at last," Cristof said. "I'm sorry, El. I wish it had worked out. But you'll find someone else. Don't let it bother you. It'll pass."

"I know it will," Eliot lied into the darkness.

"Anyway, she was a bitch."

"Do you know why that? I mean, did she say why that was the condition?"

"No," Cristof said. "I don't know. She just said it."

There was a stuttering tone, Cristof's system telling him someone was trying to break into the link.

"I'll go," Eliot said. "Talk to you later, eh?"

"Lunch next week?" Cristof asked.

"Sure. See you then," Eliot said, and broke the link.

The rain was letting up now, the sound of the drops softer, the thunder more distant. Eliot had his system link to the house, turn up the lights and start a shower. He walked to the bedroom—hardwood floors, brown stucco walls—and stripped between sips of his drink.

She would listen to his apology, Cristof said. His apology. So whatever it was, it was his fault after all. He'd hoped... hoped that maybe it had been something else. That he hadn't driven her away. That it wasn't his fault. It would have been easier if it wasn't his fault, somehow. He left his glass empty at the bedside.

The shower had been smaller before, hardly more than a stall. He'd had the house regrow it after Tania had moved it, widening it at the expense of a storage closet. It was luxurious now, with two nozzles that still sprayed the fine mist that she'd preferred. It smelled of the cedar lotion she'd used. He could imagine her there beside him, could see her wet, black hair against her skin.

"System," he said. "How many people are on my exclude list?"

"Twenty-two," the system reported in its soft, carefully asex voice.

"List them."

He let the water run over him as the system murmured the names of his enemies, the people he'd cut out of his world, never to see or speak with again. Each name was like another stone in his belly as his understanding grew of how bad the next few days would be.

❋

THE FIRST person he'd ever excluded was Margaret Huo in his second year of school. She had accused him of stealing her pen, which he had. The teacher had made him return it in full view of the class with his parents and sibs present via system link. He had excluded her the next day and cajoled his two best friends into doing the same as a show of support.

After work, he sat in the recessed seating, the windows open behind him, thinking of her. The rain had scrubbed the dust from the air, and Eliot imagined the face above the perfect towers of the city. A sandy-haired girl with almond-shaped eyes and a pen. He tried to age her face, thicken it. He tried to imagine twenty-five years softening the barely remembered skin, tugging at the eyes and mouth. He found he couldn't. The only image he could conjure was of the child he had known briefly, and he was probably remembering that wrong too.

He'd changed into a casual sweater, a royal blue that went well with his eyes. He had the system set up a screen. He breathed in deep and slow, and silently, without moving, he removed the exclusion.

When he opened his eyes, nothing had changed, except the knowledge that his world had one more person in it than had been a moment before.

"System, request link with Margaret Huo."

There were probably hundreds of matches for the name, Eliot reflected. A legion of Margaret Huos related only by the coincidence of common names. But his system knew from context and silently made the link.

She was sitting at a rough wooden table wearing a simple, well-cut cotton dress, a cup of tea in her hand. Behind her, the pale light of impending dawn glowed through a window. Eliot was surprised by how little she had changed and then an instant later by how much.

"Margaret Huo?" Eliot asked.

"Yes," she said, politely but firmly. "But I'm afraid that whatever it is, I'm not interested. Please take me off your call list, and..."

"No, I'm not selling anything. I'm looking for you. I'm Eliot Mikos. We were in second year school together. Ms. Teller's class."

Margaret put down her teacup and looked more carefully at him. A single vertical crease appeared between her brows.

"Yes," she said, a slow smile blooming on her features. "You stole my pen and excluded me."

"Yes," Eliot said. "That's the one. That's why I was looking for you, actually. I wanted to see if I could make amends."

Without appearing to move, her smile shifted, turned quizzical. Eliot found he was clenching his fists on his knees and forced the fingers to relax.

"For excluding me or stealing my pen?" she asked.

"Either," Eliot said. "Both. Whatever seems appropriate."

Margaret nodded thoughtfully and picked up her tea, sipping it. She nodded.

"I forgive you for taking my pen and dropping out of my universe. Looking back, I can't say it changed my life much one way or another."

"Thank you," Eliot said.

"If you'd like to tell me what this is all about, though..."

Eliot shook his head, laughing a little.

"It's a long story. And I don't know that it would make sense."

She nodded. Behind her, the sunlight grew suddenly brighter, as if a cloud had passed.

"I'm afraid you've caught me just before work," she said. "No time for long stories. Perhaps we'll run into each other some time, just by chance, and you can tell me then."

"I guess we might," Eliot agreed, then paused. "Thank you."

"You're welcome," she said. "Good luck, Eliot Mikos. Whatever it is. I have to say, you make an interesting beginning to a morning."

He nodded and she broke the link. The screen went grey, his own ghostly reflection looking back out at him. That was one. Twenty-one to go.

The second person he'd ever excluded was Dustin Liria. It was in fifth year, and at the time Dustin had been trying to break his ribs by kicking them. Remembering the incident now, Eliot wasn't entirely sure how to approach it. He sighed and took the exclusion off. Perhaps something would occur to him.

He removed four of the people from his list that night. When he went into the office in the morning, a package had arrived for him. An enameled blue pen, heavy and smooth, with no message.

✳

"JIHAD. HOLY war. The whole department is acting like two different hills of ants put in the same jar and shaken."

Cristof tapped his fingertips nervously on the table. There were dark circles under his eyes, the kind Eliot remembered from the mirror in his own student days. Nights spent drinking and talking and seducing that turned into mornings of hot coffee. But Eliot's memories didn't involve the same paleness of the cheeks, the haunted sound in Cristof's voice, like he was speaking from a long way off.

Cristof's room was small, close and dark, one suite of seven that shared a kitchen and communal bath. Two of the other six were in the kitchen, arguing about something Eliot couldn't follow. The whole place smelled of marijuana and cheap incense.

"It's this new thesis. Mikel Tinos. Did I tell you about him?" Cristof asked.

"He's the one who came over from political science, ne?"

"Him," Cristof agreed. One of the pair in the kitchen slammed a metal pot into the sink with a report that hurt Eliot's ears. Cristof blinked.

"Oh," he said apologetically. "Are the terrible two at it again?"

"Sorry," Eliot said, disconcerted. "What?"

"I excluded them both last week," Cristof said. "They started fucking, and ever since the place is unlivable with them in it. Come on, let's go elsewhere, eh?"

Eliot stood. Cristof shrugged on a jacket and led the way out. The terrible two glared at Eliot as he left, though not, of course, at Cristof.

The campus had changed, the same buildings regrown in the latest style of old stone and antiquity. The effect would almost have convinced Eliot if he hadn't seen them in shining and spartan neo-African designs only a few years before. He and his brother walked side by side across the quad, scattering the pigeons before them.

"He's turned the models around. He's running the '73 elections without exclusion and saying the reform party would have rounded up the liberal left and slaughtered them."

"Ah," Eliot said. "Isn't the department chair…"

"Reformist," Cristof said. "He took it very poorly. But the grant money comes from a liberal left foundation. The chair tried to kill the project, Tinos called his handlers and they threatened to pull funding."

Cristof made a gesture like throwing confetti to the wind and laughed.

They stopped at a street café just off the campus proper. A street musician stood by the door, sawing out popular tunes on an ancient violin. Cristof led the way to a dark corner where he thumbed in an order without looking. Eliot took a moment, searching for something decent in the glowing list of options, before making his choice. By tacit agreement, Eliot was the one who offered payment.

"Imagine living without our systems filtering the world for us," Eliot said as a pretty young man brought their drinks. "Going back to when you couldn't walk away, no matter how bad it got."

"Has its drawbacks if you're liberal left, apparently," Cristof said dryly.

"Yes, well. Still, it would have made my last week easier," Eliot said, not meeting his brother's eyes. "I started with old ones. From when I was young. They weren't so bad. But some of these people I stopped talking to for a reason."

The door of the café swung open and closed as a woman came in, the cheap violin music swelling and growing faint. Cristof shook his head.

"It just would have been better to take care of it all at the time, you know?" Eliot continued. "When it was still fresh. But then, I suppose Tania wouldn't have me in this position at all, if that was how it was."

"Oh, Jesus God, El. You mean you're..."

Eliot felt his smile press thin, but he held it. Raising his eyebrows, he spoke to the table in front of his brother's chest.

"I knew you wouldn't approve. But you'll see, when you get older, that walking away gets...harder. There isn't as much time as there was when I was young. There aren't as many people who..."

He waved his hand, a slow rolling motion that tried to convey all of it—lust, hope, comfort. Cristof put down his cup of sweet tea with a dull thud.

"Eliot. Please don't. Please."

Cristof's expression was, if anything, more drawn than it had been before, as if his decision was a betrayal, a failure to behave. Eliot shifted his shoulders. When he spoke, his voice was harsher than he'd intended.

"It's my dignity, brother, not yours. I'll spend it where I think it needs spending," Eliot said.

His brother shrank back from the words, and Eliot regretted them immediately.

"I have to *know*," Eliot said. "I just have to know."

The rest of the meal was strained and uncomfortable, and Eliot spent the rest of the day trying to shake a feeling of loneliness that had stolen over him.

✳

IT WAS difficult to smile, but he did his best.

"Amends?" Ariana pouted. "You want to make amends?"

"I just want to clean up some of the loose ends in my life," Eliot said, knowing as he did that the words sounded like a warning not to expect much. Knowing that Ariana would only take it as a dare to raise the stakes.

"I don't know," Ariana said in the near baby talk that made his flesh crawl. "It really hurt my feelings when you didn't want to talk to me. Ten years is a long time to make *amends* for."

"Ari," Eliot said, raising a placating hand. "It was six years, and..."

"Eliot," Tania said. "We need to talk."

Her voice was low and calm, but it hit his bloodstream with the rattling fear of gunshots. He had never taken her off his system's privileged access.

"Ari," he said, calmly as he could. "I've got to take this. I'll get right back with you."

Before she could reply, he broke the connection and Tania appeared on the screen. Her dark, serious eyes met his with an expression he couldn't read. He put his hands in his lap, weaving his fingers to keep them from trembling.

"Tania," he said. "I didn't think I'd hear from you so soon. Cristof said…"

"Yes," she broke in. "Yes, your brother's been saying a lot of things. That's why we need to talk. I've been getting panicky messages from him for three days now. I excluded him at first, but then he started on with my parents."

"I've been going through my exclude list," Eliot said. "Just the way you asked. I've still got six…well, six or seven to go."

"Eliot, you don't think I would really do that, do you?"

Eliot paused for a beat.

"Excuse me?" he heard himself say.

"I would never do that to you. Cristof thought you'd let go of me if I was being unreasonable. When you called, he'd been talking to someone about some scheme where people couldn't exclude each other. It was the first thing that came to mind. It isn't true. It was never true."

Tears filled her eyes and her lips pressed thin and bloodless. For a moment, Eliot felt dizzy, like he was looking down from a great height. He felt a smile creep onto his face, the sick smile of a man in extremis. When he spoke, his words were measured, calm.

"I didn't know what to think," he said. "I didn't know anything, really. I thought perhaps I had done something."

"I know. I'm sorry. It was wrong of me. I should have told you, but it seemed so much easier to just make a clean break. No fights, no recriminations. I would just be gone."

He tried to speak, but his throat had gone tight. Tania looked down. It struck him that she'd started parting her hair on the left. The fact had a clarity and incongruity he associated with trauma, like noticing a crack in the sidewalk just the moment before impact.

"We weren't working," she said. "I thought you knew it too. But I didn't want to fight about it, and it seemed easier to just go along. There was never a good time to talk. And then...when I met someone else...it still didn't seem like a good time."

"Ah," Eliot said. The knot in his chest released, and the sorrow behind it swelled up into his throat and eyes. "I see."

"You didn't do anything wrong," she said. "You don't have an apology to make to me. I'm sorry that..."

Eliot held up his hand, palm out. Tania, with her lovely mouth, her midnight eyes, went silent.

"I understand," he said. "Thank you for calling."

"Eliot..." she began.

"Thank you," he said again. "Thank you for calling."

He broke the link, and the screen went black. Pain filled his chest and throat like a tumor, forcing him to breathe in sips. Every time he thought it was almost over, her face on the screen came back, and he was gone again.

He had gotten as far as his bed but not so far as taking off his clothes when Ariana requested a link. He excluded her and rolled onto his side, clutching a pillow.

※

CRISTOF SAT in the quad, smoking with four other students. Eliot could tell by the slope of his brother's shoulders that he was tired. Quietly, he walked up from behind.

"I'm not arguing for it," Cristof said as Eliot stepped up. "I'm only saying that we shouldn't discount it. If the model does apply..."

Eliot put his hand on Cristof's shoulder. Cristof turned and went pale.

"Excuse us," Eliot said to Cristof's companions. He turned and walked toward the old auditorium. Cristof fell into step beside him. The air was cool, a late cold snap, one last breath of winter.

Eliot angled their path across a wide quad. An old practice auditorium stood at the edge of campus, little changed by the architectural shifts and fashions of the campus. Cristof walked in silence, hands pressed deep into his pockets. Eliot didn't speak.

The hall was in use. Voices rose in the difficult passages of song, fell away to mutterings and then rose again. Eliot, still wordless, walked to a side lobby, apart from the main entrance. He sat on an old red velvet chair and motioned for Cristof to take a seat beside him.

They sat in silence for a long moment. Eliot took a heavy blue pen from his jacket pocket.

"You want me to start?" Eliot asked.

Cristof blinked, frowned, shook his head slowly.

"No," his brother said, leaning forward and clasping his hands. "No, I'll do it."

"Okay," Eliot said.

"I was wrong," Cristof said. "I...I thought that it would be easiest for you just to let go of her, and I thought I could help."

"So you lied."

"So I lied," Cristof agreed. "It was stupid. But I did it. Did she talk to you?"

"Yes," Eliot said.

"Do you feel better now?"

Eliot frowned, considering. The blue enamel pen caught the light like a shard of sky.

"No, not really," Eliot said. "But I will. And that's about the best I could do this time. Did it ever strike you as condescending to decide you know my life better than I do?"

"You mean before the fact?" Cristof said, and despite his discomfort, a laugh stole into his tone. "No. The last week, I've been over the point in detail, though. I wanted to apologize. I would have, but I was afraid to link to your system. I thought, you know, you might have excluded me."

"I did, for a while," Eliot said.

Cristof looked up, a question in his face.

"I took it off again," Eliot said.

A woman sang three notes of a falling trill, the sound echoing in the tall air. Cristof shifted in his chair.

"Forgive me?" Cristof asked, his voice quiet, dreading, hopeful.

"No," Eliot said. "I tried to, but...No, I don't. I don't trust you right now, Cristof. I feel betrayed. I don't understand how you could treat me that lightly. You made this a lot harder than it should have been. And it was bad to start with."

"I'm sorry," Cristof whispered.

"I know," Eliot said.

"Don't go?" Cristof asked, desperation in his eyes. "Look, El, I know I've been a shit, but please don't put me on your list. Give me a chance and I'll make it up to you. I swear to God..."

Eliot hushed him gently and put the pen back into his pocket.

"It's okay," Eliot said. "I'm not going anywhere. I promise."

"I'm sorry I screwed up," Cristof said.

"We'll deal with it," Eliot said. "Give it time, we'll deal with it. I just went through just about everyone I never wanted to talk to again, and most of the time...Did Tania tell you why she did it? When you talked to her?"

Cristof shook his head.

"Because it was more convenient for her. Easier than having a hard conversation with me. Easier than working it out."

"I'm sorry..." Cristof began.

"It doesn't matter," Eliot continued. "The important thing is that I did the same thing to all the people I excluded. Cut them out and gave up on actually solving anything. I'm just the same as her. I let all those people be dead to me because it was easier at the time. I don't want that anymore."

They were both silent for a long moment. Behind them, music began to fill the cold, winter air.

"And anyway," Eliot said, "you're my brother."

Cristof sat forward. His hand was warm on Eliot's wrist. For a moment they sat, holding hands like children.

AS SWEET

I WAS IN THE middle of my lecture when the woman appeared, fading in like a cheap special effect at the back of the classroom. She stood there, arms akimbo, for a long moment. She was older than me by perhaps five years of hard living, ten years of watching her weight and hitting the gym. Her temples were touched with grey. She wore clothing that reminded me of the Italian peasant blouse Jules had bought me when he was in Rome three years before. "A very old fashioned cut," he'd called it.

The kids looked up at me, more interested in my sudden silence than the words I'd been speaking. A couple looked to the back, but their gazes skated over her. She raised her eyebrows and motioned me on with one thick-fingered hand.

"Um," I said. "Well, let me show you what I mean. Everyone open your books to act one, scene two. Eric, you read Benvolio. David, you take Romeo."

The pages opened with the hiss and slick of new paper. One of the girls in the fourth row—Melissa Garcia, with her hair perpetually in her eyes and spiderwebs drawn on the back

223

of her hands in black pen—sighed. They were already bored. The woman in the back of the room smiled. There was a sorrow in her eyes and a profound amusement.

"Start where Montague leaves," I said.

I'd chosen Eric and David because making them read was the only way to keep them from talking. They smirked and fidgeted. Eric began.

"Good morrow, cousin," he said, and it sounded almost natural. They pressed on, David stumbling over unfamiliar ground, getting lost so that he was reading one word after the next without trying to make them make sense. Eric's mouth found its way around the syllables in a way that approached playful. Eric was always closer to a Mercutio.

The woman in the back listened while a halting, inarticulate Romeo lamented and my too-clever Benvolio subtly mocked me, my little fluorescent-lit, chalk-dusted classroom, and the whole world with the way he delivered his lines. I stood, pretending to listen, watching her features, trying to convince myself that I was hallucinating.

"Farewell," David said, "thou canst (he pronounced it can't-st) not teach me to forget."

"I'll pay that doctrine or else die in debt," Eric rejoined.

"Okay," I said. "You all heard it. Now. Tell me what happened."

The kids were silent. Adolescent eyes searched out the corners of the floor and ceiling. I crossed my arms, not realizing right away that I was mirroring the woman, but then too self-conscious to undo the gesture.

"Come on," I said. "He's talking about a girl, right?"

"He's breaking up with someone," Miguel, thin-faced and dark-eyed, said.

"Right," I said. "That's exactly right. And who is he in love with? Come on, you all read the first act last night, didn't you? Is it Juliet?"

"No," Eric said. "He doesn't even meet Juliet yet."

"That's right. It's someone else. Her name's Rosaline, and she doesn't show up again. Can anyone tell me why Romeo's breaking up with her? Alice?"

"Because she doesn't want him," Alice grudged.

"Be more specific," I said.

Alice shrugged and looked away. I narrowed my eyes, as if I was judging whether to do something, to tell them some secret. It was the same thing I always did, a scene I had already played. I walked the four steps to my door and closed it, cutting us off from the hall, the school, the possibility of prying ears. When I stepped back up to the blackboard, I had their attention. Hers too.

"Then she hath sworn that she will still live chaste?" I recited from memory, then lowered my voice to answer for Romeo. "She hath, and in that sparing makes huge waste."

I paused, smiling a secretive, complicit smile, raising my eyebrows just a little.

"She won't put out," I said.

They blinked, they giggled, but they started really listening. They do every year. Every year they think that I'm too old, that I was born and raised before the discovery of sex, that Shakespeare is about the arid land of school. And every year I floor them. I haven't been caught at this yet.

"Maybe she'd sworn herself to be a nun," I said. "Maybe she just didn't want Romeo. Maybe she's waiting to get married."

"Maybe I got lucky," the woman in the back said softly, to me because no one else could hear her. Her voice was rich and soft as cream in coffee. "Or maybe some part of me knew he was trouble. Sometimes children are born wise."

I met her eyes and she cocked her head. I was quiet so long the kids got nervous.

❋

THE BALLROOM is filled with the finest of Verona, young flesh dancing itself to exhaustion and delight. It is part of a single movement, a single roving party that moves through the world from the first delighted squirming of an adolescent mammal to the shocking sexuality of a waltz, the drug-soaked artificial ecstasy of a warehouse rave. There is only one dance, reaching back forever, wearing out and wearing down the dancers, shifting from place to place like an invisible cat placing careful paws as it stalks through history.

He is there, his clean, clear skin, his brooding, romantic face. He isn't allowed, and he is there anyway, in the flicker of firelight and the smell of sweat and wine. His fellows, his gang, his homies, his vatos stand with him, all with an affected casual air. The way he holds his hips, the coltish awkwardness and power of his movement, mark him as one of a species of countless young men, a moment of manhood's arc caught in strobe.

From behind a low curtain, red velvet soft against her fingertips, one girl watches him. She already knows what his lips taste like, she knows the feeling of his hand between her thighs. And she watches him watch the crowd, watches his eyes seeking, looking for someone, looking for her. And she sees it when he finds her, only it isn't her at all.

She shifts her gaze to follow his. The girl on the dance floor is beautiful, black hair in her wild eyes. When she laughs, the crash of it carries over the air like shards of glass striking pavement. When she dances, her hips shift more than the others, her hands caress the air more carefully. When she bounces up on her toes, arms high, her small, recent breasts threaten to crawl up out of her dress. She is thirteen.

Behind her curtain, the watcher shifts back to him. His face is shut, his attention focussed to a single point which was once her own mouth and never will be again. His friends around him are looking more nervous by trying harder not to.

They can feel that something has happened, even though they may not know what.

The watcher lets the curtain fall on the drama that has just passed her by, her fingers trembling. She regrets now that she stopped him, that his cock never filled her and never will. She weeps in the darkness to be left behind. Perhaps if she goes to him now, perhaps if she offers herself now, it might not be too late. But she doesn't.

And the old woman in the back of her mind, the one who was always there, will always be there, the one who was born with her, closes a pair of interior eyes and breathes relief.

✳

JULES CAME home later than usual that night, held up at the office over some minor local area networking disaster. I was half way through my dinner—a BLT, a little sliced fruit, a beer—when he started warming up a can's worth of Manhattan-style clam chowder. The wrapper of last night's frozen lasagna peeked shyly out the top of the trashcan until he smashed it down.

"So what news?" he asked, his back to me. His wide shoulders shifted, his bald spot shone in the unkind light. "Are they literate yet?"

"No, not yet," I said, completing our usual schtick. The humor drained out of the words two years ago, but we still said it. "And you?"

"More of the same," he said, still not looking at me.

Jules had been a prettier man when I'd met him. His age was starting to show, not only in the baldness that he had to call early instead of premature, but also in the width of his waist, the time it took him to shrug off colds and heal scrapes. My lover is a middle aged man, I thought. And I'm six months older than he is. When did *that* happen?

"Actually," I said, "there was something strange."

Jules turned, still stirring his soup, to look at me. I leaned back, prepared myself, and told him the whole thing—the visitation, the woman's gnomic pronouncement, the way she'd vanished like waking up from a dream when the bell rang to end class. When I was finished, he was almost done with his bowl of soup, the scent of my bacon washed away by the disturbingly intimate and oceanic smell of hot seafood.

Jules shrugged.

"Weird things happen all the time," Jules said. "Did I tell you about the time I heard a ghost?"

"It was at your mother's house," I said. "Just after your dad's funeral."

"You see," he said, as if his old anecdote explained mine, as if I made sense when considered in relation to him.

"Well, if I'm going to be haunted by a character from a play, it could at least be one with a speaking part," I said, picking glib as the graceful way out.

We watched TV for a while, his arm around my shoulders with the casual feeling of habit, then I showered and he checked his email. It was another perfectly normal, average night in my life. As the warm water slid over me, washing away some thin, sticky, ectoplasmic residue of the day, I wondered if Jules ever wanted out of the marriage, if he ever dreamed of packing a bag, throwing it in the back of the car and heading out, half of our savings in his pocket, to find some new life, some cute waitress with a kink for balding network administrators. Which was the same as wondering if his fantasy life mirrored mine.

We met, Jules and I, when he'd been working for the school system. At twenty-eight, I had just ended a depressing, destructive relationship with a married man and was at low ebb. For three months, I'd been smiling wanly at nothing and looking through crowds, hoping to recognize a stranger.

And then Jules had smiled and flirted with me, and I was his for the asking.

Not that he asked. Not right away. For two months, he would swing by the school to check on some hardware, or take off some virus that had struck the mechanisms dumb. He mentioned that he had never felt the urge to have kids. I confessed similar emotions. We'd flirt, smile, and I'd spend my evenings alone with a sick longing that I cherished because it was infinitely better than pain. I told myself that I was too late, that he was just flirting to be polite, that he couldn't possibly want someone like me—someone worn at the edges and old. I'd thought of myself as too old then, for Christ's sake, what was I thinking now?

When he did ask me out, it was a good dinner, half a bottle of decent wine, and into bed. We never even got to the movies. For three months, we screwed like teenagers. Every time he looked a little surprised and delighted, like I was an unexpected present. By the time my hormone haze faded, I liked him. It was almost two years after I first whispered I love 'you that I decided it was true. And that was six years ago.

I killed the water, stepped out of the shower. The image in the mirror didn't flatter me. The gym was changing my body, but slowly, and it made me look like a stronger middle-aged woman not a younger one. The tone of my muscles was good, my legs still had their shape, but somewhere along the way, my skin had gone slack. My neck had wrinkles. There were veins on my calves.

If Jules left me, this was the body I'd be using to lure someone new into my life. This face, growing crow's feet and pale lips, would be my billboard: Love Me! I'm Not Dead Yet. If Jules left me, or if I left him.

I knew I wasn't unhappy, but I wasn't happy either. I missed the electric jazz of a first kiss—any first kiss. I hated the thought of going it alone again, but when I pictured Jules and told myself he was the last man I would ever love, I wondered whether lifting those weights, attacking the imaginary flights of stairs, wasn't something like a prayer.

Some children are born wise, the vision of Rosaline had said.

"Yeah?" I said to the woman in the mirror. "Well bully for them."

✳

THE RUMORS and whispers run fast as voles, shuttling back and forth through time, across stories. In the barber's shop with its scissors and razors and instruments of surgery. In the coffee houses with their strange smelling smokes and Arabic poetry. On the campus of the university, in the letters from the battlefield, on the wind anywhere the wind goes and as long as the air is moving. If some of the murmurs are about flesh long dead, it hardly matters. The shape of the tale is the same.

That dark-haired boy, he was outside her window last night. They were talking. I hear they're lovers.

It isn't true. I heard yesterday she's engaged to someone else. A guy in the army.

He got a tattoo of her name. I saw it.

There was a fight. Her cousin is in the hospital. Critical condition. The police...

It was drugs. They were all into drugs, all those kids.

She keeps liquor in her school locker. All kinds of it, in mason jars. She'll sell the combination for twenty bucks to anyone who promises to be discreet.

It's his family. His father's violent. Child protective services would have come in if the kids were a little younger.

Didn't you go out with him once? What's he like?

And on behalf of all the discarded first lovers in the history of the world, she raises her eyebrows, shrugs. She has very little to say on the matter. No one wants to hear how it

230

pricks a little each time the question is asked. *Her* heart is not at issue.

Instead, she writes in her diary, sips milky tea, stays up late with her friends walking along the river and listening to bards sing of perfect love never attained, or captured and then lost. The memory of his mouth against hers fades slowly. His passion for her is forgotten by everyone until the ghost of it is hers alone, like a dream remembered but never retold.

She tells herself that it wouldn't matter if she did speak; her words would carry no more weight than the well-crafted lies falling from other lips. Truth forgives her nothing, grants her no weight or authority.

She tells herself it is not her story.

※

ERIC, MY too-clever Benvolio, sat glum and resentful beside his father while Mr. Makey, the vice-principal, outlined the problem. Fighting, cutting class, a little vandalism. Eric's father, Gary, listened with an expression that seemed a grim mirror of his son—the same sharp face, the same light eyes. The twenty year difference between them reminded me of pictures of a single man, across time. I could see what Eric would look like as he aged, or what Gary had been in high school, scowling as his own father had listened to a litany of his minor sins. They even moved their hands the same way.

"So you see," Makey said, "we're worried that his academic standing will slip, and..."

Gary glanced over at us, a Greek chorus of teachers, our lips pressed thin. I apologized with my eyes. It was clear how angry he was with Eric. And how hurt.

"Thank you," he said. His voice was musical and rough—a cello with a bad buzz. "You did the right thing. I'll take care of it from here."

"I wonder if there's anything we can do to help," Makey said. "We can arrange extra tutoring. And, well, I don't like to mention it, but we have counselors here if there's some trouble at home..."

Fucking vulture, I thought, *Couldn't you at least wait until you were alone with them?* And a flicker of amusement seemed to pass over Gary's face. I looked down.

"No, it's all right. I'll take it from here. But there is one thing you can do."

Makey leaned forward, frowning his *listening thoughtfully* frown. I thought I saw Gary suppress a smile. Makey's absurdity was lost on Eric, but his father and I shared an appreciation of it.

"If you teachers here could give me an idea of what exactly it is he's supposed to be doing. Straight to me, just so that it doesn't get lost on the way home by accident."

"I think we can do that," I said. Makey scowled, but the others nodded.

"Thank you," Gary said, to me.

There were pleasantries and meeting's end handshakes all around, except for the condemned boy of course. Gary's hands were surprisingly rough. I wondered what he did during his days. Father and son left together, Eric's head bowed, Gary's hand on his son's neck like a man walking an escaped dog back to its pen.

"I wish he'd agreed to counseling," one of the chorus murmured.

"Is the mother around?" I asked. "It seems to go better when we can get the whole family together."

Makey raised an eyebrow, reading some ulterior motive into my question.

"She took off three years ago," the math teacher to my right said. "I had Eric's sister in my class that year."

"And there's a history of alcohol abuse in the family. It's that kind of tragedy that can rip a family apart," Makey said. "Ah well, we do what we can."

The after-school halls felt deserted. What voices there were fell to murmurs that still managed to echo. I unlocked my empty classroom, sat at my desk, pulled a stack of grammar quizzes in need of grading out from my satchel. I'd budgeted two hours to finish sixty. An hour and a half in, I was just finishing the twenty-eighth. I put down my pen and rubbed my eyes with the heels of my palms until yellow and green ghosts blossomed.

Jules was home before I was, stretched out on the couch, his feet still in their shoes. A bottle of beer was sweating itself a puddle on the coffee table without the benefit of a coaster. On the television, Mr. Data cocked his head like a starling and said something naïve to Captain Picard.

"Hey, you," he said as I came in the room. "They literate yet?"

I didn't answer, just took myself upstairs and drew a hot bath. My skin was sweat-sticky when I pulled off my clothes, and the water felt like heaven. Closing my eyes, I could see Gary leaning against the desk, frowning, smiling, considering me with perfect pale eyes. I could feel the rough skin of his hand against mine. I wondered what his lips would feel like.

It was stupid. It was doomed. It was temporary; a good night's sleep and it would pass. I was too old for this shit anyway.

It was so soon. I hadn't thought it would come so soon.

✳

IT IS summer, and she is walking alone. It isn't a wise thing for a woman to be alone, but the judicious abandonment of good sense is also a kind of wisdom. The day is bright and the tempers of the city's great houses are focused on each other, not on minor players like herself. So she walks through the market, trading a tiny silver coin for honey cake. It has rained earlier, and the streets still smell of water-slaked stone.

The city is Verona, and it is also New York. All the
Alexandrias, all the Springfields, Santa Fe, Berlin, Kyoto, all
touch corners of the city. Some contribute a sound or a scent
or a building but most often only the invisible sense of the
cosmopolis, the eternal city of which even Rome is only a
shadow. And, as she walks to the river, the sun warmth making her flesh feel heavy and pleasant and slow, she thinks of
the boy she wanted once, in what seems like another life.

He is banished now, sent away to Mantua or Liverpool
or Denver. Blood is on his hands, while her fingers are only
a little sticky with honey. How easy it would have been to
be sucked into that horror. Death and murder and tears followed him, and she might have too—followed him like any
of his little plagues—if he had asked. And this perfect afternoon would have been spoiled by the pain of loving him. The
thought leaves her bemused, like remembering an old illness
but being unable to conjure the sensations of being sick. *I had
a fever, once, and it brought terrible dreams, but I've forgotten
them all.*

She takes herself down to the river where the booksellers
have their stalls, rows and piles of uncut pages. She washes her
hands in a fountain before buying a thin book of poems from
a grey-haired man.

The stone quays by the waterside are full of people enjoying the touch of the sun, the sound of the water. A young man
with crow-black hair sits at the water's edge, bent over a tab-
let of drawing paper, crayon in hand. An old woman calls out
from the top of the bridge. Pigeons coo and strut, playing at
being doves.

She sits on a wooden bench with just a touch of shade to
it. The poems are printed with a pale ink, sonnets to love,
and to food, and to the constant presentiment of death. Boats
passing on the water, children laughing, nurses and mothers
scolding, men arguing and boasting—all these things fade into

a comforting, golden flow. She is hardly aware that she is being lulled to sleep until the artist approaches her.

"Excuse me," he says.

She blinks awake, shakes her head to clear it. The man is younger than she is, though by very little. His eyes are perfect black, so dark she cannot make out where the iris and pupil meet. He bows to her, just slightly.

"Excuse me," he repeats. "I did not wish to interrupt, but I wondered if, as you are here and by far the most deserving to be immortalized, I might be permitted to take your likeness?"

He is dressed in common clothes but his voice betrays his education. He has lovely teeth. She casts a glance at his paper, his fingertips tinted red and grey.

"You flatter, sir," she says. "I think you wish to draw me because I am stationary and convenient."

He blushes now.

"But," she sighs. "You may as well. I shall be staying here long enough for a sketch, I suppose."

"You honor me," he says. "Leonardo Urbino. Lately of Padua."

"Rosaline," she replies.

"Then I shall call you Rose," he says, nods, steps back a few paces, and sits down insolently in the middle of the walk, blocking the foot traffic.

There they sit for hours. He completes three sketches, and she reads her book through twice. When the church bells toll four o'clock, she stands. He takes her hand, kisses it, and presents her with one of the drawings.

"Thank you," she says, considering her own face, the shape of her eyes as seen through his. He has made her beautiful. She begins to say something, but fails, shakes her head.

"Thank you," she says again.

✳

IT WAS four-thirty on Thursday. I sat in my classroom, telling myself I wasn't stalling. There were just things I had to do, and if I did them here I wouldn't have to carry the papers home and back. The memo from Makey and the manila envelope I'd prepared were on my desk, on the corner, looking casual. My chair was unusually hard and uncomfortable. I kept fidgeting.

Fifteen more minutes, I told myself. Then I'd take the damn thing up to the front office and leave. It wasn't the first time I'd made the resolution.

Gary showed up ten minutes later, rapping gently on my door. His hair was combed back, a style his son imitated, and he held a handful of folders and envelopes. My heart ticked over into fight-or-flight.

"Excuse me," he said. "I'm Eric's dad, and..."

"Gary," I said, standing, smoothing my skirt against my legs. "Come in. I'm sorry I didn't have this up to the front office yet. I was just heading out."

"Oh. No trouble," he said.

I picked up the envelope and handed it over, a little awkwardly. He had the opportunity to brush my hand, but he didn't.

"It isn't much," I said. "Grammar and a reading assignment."

"Well, with all of you giving him something, I'm sure he'll be plenty busy," Gary said. "I wanted to thank you for taking an interest in him. All of you. And for letting me know there's a problem."

"You're welcome," I said. Then, "How's he doing?"

"Still a little bit of fever, but he'll be fine. Just needs a little more rest. He's a strong kid."

I smiled. He smiled back. We held each other's eyes a half-beat too long.

"Um," I said, "I was just..."

I made a vague gesture toward my purse.

"Walk you to your car," he offered. My pulse stepped up its tempo. I thought I was blushing, but I couldn't be sure.

"That's very kind of you," I said.

I gathered my things, locked the door, and walked out, Gary beside me. Twice—once as we stepped close to each other passing through the main doors, and again when we reached my car—I caught the scent of his skin, sweat-salt and musk. He walked the way Eric did too, only a half-beat slower and much more assured.

"Well," I said, opening my car door. "Tell Eric to get well soon for me."

"I'll do that," he said. His gaze flickered to my hand on the door frame, to my wedding ring, then back to me. Another too-long moment, then a wry expression—sorrow and amusement both—and he nodded.

"Be seeing you, then," he said.

"Bye."

I sat in my car, fiddling with the radio until my hands stopped shaking. I was being stupid. I was playing with fire. I felt giddy and light-headed and bone-deep delighted in a way I hadn't in years. All the way home I imagined other endings. Hey, I could have said, I was just going to go grab a cup of coffee...Or, Here's my phone number. In case Eric has any questions about the work.

Maybe I was flattering myself, but I had the feeling that if I'd pushed, if I'd wanted to, I could have spent the evening with slow, rough-skinned Gary, could have touched his hands again.

I could have broken Jules' heart. I could have been out right then, breaking poor, sweet Jules' heart. Jules who hadn't done anything wrong but not stay more exciting. It wasn't fair to him.

I wondered whether, if I tried, I could turn my back, decide through force of will to be a better wife. I didn't think I could. And even if I could, I wasn't sure that I wanted to. The rush was too lovely.

I had never seriously thought I had it in me, this kind of betrayal. The intimation that I did horrified me. And the delight and the horror didn't cancel out, they only sat beside each other in my mind while I drove.

He wasn't home when I got there.

She was.

She sat at my kitchen table, drinking a cup of coffee from one of my good blue mugs. When she looked up at me, her eyes were dark, her mouth strong. The lines in her face made her almost too expressive, like a stage actor whose makeup exaggerates so that every smile and frown can be seen from the back row.

"What do you teach them?" she asked, as if we were already in the middle of our conversation. "What do you teach *about* them, ah?"

I closed the door and sat down at the table. She rose, poured a mug of coffee, put it on the table in front of me with a clunk. I scalded my tongue sipping it.

"He was a crazy little boy, and she was a stupid girl in a time when it was very dangerous to be a stupid girl," she said. "And this is your love story? *This?*"

Rosaline made a disgusted face and brushed the air with her fingertips, shooing away a fly. I didn't know how to talk to a hallucination.

"Look," I said. "I've got a lot on my mind right now, and Shakespeare just isn't the top of the list."

"Love, betrayal, passion, tragedy," she said, ticking off fingers as she did. "And you. You *teach* them this. Leonardo and I had four children. Passion? Yes, there was passion. He was beautiful. And then he wasn't as beautiful and there wasn't as much passion. But there was something else, something you don't teach. Something you *can't* teach, ah? We kept house together for forty years. And *they* are the great lovers?"

"They're tragic," I said. "It makes a better play."

"If they had lived, they wouldn't have stayed together, you know. Five years, ten at most. Separate bedrooms. Separate houses. They make a better play this way? Dead? Fine, but the world is *not* a stage, my dear, no matter what anyone says. You are teaching lies."

Her voice was harsh, and my head felt like I'd packed it with cotton. I was tired of being hectored by visions. I looked out the window, hoping to see Jules drive up, hoping a real human presence would end this conversation.

"Why do want him home?" Rosaline demanded. "You want rid of him, don't you? All your daydreams about leaving, or having him leave. You want the hot and quick again. You want to be able to love whoever you love, and no guilt about Jules."

"Say I do. Okay? Just say I do. Would that be so fucking wrong? Would wanting that feeling again make me such a god-awful person?"

"No. Only young. But, if it's so important to you, fine," she said with a sigh. "He's dead."

"What?"

"Jules," she said. "He's dead. He was going to a meeting. A linux users group, whatever that is. A man in a truck was arguing with his little girl and didn't see the stop sign. Jules died in an instant. The police will call you as soon as they get him to the hospital. An hour maybe. You're free."

I didn't know what to say. I blinked. And I knew, I knew in my bones, it was true.

"Congratulations," she said, disgust in her voice thick as a river of mud. And then she was gone, and I was alone with a kitchen and two coffee mugs. I started by washing the dishes. I didn't intend to, my hands just started doing it, and I let them. The house seemed unreal, attenuated.

Jules was dead.

I'd have to cancel our dinner reservations next week. The thought crossed my mind like a victim of a car wreck noticing that her purse is out on the pavement, that it has blood on it. So this was shock. How odd.

When I was able to feel anything again, it started in the back of my throat, then spread down to my chest and stomach. It didn't feel like sorrow or loss. It felt like nausea. I even went to the bathroom and knelt in front of the toilet, cool porcelain against my palms.

Jules, with his thinning hair and his little pot belly and his way of merrily switching from opinion to opinion without bothering to think in between, was dead. The dangerous, thrilling thoughts of Gary seemed like a dream I'd had as a child. I could barely remember them now.

The pressure in my throat filled until I was sure I was going to retch, but what came out was a high keening wail. I watched my weeping from a distance, like it was happening to someone else, like it was a storm.

Oh, I thought, this is going to be bad.

Then the sorrow reached up from my body and sucked my mind in. I didn't hear the car drive up, or the front door open. The first thing I knew was Jules, standing in the doorway of the bathroom. His eyes were wide, his mouth in a comical "o" of alarm. I pressed a teary, snotty palm to my mouth, dragged my hair out of my face.

"What happened?" he asked.

"You're alive," I said. It was the only thought I could manage.

"Ah," he said. Then, his brow furrowing. "Is that a problem?"

My laughter was no more rational or comforting than my tears. Oh, but it felt better.

❋

SHE SITS in the back during the funeral, only coming up at the end to view the bodies, to pay her last respects. Both families are weeping before the caskets. The boy's face has been tinted a little green by the poison. She tries to remember what those pale lips felt like on her neck, what the sound of his voice had been, soft whispers in a dark corner of the gardens that had turned her blood to wine. Could that really have been her with his scent on her skin?

The girl is paler. Her dress is black and formal, a tiara of silver shines from lustrous hair, and thin, string gloves web the backs of her hands. Death makes her look somehow triumphant. No mere poison for her. Who would have thought she had it in her? How did a little girl without the bravery to openly refuse her father muster courage to drive a blade into her own heart? What kind of love gives that strength and that self-hatred?

She wishes she could touch the cool flesh. Perhaps there might be some last communication, a recognition between two girls who have loved the same boy. Instead, she walks back down, past the clouds of expensive incense, past the two enemies weeping together, now that it is too late. The burial will take place on hallowed ground. There is too much gold in the purses of the front rows for these suicides to be thought of as sin. These children cannot be responsible. It is evil luck, mischance, an accident of the stars. Worse, it is something romantic, something noble.

Leonardo sits on the pew, waiting for her. His face is all concern. She sits beside him, her hand in its black lace glove seeking out his fingers. He holds her hand as if it is fragile. As if she is fragile. Sweet boy. She is the survivor.

The priest, himself all tears and woe, calls the congregation to kneel and pray for the souls of these poor dead children. She slips to her knees, but will not let go of Leonardo's hand. He tries once to pull away, to place palms together in prayer, but she will not let him and he stops trying. The low sound of weeping, like a summer brook, babbles distantly in the vaulted space of the cathedral.

Thank you, she thinks, projecting the thought out to God. Good Christ, thank you for my escape. And find it in your heart, Lord, to condemn the souls of the families who would ennoble these deaths and the poets who would tell this story as if it were about love.

"Are you well, sweet?" Leonardo whispers in her ear.

She considers, leans over.

"I am breathing," she says, resolutely, "and I am holding your hand."

✳

I WOULD have thought that the vision and her ugly trick would have stopped it. But two weeks later, I was still thinking about Gary, still recalling the half-sad smile in the parking lot. I caught myself talking to Eric more, as if being closer to him was a safe way to be closer to his father.

No, Rosaline's lies hadn't cured me, but they had changed the game. It was Sunday night, and Jules and I were at the house. I sat at the kitchen table, preparing exam questions on Huckleberry Finn and eating vanilla ice cream with Oreos. He was in the living room, sitting on the couch and working with a new computer. I could hear the staccato clicking of his fingers and the occasional fast tapping of his foot against the coffee table when he paused to think.

Oh well, I thought, putting down my pencil. Might as well get it over with.

He looked up when I walked in the room, his face interested but still distracted. I took in a deep breath.

"Okay," I said, walking across to him. "So what happens if I fall in love with someone else?"

Jules blinked, ran a hand over his broad scalp, and seemed to deflate. I bit my lip. His eyebrows lifted and he sighed, turning off the monitor. I leaned against the mantle, half-aware that I was mimicking Rosaline's posture.

"Ah," Jules said. "Is that what this has been about?"

"Sort of," I said. "No. Not really. I mean, I'm not seeing someone on the side. Nothing's happened. It's just…"

Jules crossed his arms, but it didn't make him seem angry. Only sad.

"You're bored with me?" he asked. "I mean, if you're bored with me…"

"No," I said, waving the comment away. "No, you're fine."

"Is it about having kids?"

"No. Jesus, no. It's not about you. I just that I keep thinking that we're it. That you and I are the end of it. A few more decades of hanging out, watching TV and trading gossip and then death. I'm never going to have that mad fling down in Mexico with the dance instructor. I'm not going to stay up until four in the morning telling my life story to someone who's never heard it. I keep thinking I've had my last first kiss. And it's oppressive."

Jules looked at the ceiling. His expression was thoughtful now, careful, considering. I had thought he would cry, accuse, get pissed. That would probably have been my reaction, if he'd been the one asking the question. To him, it was another problem to consider, only different by the one small tear at the corner of his eye—hardly there before he wiped it away—and the tiny tremor of his hand. He was so beautiful in that moment, my middle-aged, balding, heartbroken, computer geek husband, that I could have cried.

"Mid-life crisis?" he asked. "I mean, is that a fair shorthand description?"

I nodded slowly.

"Yes," I said. "That covers it."

"I don't guess getting a Lamborghini would help?" he asked hopefully. I laughed. We were silent for a long moment, the humor giving way to the depth and danger of the conversation we were actually having. I wished that the rest of my life could be in those seconds—quiet and profound and humane despite the pain.

"I admit I kind of thought it was something like that," he said. "So. Okay. What happens if you fall in love with someone else. Right. Well…"

"It's not that I don't love you," I said, "What we have is very important to me. You're very important to me. I'm not looking for a way out, I just…"

I ran out of words and had to make due with a gesture—my hands open to him, asking for help or forgiveness. Or permission.

"Okay," Jules said and visibly steeled himself. "Well, I'm going to have a problem if you fuck him."

I coughed out a laugh.

"I can't believe you just said that."

"Well, I would," he said, defensively. "And it extends to all kinds of sex. I think I'd react poorly to you necking with him too. But I understand where you're coming from. This happens all the time. I mean, I think every couple has to deal with this."

He shrugged and opened his arms, palms up.

"People seem to get through it, though. So I guess we can too. Can't we?"

"So it would be okay with you?" I asked.

"Oh no," he said, smiling and leaning forward. "No, sweetie. The idea scares the hell out of me. Makes me feel like I'm waiting for biopsy results. But what can I do? Tell you what you're allowed to feel? Like that would work."

"Would it help if I showered you with affection and promised you were the most important man in the world to me?"

"Wouldn't hurt," he said. "That and really, really, really, don't fuck him."

"Okay," I said. "I can work with that."

He held out a hand to me and I took it, lowering myself into his lap. We sat there, his arms around my waist, mine around his shoulders.

"That's it then?" I said. "What about all the high drama?"

"Advantage of being grown-ups," he whispered. "Fewer hysterics. Feel better?"

I nodded.

"Good," he said.

"You?"

"Nope, still terrified," he said. I kissed the top of his head. His scalp was so warm. I lay my cheek against him and rested my head on his.

"I love you," I said.

"I love you too," he said. "One other thing?"

"Yeah?"

"Don't die first."

✳

IT IS summer, warm and fragrant. The apples on the tree are bright green and she knows that despite their beauty, they would still be sour and chalky. She kneels in her herb patch. She has kept this patch of ground—this house and its gardens—for forty years. Time has thickened her just as it has made Leonardo thin. Her eyes are still good, though. Nothing broke Leonardo's heart like the clouding of his sight. He has not drawn a picture in two years.

Broad-leafed basil and lemon mint grow together in the small, stone-lined plot. Her fingers pluck out weeds, reaching just below the soil to pinch their roots as she pulls. The earth feels good to her, and today her knuckles do not ache. She plans to walk down to the village later and trade a few eggs from her chickens for a bottle of wine and bread for dinner.

Her hair is tied back, graying now at the temples. The style looks severe. She tells herself she is an old woman and past vanity, but then she laughs. Age suits her, rather. It is as if she has finally grown into the woman she was at birth.

When the weeds are all on the pathway, their pale roots looking naked in the afternoon sun, she stands and brushes the dirt from her hands and knees. She gathers the dying plants, plucked untimely from their beds, and throws them in the rubbish heap. They remind her vaguely of something, but she doesn't pursue the thought. Centuries will come and go, she thinks. But there will always be weeds.

The house is on the south side of a low hill. Wind chimes play soft mindless tunes. Far off, she hears the church bell toll the hour.

"Leon?" she calls as she steps into the cool of the front room. "Are you here?"

She sees him sitting at his favorite window. The old tortoise shell cat is in his lap. She smiles and turns to go, letting him sleep, then frowns, looks back. His face has become more interesting with age, but the flesh hangs slack now. She can see the nubs of his lower teeth. His eyes, his poor, milky eyes, are closed.

"Leon?" she asks again, her voice trembling. The cat jumps down.

She hangs her head, takes his cool hand in her own. The fingers are stiff. She nods to herself, and two thick tears drop from her eyes, then two more. She leans over and kisses his white hair.

"Good-bye, Leon," she says, her voice breaking. "You are a very good man. And I will always love you very much."

She pats his hand, wishing he could feel it. Perhaps she should have kissed him before she went out to the garden. She wishes she had. It is a silly thought.

"I will miss you, husband," she says.

She sits with the body for a time. The sun shifts, sliding across a fraction of the sky. The cat returns, rubs against her ankles to be pet. She sighs, stands, and dries her tear-streaked face with a dish towel. Then she sets out. The village is a fair walk for an old woman. She will need the fetch the priest.

✳

THE RECEPTION after the awards ceremony was well attended. The students spilled out onto the newly-cut grass, bathing in the warm glow of sunset, while teachers and parents stayed mostly indoors or ventured out as far as the concrete steps. Jules was inside, in a deep discussion with one of the math teachers. I sat outside on a chair I'd pulled out from the office, shelling scarlet-dyed pistachios. I cracked one open and popped the nut into my mouth. A small pile of concave red shells nestled in a handkerchief on my lap. Gary leaned against the wall, his hands in his pockets.

We watched his son in a crowd of friends and fellow-graduates, pretending that it wasn't a big deal, that the paper in his hand didn't mean anything, beaming despite himself.

"You did a good job," I said. "I didn't think he'd pull it out."

"He needed some discipline," Gary said. "He's the last of them. Three kids, and every one of them's going to college."

"You must be proud."

"Yeah. Well, they had good teachers."

We were silent. He looked inside, stepped away, and came back with a metal wastebasket. As he set it beside me, he pointed at my snack.

"Mind if I...?"

I handed him a few pistachios. Our fingers touched, maybe more than they needed to. He cracked open a nut. I was better at it; he had to look at the shells. I considered his mouth. I will never kiss him, I thought. The idea didn't offend me, but it didn't sit perfectly still either. I tried again. I will not kiss him today. That felt solid.

I turned, looking along the side of the building. There, in an alcove where they thought they were hidden from view, Eric had his arms around Melissa Garcia.

"Looks like he's made a friend," Gary said, following my gaze.

"Looks like," I said.

"Bad time to get involved with someone, right before you head off to college," Gary said, something in his voice not quite disapproval.

"True," I said.

"It'll only end in tears."

I dropped a loud handful of shells into the wastebasket and rubbed my red-stained fingertips on my handkerchief.

"They all do, eventually," I said, softly.

Gary looked over at me, caught perhaps by the tone of my voice. I cracked a half-smile and shook my head. Below us in the fading light, the boy leaned over and kissed the girl as gracefully as he could when they were both still new at it and awkward.

THE CURANDERO AND THE SWEDE:
A Tale from the 1001 American Nights

THE NIGHT I TOOK Abby to meet my Atlanta family, we spent about three hours beforehand going over the rules. The dress sleeves had to cover her tattoo at all times. She couldn't say anything snarky about the casserole, even if it totally deserved it. Her analysis of Bill Clinton as reincarnation of Elvis was funny among our mutual friends, but wouldn't go over well with Oma Hauptmann. It would to be hard enough for the family to accept that I'd proposed to a Yankee girl without rubbing their noses in it. Abby's smile got more and more fixed, and her eyes started to get the glazed look of a deer facing a semi. When we pulled up at Aunt Mary's, I'd started to think the whole thing might have been a mistake.

Abby squeezed my hand hard as we walked up the drive.

"This is going to be all right," she said, as if she was telling me. And all through the meal, the announcement, and dessert, it was. Then the time came in the dance that was unspoken family tradition for the women to kick the men out onto the porch.

The late August heat had convinced Aunt Mary to pull out the wading pool and fill it with the garden hose. All the kid cousins between five years old and fifteen were shrieking and splashing and hopping in and out of the water in the darkening twilight. Inside, Mama and Aunt Mary led the rest of the family in singing hymns while Oma Hauptmann cleaned away the remains of the wrapping paper and snuck the last few squares of sheet cake. Between these two celebrations, one pagan and the other pious, was the back porch and Uncle Dab.

"So, boy. Engaged, are you?" he said with a wide grin. "Big news."

I craned my neck. The harmonies of Christian praise floated in the dim air like pollen. I could just make out Abby's voice, still finding its place within the music. The back window showed a small slice of the living room, but her lemon-creme meeting-the-family dress wasn't there. I hoped the tattoo hadn't slipped. Abby had a way of unconsciously pushing up her sleeves.

"Yeah," I said. "I s'pose it is."

Uncle Dab lit one of his little black cigars then leaned back, white hair haloed by smoke.

"I ever tell you about how I met Mary?" Uncle Dab asked.

"The grain boat that caught fire, and her father's truck," I said, nodding. It was one of Dab's favorite stories, but he'd told it more times than I could count. It was always full of comedy and romance and smart-mouthed remarks made at just the right time. I knew from my mother that it skipped over the fact that Mary had been pregnant by someone besides Dab at the time and had lost the baby.

He took being cut off with good grace, nodding and smiling as if he'd gone through the whole adventure. One of the older cousins—Paula or Stephanie—laughed, the sound carrying over the piano. I wondered what questions Aunt Mary would ask Abby once the music stopped, and how Abby would answer. Dab drew on the cigar, the ember flaring, then considered me.

"So why don't you tell me about how you met the love of *your* life?" he said.

"There's not really much to tell," I said. "When I got back from Macon, I took a job at Paul Keneson's place. Abby worked there too, and one thing just led to another."

I shrugged. One of the older kid cousins shrieked, clutching her recent breasts with one arm and splashing a younger boy with the other. The droplets caught the gold of the sunset. Dab, settled in his chair, smacked his lips once, and nodded. I had the sense that I'd disapointed him.

"You know, there was this fella I knew back when I was working at the machine shop," Dab said. "We called him the Swede. Little fella, maybe five foot five. Five foot six on a good day. Blackest man I have ever known. You know how most folks we call 'em black, they're anything from dark brown to one of what Gram used to call *high yaller*? Well, not the Swede. He was black like a dog's nose. So black, he was damn near blue.

"He used to tell it that his people escaped as soon as the slave ships dropped anchor, headed up north until it got so cold they just froze in place. Could trace his family back seven generations without a single white person. He was the first one in his family to leave Minnesota. Nice fella. Good machinist, too. Anyway.

"He'd been down here about six years when I knew him. Had a girl he was seeing name of Corine. She was pretty. Had this line of dark little moles, just like pinpricks, all along her jaw. Made me think of the sort of bangles they put on women's veils out in Baghdad. She'd come by the shop sometimes, and we'd have to make him stop working until she went away for fear he'd get distracted and lose a finger.

"He'd been seeing her for maybe six months when Martin Luther King got killed. That was before you were born, so I don't expect you'd understand it. And, honest to God, I'd never say this outside the family, but the Blacks have got a whole different country they live in. Even someone like the Swede who worked with us and drank beer with us and all? Now I was sorry to hear about it when King died, and I'm not ashamed to say it. But it wasn't that much to me. For the Blacks, though..."

Dab shook his head.

"It was different for them. What with everything else that was going on back then, King's getting shot was like Kennedy in Dallas and the planes in New York all wrapped up in one. The Swede was living in one of them shotgun houses over by the bend in the river. Little place with five rooms all back to back in a line, and it always smelled like old cabbage. I never did know why. When it happened, he was in the front room drinking a beer and listening to the radio news. Corine was in the back, sleeping a little. He heard about it and just finished off his beer, went back, and told her. She didn't believe him at first, and then she did.

"Thing was, the Swede didn't talk much about it. He just nodded and sucked his teeth and had another beer. It was like he'd heard about a team losing a baseball game. He came into work next shift, you wouldn't have known a goddam thing had happened. I figured that he was just taking it like me. Sad to hear it, but you know how it is. Life goes on.

"It was Corine who saw different. She was spending nights with him. They weren't married or nothing, but there was an understanding between them. So anyway, she was seeing him in his altogether on a regular basis, and none of us sure as hell were, so she was the one that found the bumps.

"Now later on, I saw it a little myself, and I've seen my fair share of rashes and bites and whatnot. This was different.

Looked like the Swede had marbles under his skin. Big, angry-looking lumps. And thing was, they *moved*. Each one of them shifted and kicked like a baby. Started right at the top of his plumber's crack like he was gonna grow a tail, and every week or two there'd be a little new one staring up. Climbed up his spine, one at a time, and out around his sides and down his legs. He said they didn't hurt or itch or nothing. They were just there.

"Corine didn't think much of that, I can tell you. She'd had a sister who died of cancer when she was young, and she looked at those bumps and knew that wasn't right. She'd hound him and pick at him and yell until the Swede went to see some doctor.

"Thing was, this was the end of the sixties, start of the seventies. We were all making pretty good money, but it wasn't great, and he was a Black. Maybe that doesn't mean now what it used to, but they didn't have a lot of trust for what you'd call the medical establishment. They hadn't found out about what those doctors were doing down in Tuskegee, but they were't dumb. The Blacks knew that white doctors didn't care all that much about a Black fella's bumps. So the Swede went to a few, and they told him to rub grease on it before bed or to stop drinking liquor or whatever other easy advice they found to hand. Nothing ever came of it. The bumps just kept spreading out. As far as the Swede was concerned, it was just part of who he was.

"It didn't all come to a crisis, as you'd say, until just after Thanksgiving...well, we'd just got Nixon out of the White House, so that'd make it seventy-four. Corine and the Swede were at his place one night, and they were curled up together in bed. It was cold that year, so they were laying right on top of one another, and the way it was, Corine had her ear right up against one of the Swede's bumps and it called her a cunt. Soft little voice, but full of hate, and she always swore it spoke as clear as you or me.

"You can imagine that was the end of that. Corine got her things in a suitcase and went to live with her sister. Nothing the Swede said drew any water with her. He had to do something, but he'd been to all the doctors any of us knew about. Poor ess-oh-bee didn't know where to turn.

"Now it happened the Swede knew a guy right around then who'd been a trucker down in New Mexico the year before. Steve Williams, his name was. He wasn't a bad fella, but he'd had some trouble with getting drunk and stoned and fighting and such. Spent a few months in prison and it made it hard to find steady work. So Williams was pretty happy to get a job hauling fruit from Albuquerque up to the Four Corners area.

"Now you've heard about route 66, but what you might not know is there used to be a route 666 coming off it in Gallup and heading up all the way to Colorado. Long, thin road with a whole lot of dead people. The Devil's Highway they called it, and a lot of people wouldn't drive the route because of it having a bad reputation. Williams wasn't what you'd call a religious fella. He figured 666 to be the number before 667, and Devil be damned. And maybe there was something to that, because what happened to him didn't have much to do with the Devil or Jesus either one.

"He'd been going up from Albuquerque on a night run. Now that wasn't something he usually did. The highway there was two lane, and no barrier in between, so a trucker got sleepy or drunk, there was nothing to keep him from slipping over into oncoming traffic. And more than that, it was a damn lonesome piece of road. Between Gallup and Farmington there was about a hundred miles of reservation. No lights, not many gas stations, and what there was didn't stay open late. This was right before the CB radios got popular, so there wasn't even people to talk to. But the cargo had come in to Albuquerque late, and it had to be delivered by morning, so Williams gassed up and headed out.

"It was the first part of summer, and a black night, no moon to speak of. Williams was tired, and truth to tell, he was feeling a little sorry for himself. His lady friend had taken off a couple weeks before, and he didn't have much prospect of getting her back. There's nothing like an empty road and cold and darkness to make a man feel the loss of a woman. Well, he was about an hour out of Gallup, and he saw a girl by the side of the road.

"With his headlights the only thing out there, it was like she'd just popped up out of nowhere. She was an Indian girl, as you might expect out there on the reservation. Maybe eighteen, maybe nineteen. Well, he figured she was hitching, and if she wasn't, she might still rather not walk all the way to Shiprock. He could use the company, and if it was a girl with a sympathetic ear, well then all the better. He pulled the rig over to the shoulder and stopped.

"Now a rig that size in that part of the country? It kicks up a fair cloud of dust when it stops, so Williams wasn't all that surprised that the girl didn't come running right when he opened the passenger's door. He just waited until the dust thinned out. But even then, no one came up. She wasn't in the mirrors either. Williams hopped out and looked back at where she'd been, but there was no one there, and not even a weed thick enough to hide behind.

"He calls out a few times. Says as he was just heading up to Shiprock, and thought she might want a lift. No one so much as spits at him.

"He climbs back up in his rig, gets ready to head back out, and then all of a sudden, he gets this sick feling. Starts thinking *What if I hit her and just didn't notice? What if she's under the wheels right now?* So he climbs back out and looks around, slow and careful. But she isn't there. Eventually, he gives up and heads back out.

"And that might have been the end of it, but it wasn't. That night, Williams had a dream. A nightmare, and a bad one.

"He was in the desert, and he knew the way you do in a dream, that he was walking away from the place he wanted to get to. Heading east when home was west, like. Every time he tried to turn around, though, someone hit him. Spun him back east. It wasn't a short dream. It was one of those kind that go on all night, so all night Williams was driven across the desert like an animal. Sometimes his friends and family were there with him, getting whipped just like him. Sometimes he was all by himself. And he started feeling a powerful hatred for the fella that was hitting him. Then just a little before dawn, he turned and got hold of the guy. Said afterwards that he could feel the cloth of the man's shirt in his fist just like it was really happening. Thing was, the fella he'd grabbed onto looked just like him. It *was* him.

"Now you might think that would have woken him up, but the dream wasn't done with him yet. He took a knife, and he started slashing this guy, started killing him. He could feel the knife catching against the bones, could hear the fella trying to breathe. Smelled the blood. He knew it was himself he was killing, and he just didn't care.

"Well.

"He woke up in the back of his rig, just like he'd gone to sleep, and the first thing he thought, sober as a Baptist judge, was *Holy shit, that girl's going to kill me.*

"Now Williams wasn't the superstitous type. He got up and went out, ate his eggs and bacon and drank his truck-stop coffee, and tried to laugh it off, same as anyone would. He told himself that whoever she was out on the road, she'd spooked him with that vanishing act was all. He'd had a bad night of it, and be done.

"It was about a week later he saw the girl again. It was broad daylight this time. He was heading back south, going into Gallup this time, and there she was standing by the side of the road. She didn't have a thumb out or nothing. She was just standing there, watching the truck come on. Williams got a cold feeling on his neck, and his heart starting tripping over like someone'd pulled a gun on him. He was a big fella, and he'd been in his fair share of fights, but that Indian girl just standing there on the side of the road looking up at him... Well, she scared the piss out of him. He gunned the engine and sped straight past her, fast as he could. Thing was, five miles on, there she was again. He passed that girl four times before he got to Gallup. He sat in a booth at the truck stop for three straight hours, not wanting to get back on the road. He was afraid to be alone, you see. If he hadn't been more scared of being caught on the road after dark, I expect he'd never have left.

"Well, he got back to Albuquerque and went to his boss and said straight up that he was never doing that run again. If it meant quitting, then he'd quit. The boss didn't like that much, but Williams was a pretty good driver otherwise. They worked out a different run for him, heading south to Las Cruces. Williams thought that was the end of it, but he was wrong again.

"The dream kept coming back, you see. First every week or so, and then more and more often, until by the end of September, he wasn't getting any rest when he slept. He'd wake up in the morning half sick with dread and half still feeling the joy from killing the other version of himself from the dream.

"It was September fourth of '70 that he ran his rig off the road. He had his heater on in the cabin, and the radio was playing something soft. Country music or some Fleetwood Mac or some such. And then just like that, he woke up going eighty on the shoulder and heading for a ditch. He wrestled the truck down slow enough that when he hit, it didn't kill him. But it messed up the rig, and he had to wait half a day to get someone out there to tow him.

"He was sure of it now. That Indian girl, whatever she was, didn't care whether he was driving old 666 or not. She'd seen him, she'd heard his voice, and sure as kittens in the springtime, she was going to see him dead.

"Now back in those days, there was a fella used to hang out at a diner in Abiquiu. An anglo, which was strange enough in that part of New Mexico. What's more he was a queer too. The locals put up with him, though. I won't say they were afraid of him, but they had respect. Said that when a man was different one way, sometimes he was different other ways too.

"The way it was, someone needed advice about spirits or how to get someone to fall in love with them or whatever, they'd go to this little greasy spoon out in Abiquiu, sit at the back table, and the queer would tell them things. Sometimes it was things they wanted to know, sometimes it wasn't. Sixth of October—same day the Israeli airforce starting bombing the shit of Egypt—old Steve Williams got his rig back from the shop and drove in to Abiquiu.

"By then, Williams didn't look like the big, tough ess-oh-bee he used to be. He hadn't slept for shit in weeks, and he was scared all the time. His skin had that grey look meat gets right when it starts to turn, and he had the standing shakes. The place was a pit. Smelled like they were still cooking in last month's grease, and the linoluem tile was all chipped and bleached out from the sun. And there at the end of the aisle back by the men's room, was this fella in a white silk shirt and a great big blond pompadour haircut drinking a cup of coffee.

"Williams walks up and the queer smiles at him and nods to the bench across the booth, just like they were old friends and he'd been waiting on him. Afterwards, Williams said that sound changed when you sat down with the queer. The radio from the kitchen, the bells on the diner's door, the tire noise off the highway. Everything got soft, like they were farther away than they really were. The windows looked out on the parking lot, but they were so greasy, everything out there was in soft focus, like when they'd shoot through gauze in the old movies. The only thing that seemed real was the queer and his cup of black coffee.

"*You've seen her* is what the queer says, first thing out. Williams hadn't even told him anything, and so the queer comes out with this, and Williams just nods.

"*That's going to be hard for you*, the queer says. *She's angry.*

"So Williams says *Thing is, I don't know what she's angry at me for.*

"The queer smiles just like a woman and puts his hand out, touches Williams on the wrist and says *Of course you don't, sweetie. You never even heard of the Long Walk.*

"And so the queer tells Williams about it. Way back in the middle 1800s, there'd been a couple decades worth of playing cowboys and Indians for real. Lots of dead people on both sides, and lots of anger. Well, come 1863, Kit Carson got sent out to accept the surrender of the Navajo, only when he got to the place he was supposed to be, no Navajo showed up to surrender. Carson took it personal. Next few years, he started burning Indian crops, starving them out, and eventually, they did start giving up. That's where the Long Walks came in.

"Back then, the Navajo were all through northern Arizona and New Mexico, on up into the south part of Colorado. Well, the government's bright idea was to get them the hell off that land. Break their connection to it. Turn 'em into exiles. So they started herding them off to Fort Sumner and the Bosque Redondo. Three hundred miles on foot. Hundreds of them died along the way, and when they got where they were going, it was like a little slice of hell. Nine thousand people squeezed into forty square miles. Not enough food. Not enough water. Maybe the men at Fort Sumner didn't like the Indians. Maybe they just didn't care one way or the other. Either way, the starving never stopped.

"Now the story was that in the middle of this internment camp, there was a group of people—women mostly, but some men too—who were trying to do something about it. There's this journal from one of the soldiers at Fort Sumner that talks about a girl named Sahkyo leading some kind of pagan ceremony in the summer of 1867. The details were scarce, but you can tell from the tone of it that the fella was disturbed by it. Said there were sounds coming out of the woods after that. Voices, but not the kind you'd hear from people. And lights at night where there wasn't anyone to make a light.

"Well, the general at Fort Sumner cracked down. Fifty Navajo got killed over it, including the girl Sahkyo, but things only got worse. There were rumors about Indians whose shadows moved even when they were standing still. Soldiers started dying in strange ways. One fella hung himself from the rafters in a stable, only there wasn't a ladder to get up there. The official story was he'd climbed up the side of the wall, but them soldiers who went and kept the Indians in line said the story in camp was he'd been hung by the spirit of Sahkyo.

"One way or another, it was about a year after they did whatever it was they did that night that the Lt. General W. T. Sherman signed the treaty of Bosque Redondo and sent them back. That started another Long Walk, but this time, they were going home. People said they saw Sahkyo walking with them.

"*There's power in a return from exile,* is what the queer says. *It makes a spirit stronger, but it does not bring peace.*

"And Williams says *What's it got to do with me? I didn't put anyone off any land.*

"So the queer sighs and nods and looks out the window. He's looking real sad. And he says *Violence and death have narrowed her. Only revenge has meaning for her now.*

"Now Williams was just about shitting himself right there. The queer's telling him there's a hundred-year-old ghost has it out for him? Well, he knew that, but all this talk about vengeance and that soldier hung up from rafters and no way to get up there was bad enough. But more than that, he understood the dream now. He was dreaming this Sahkyo's world, what she went through. And he'd felt just how happy she was going to be watching him die.

"So he asks the queer *What the sweet fuck am I supposed to do about this?*

"And the queer says *Give her mercy meaning as well.* And then he picks up a copy of that morning's newspaper and hands it to Williams. Says *You'll need this.*

"So Williams walks back out of the diner and into the parking lot, gets in his rig and heads off. He didn't have the first idea what he was going to do, except he was pretty clear that running wasn't going to help and whatever this girl Sahkyo had turned into, she was way stronger than he was. For about eighty miles, he didn't even think about that newspaper or why the queer thought he'd need it.

"Well, there wasn't any question that he was going to have to face her down, and most likely on her own territory. Williams, he put up at a hotel outside Española for about a week, thinking and stewing and not sleeping if he could help it. The dreams kept after him like hounds on a possum. Time came, he decided he couldn't let it go another night or he'd be too tired to drive at all. He tanked up on coffee and diesel, and headed back out to Gallup and the Devil's Highway.

"At first, he thought she wouldn't show up. Thought he'd just be driving up and down the highway until he dozed off and she killed him. He just gritted his teeth and kept going. It was tough work. His eyes felt like there was grit up under them, and the engine noise started sounding like it was trying to say something, distract him. She didn't show up until almost midnight.

"Then, bam, there she was, standing like before right at the side of the road. He uses the engine brake, and the rig starts jumping and screaming like it's about to come apart, he's trying so hard to slow down and pull 'er to the shoulder. But he does it, and he jumps out, and she's gone. Just like the first time.

"Thing is, this time, he knows her name. So he walks back into the dust and he yells out *Sahkyo* and the third time he says it, there she is.

"So he's seeing her up close now, and there's no way he can pretend she's alive. Her skin's all pale and thin as paper. Her eyes are moving, but they're black all through. There's things moving in her hair. She's standing there by the side of the road all red from the back lights, looking at him, waiting, and he knows if he wants to see morning, he'd better talk pretty damn fast.

"*Look, Sahkyo* he says *I heard all about what happened to you and your people and all, and I'm real sorry about it. But I didn't do it.*

"The girl just looks at him, doesn't say a damn thing. He can feel the hate coming off her like hot off a fire. So he holds out the newspaper the queer gave him. Right there on page one above the fold, it's all about the Israeli airforce pounding the shit out of Egypt. The girl doesn't look at it, but Williams holds it out to her all the same.

"*You're pissed off I'm on your land, right?* he says. *Here's the thing. I ain't got no from to go back to. Maybe my grandpa or his grandpa came here from off in Europe someplace, but I'm from America. I'm from here, see?*

"She takes a step toward him, and all he wants in the world is to run like hell away from there. But he holds his ground and says *Maybe you kill me, okay. But what good's that do? You're gonna make all this around here just as messed up as they are over in the Middle East. That what you want for your people? Have 'em still fighting a thousand years from now?*"

Now she looks down. I don't figure she can read English, but she looks at the paper all the same. Williams starts to get this feeling that maybe he's getting to her, so he keeps going. *Your people got fights enough right now,* he says. *You don't let go of the old ones, we're gonna be doing this forever."*

"Now maybe he scored a point with her by showing how the Jews were still fighting thousands of years after they got back from their exile, or maybe she was just tired, or maybe a ghost loses its power when you face it down and the newspaper and the Jews and all that were just something the queer gave Williams to give him courage. Either way, Sahkyo turned away from him and walked out into the night. Williams never did see her again, and he never had the dream again neither.

"Now it's true when he took his shirt off that night, he found a handprint on his chest right over his heart. It was black as ink, about the size of the girl's hand, and it never did come off. But that was the worst he got out of it, thanks to the queer.

"So when his bumps chased Corine off, the Swede started thinking maybe he could find someone like that to help him out too."

The back door swung open, old wood barking against the side of the house. Uncle Dab looked back over his shoulder as my little sister Joanie led the women of the family out into the thick night air. Abby's lemon-creme dress seemed to glow in the darkness as Aunt Mary walked with her. I sat forward, trying to interpret Abby's expression in the dim light. The kid cousins, water-soaked and grass-stained, swarmed toward the women and were shooed away into the house. A dozen bare feet pounded across the boards of the back porch.

"Satellites," I said with a sigh. "She pulls us out two or three times a week to look for one."

At the edge of the lawn, Joanie was pointing up at the star-filled sky. Abby and Aunt Mary and the others were following her gaze. Eight grown women peering up into darkness. Abby raised her hand as if to shade her eyes, and the engagement ring glittered on her finger. Auny Mary leaned over and said something to her in particular, and Abby shook her head. Her sleeve was riding up, and the smallest arc of ink showed at the edge of the cloth. I bit my lip. Dab sucked on his cigar and chuckled.

"You ought to tell your sister how smart she is, doing something like that," Dab said.

"It's not hard," I said. "There are websites you go to, just give them your latitude and longitude, and they give you times."

"You ought to tell her anyway," Dab said. "More times you tell something, the more it gets true. Ah! There. Look at that, will you?"

In the high, dark arch above us, a star caught fire. It moved slowly across the sky, slower than a meteor and never consumed by its own flame. The women of the family murmured admiration, and Joanie grinned as brightly as the star. Abby looked over at us, followed my gaze, and tugged her dress back into place. She mouthed *Thank you* and I touched my finger to my eye in our covert sign that meant *I love you.*

"Beautiful," Uncle Dab said, still looking at the sky. "That's just *beautiful.* Now then, where was I? Oh yeah. The Swede.

"Well now, the Swede started off looking for someone who could give him a hand. Thing is, folks like the queer aren't common. Oh, there's people who say they've got the hoodoo or the Holy Spirit or what have you, but most of those are liars and thieves who're just too small-time to start a bank. I'd like to say it didn't take him too long, but the fact was the Swede took the better part of a year going one place and another.

"He got his energy balanced and his aura looked at and one thing and another. There was one time he had this guru fella who had him eating nothing but onion soup for the better part of a month. Poor old Swede had the shits so bad, he couldn't get through half a shift without the foreman giving him hell for being in the john all the time. He even took a week off and drove to New Mexico to look for the queer. Found the diner all right, but by then something must have happened, because there wasn't anyone sitting at the back table. No one out there would talk about it, so he had to just come on back. Must have taken him five or six months before he found someone that could actually help out.

"There was this Mexican fella had a reputation for performing miracles, but so did a lot of people the Swede had already been to. This one called himself a curandero and worked out of a little shop, down where all the Mexicans live. Going down there was just like stepping into Juarez. All the signs were in Spanish, all the flags were Mexican, and you didn't find many cops around.

"Well, the Swede was just about covered in bumps by this point. All over his back and his legs and his belly. Crawling up his neck now too, and there were nights he said he could hear them talking, just like Corine had. So even though the Swede wasn't one to think much of Mexicans as a rule, he took his balls in hand and went down.

"The place was really little, and it had a Mexican butcher on one side of it and bail bonds office on the other. Swede said the place smelled like hot chocolate and blood. And dark? It was so dark in there he couldn't tell what might be in the shadows.

"The curandero was a big fella. Fat, and I mean huge. Maybe three and a half, four hundred pounds. Tell you something about people that fat? They're strong. They got to be.

"So anyway, the Swede walks in and there's this fucking mountain of a Mexican in a Hawaiian shirt the size of a tent, talking Spanish into the telephone too fast to follow. The Swede waits a minute, but the curandero just starts waving his hand at the Swede like he's saying *Look around, look around. I'll be right with you.*

"The Swede's eyes are getting used to the dark by now. Things start coming into focus. And the crap that's in there just about makes him walk back out. There's a stuffed cat with all the fur gone laying there, covered in dust. There's something that looks like a snake, but it's made out of silver, scales and all, and it's moving so he can't tell if it's a clockwork or something alive. The thing that catches his attention the most, though, is this mason jar. Looks like it's full of whiskey, but there's something white floating in it. Looks like a little girl doll made out of smoke. The Swede picks it up, and turns it, and he sees how the little doll doesn't have a back to it. Hollow as an Easter rabbit.

"The curandero gets done with whoever he was talking to, hangs up the phone, and says *What can I do for you, sir?*

"Well, half of the Swede's brain is saying put down the bottle and get the hell out and I mean now. But the other half is thinking that maybe this one's the real deal. Between the two ideas, the Swede sort of freezes up, doesn't say anything.

"The big fella comes toward him. He's got to outweigh the Swede by something like three to one, and he's a head taller to boot. He sees what it is the Swede's holding, and he nods like he's agreeing with something the Swede hasn't even said yet.

"*I remember her* is what the big fella says. *Must have been ten years ago now. You here about her?*

"The fella's voice is low and deep, like a pitbull that's just starting to growl in the back of its throat. The Swede shakes his head and puts down the mason jar. The little smoke doll inside starts swishing back and forth a little like maybe she's dead and drowned. The curandero puts his hand over it. One hand, and it covers the whole jar lke a gumdrop. *That's too bad*, he says. *I wanted to know how it came out.*

"Well, by this time the Swede's lucky he can say anything, and he sure as hell can't come up with something clever. He just repeats the last few words he's heard. *How it came out?* Like it was a question.

"The big fella puts the jar back on the shelf where it was before and leans against this old wood table, and he sighs, and he starts telling the Swede about this girl.

"This was back when the curandero was out west. California, not too far from San Jose. It was winter then, and even a little snow on the ground. Got dark early. So when this girl came into the shop right before he was fixing to close up, it was already dark as night outside. Thing was, the girl was an anglo. Now he wasn't stupid. He knew a white girl all by herself coming to see a Mexican witch doctor…well, it wasn't a sign that things were going too well for her.

"Girl was maybe fifteen. Reddish hair and green eyes, and thin, but not skinny. Had that look kids get when they've just about done growing up, but haven't but just started growing out, if you see what I mean. Well, this would have been the early December of '62 or '63, so he pretty much knew on sight what was going on. He waved her in, gave her a chair and a cup of coffee, and waited until she worked up the guts to tell him how she was pregnant and she needed to get it taken care of before her daddy found out. Took her about twenty minutes.

"Well, it was what you might expect. Girl had fallen for some fella. Said he loved her and she believed him. Hell, it might even have been true. At the time, at least. Then things went too far, and now she was ruined. If her folks found out, they'd kill her. It was the old, old story, and we all heard it a hell of a lot more back before girls got the pill, let me tell you.

"Anyway, he listened to the girl talk, didn't say anything one way or the other. Oh, he maybe nodded now and then, kept things on track. And when she finished up, she took twenty dollars out of her pocket and gave it to him. Some of it was in quarters. Probably everything she'd saved since she was a baby. Girl never cries. All through this, never sheds a single tear.

"He thinks about it, and he looks at her, and then he goes into his back room and gets this mason jar ready. It's whiskey and a little blood. He brings it out to the girl, puts her hand in it and they say some words together. He tells her about this particular statue of the Virgin Mary. It's a fair way from where they are, at an old church no one used anymore. He draws her a map on a piece of paper and everything.

"*It's easy to find, he tells her, because almost all the statues of the Madonna, she's wearing a blue cloak. This one, her cloak is red.*

"He tells her she needs to sleep with the jar in her bed with her for two nights, then on the third night, she's got to break an egg, pour in just the white, and then bury the jar at the Red Virgin's feet. That night, she's got to sleep in the churchyard, and then dig the bottle back up and bring it to him.

"Well, the girl doesn't talk back or complain or anything. She just picks up the jar and walks out into the night, so he finishes closing up. Keeps the twenty dollars, too. Man's got to make rent.

"Well, three days passed, and the girl didn't come back. The curandero, he kept expecting to see her, even stayed late a couple days, just in case. Then when she didn't show, he figured maybe she got cold feet. Changed her mind. But then Christmas Eve rolled around, and there she was at his door, this jar hugged under her coat. He didn't say anything, just let her come in. When she took the jar out, the egg white was there floating in the whiskey, all cooked up. And it looked then just like it did when the Swede picked it up. A little hollow girl.

"So the girl, the real one, she nods at it and asks *Is that her? Is that my baby?*

"And the curandero shakes his head and sits down and says *No, miss. That's you.*"

In the darkened yard, my sister laughed too loud, the sound forced and abrasive. Abby crossed her arms, her mouth in a half-smile that meant trouble. I shifted forward in my chair.

Dab's cane slapped my thigh. His eyes were narrow and angry.

"I'm starting to think you ain't listening to me, son," he said. "I'm not telling you all this just to hear my own voice."

Then why are you doing it, I wanted to say. But instead I squeaked out, "Sorry. Go on."

"That's better. You see the Red Virgin had power and a history, but when the curandero sent the girl out to Her, he never said that it would kill out the baby, because that would have been a lie. Not that he couldn't have done the thing, mind you. Nor not that he wouldn't. He'd done worse things than that before. Only he wanted to do the girl a favor, even if it was the hard kind.

"Way back when the Spanish were running the missions up the coast and King Ferdinand was kicking all the Jews out of Spain, there'd been this sculptor name of Severo Muñoz lived there. No one local knew quite why old Severo had left Spain and come out to live at the ass end of the world, but there were plenty of guesses. He wasn't a good man. Drinking and whoring and beating folks up…well, that was pretty much the standard. Severo was something past that. He'd killed about a dozen folks that everyone knew about. Raped a few. Did things to the Indians thereabout just because he could.

"Thing was, Severo was damned good at what he did. The Governor of New Spain, down in Mexico City, he'd seen a fallen angel Severo'd carved out of a block of pine bigger than a man and he'd liked it. Well, Severo gave that angel to the Governor, and afterward the law wouldn't touch him.

"The way the story went, God watched over the mission at San Jose, and one day Severo was drunk and happy and full of himself, and he had the bad luck to sin when the Lord was in a playful mood. It was a Sunday, and the priest was up saying Mass and all. Severo's in the front pew, drunk and breaking up the service. He'd start talking to the girls next row over or take down his pants and give his nuts a good scratch or what have you.

"The priest put up with all this as long as he could, but right about the time they're gettig ready to hand out the Eucharist, Severo cuts the cheese so loud, the whole church is ringing with it, then he gets the giggles and starts slapping the pew and howling. Well, that's it. The priest puts down the wine and starts cussing Severo out. Says how it's the house of God, and Severo's defaming the sacrifice that Jesus made on the cross, and he tells old Severo to get gone.

"Severo stands up and gives him the bird. He says *If this is the house of God, then let God cast me out of it.* And everyone gets real quiet. The whole congregation is ready for lightning to come down or the floor to crack out from under him. The priest gets all red in the face, and Severo just holds out his arms like he's shown up God as a pussy that won't take him on.

"Later on, Severo said he heard someone laughing. No one else did. Everyone else said it was dead quiet, but Severo heard someone in the back laughing his head off, didn't know who he was. After, he figured it for Jesus laughing because He knew what was coming next.

"Well, the priest limped through the rest of the mass with Severo spitting and calling him shitty names. People start heading out, and there were a bunch of them waiting just outside the church. Men mostly, and they looked pissed. Now Severo was dumb, but he wasn't stupid if you get what I mean. He figured he'd head out the back way, keep himself from getting jumped. Only out back was where God was waiting for him.

"They knew the dog was Jesus because when all those fellas waiting out front to beat the snot out of him heard him screaming, they went back and killed it. Dog had a cut on its side and a bunch of scabs all around its head, and all four paws were raw and bloody like someone'd driven nails though it. Now that might have just been the rabies, but happening when it did and all, no one doubted it was divine retribution. Not even Severo.

"Rabies, now. That's a bad way to die. Can take a couple of weeks between getting bit and knowing you got it. Starts with a fever and just feeling generally sick. Then a fella gets where he can't drink water. Gets anxious and confused. Delirious. Crazy. Then dead, and honest to God, sooner's better than later for that. Well, Severo started showing symptoms just two days after he got bit, and he knew he was screwed. He had maybe a few days left in the world, and he was going to be suffering every minute of every one of them. And he also knew that hellfire was waiting for him if he didn't get right with God. He didn't put it off or beg for mercy or anything like that. Severo was a bad, low, vulgar man, but he was an artist.

"He got the biggest block of stone he could find on short notice, and all his tools, and he laid in to make a tribute to the Virgin Mary like an apology to the Lord for how he'd lived his life. Worked all through the day and night. People started going to watch, part because no one liked him and part because everyone had this uneasy feeling that something holy was going on. Well, about the fifth day after he got bit, Severo started talking while he worked. Strange voices, like they weren't really him. Singing and gibbering, declaiming on religious doctrine and talking dirty. People said it was the Devil leaving Severo's body. Said they were watching him turn into a saint.

"So by the time he finishes the statue, he's pretty much gone, but She's beautiful. There's this radiant, serene Madonna born out of a dying man's madness. Just at the end, he paints her but instead of blue, he paints her red, and then he collpases at her feet. Last thing he says is *I have seen myself in Her eyes.* That's what they put on his grave. *I have seen myself in Her eyes.*

"Ever since then, strange things happen around the Red Virgin. The curandero, he tells the girl about some of those too. There's the fella right around the turn of the century about to get married and the Red Virgin shook her head at him. Turned out the girl he was sweet on, his daddy'd been messing around with her mother. Red Virgin kept him from getting hitched up with his half-sister. Or this old fella just after World War II who came back with shell shock, didn't know who he was until he spent a night sleeping at the Red Virgin's feet.

"What the curandero tells the girl is *That statue is a mirror. Sometimes we all forget who we are. Or we get blind to it.* And he points to the hollow girl in the mason jar. *This is what you've become.*

"Now the girl looks at it, knowing now what she didn't know before, and she nods. Her face is blank, just empty. The curandero knows she's right on the edge. Maybe she's going to kill the baby like she wanted at the start. Maybe she's going to hold on to it after all. And he just sits there with her. He knows that the girl's screwed either way. She can't win. Best she can do is lose a little less one way than another.

"Well, what she says is *Give me another one.* The curandero doesn't ask for money or what she's going to do. He just goes in the back, gets a second jar, puts in the blood, puts in the whiskey. He brings it out, and they say some words over it. And then the girl goes out with it, and she never comes back.

"*That's why I was hoping you knew what happened,* the curandero says. And the Swede shakes his head. All in all, they've been talking for maybe an hour at this point, and somewhere along the way, the Swede's stopped being quite so scared. He can come up with things to say now.

"So the Swede says *You didn't cure her, though. She came to you for something, you didn't do it.* And the big Mexican gets this soft look on his face.

"*She came to me looking to be healed* is what he says. *I never heal anybody. I only do what I can, and then God heals them or else He doesn't.*

"And that, it turns out, is exactly what the Swede needed to hear. He said it was like he'd been twisting and turning trying to make a piece fit where it was supposed to go, and that what the curandero said was what made it all click into place. After that, he could tell the big fella about Corine and about the bumps and how they'd been spreading and talking and moving. The curandero had him take off his shirt, and he looked at the bumps for a long time, went and got a stethoscope just like he was a real doctor and listened to them talking.

"Then the curandero put down his stuff and just talks to the Swede. Talks about Corine and what she was like, how he felt about her, what it felt like to fuck her, what it felt like to wake up with her, what it felt like when she was gone. They talked about the boys back at the machine shop, and what it was like working with whites. They talked about Minnesota and Africa and the south. The curandero got a coke for the Swede and a big bowl of beans and chile for himself, and they sat around and chewed the fat just like they were old friends.

"Time comes the curandero finishes his beans and he leans back in his chair and he says *You have been injured. What your body's doing is trying to deal with the rage and the anger.*

"And the Swede crosses his arms and he frowns real hard and he says *How do you figure? I didn't break anything or get hurt. I'm not mad at anyone in particular.*

"The curandero shakes his great big head and he says *You are a black man in America. That's injury enough.* Well, the Swede doesn't quite know what to say back to that, but he's gotten to where he likes the big Mexican enough to let it go. The curandero, he keeps talking. He says *I can help you with the rage, but the hurt that caused it in the first place? That's for God.*

"And the Swede points to the bumps on his arms and says *Will it get rid of these?* And the curandero says it will, so the Swede claps his hands and says *Let's get to it.*

"The curandero, he goes and roots around in the back. There's noises that sound like knives getting sharpened and someone singing that wasn't the big fella. Smells like rain and overheated iron. Well, it's only about ten minutes before the big guy comes back to the front dragging this massage table. You know the kind with that head rest you can look down through it? Like that. And he tells the Swede to get naked and lay down on the table with his face on the rest looking down.

"Two hours before, the Swede had been too scared of this man to talk straight, but now it's like they're old friends. Brothers. The Swede shucks off his clothes and lays himself down, and the curandero comes and starts putting little weights on all the bumps all over his back and legs and arms and neck. Curandero's muttering something in Spanish under his breath. So the Swede winds up with these little weights everywhere, he's maybe got ten, fifteen pounds all told, and the curandero stops and sits back.

"*Okay,* the big fella says, *this part is going to hurt some.* And the Swede figures he's going to press on one of the bumps or cut it open or some such. He nods and he gets ready for it, but he's got it wrong. That wasn't the kind of hurt the big guy meant. Instead, just like that, the Swede feels this sorrow rising up in his chest like a flood. He starts crying like a kid whose momma just died, and he can't even say why.

"And the thing is, he never stopped. Last time I saw the Swede was three, maybe four years ago. He's all white hair now, just like me, and he's still crying. Not bawling, but weeping a little all the time, like he's got a slow leak. The bumps went away, and Corine came back. They've got three kids and something like eight grandkids. Love each other no end, got a nice house and good lives, but the Swede can't stop crying. And I'll tell you now, I expect when he dies, his body'll keep right on weeping even once he's done with it."

Uncle Dab paused, looking at the spent stub of his black cigar. He looked out to the edge of the lawn where the women still stood in the darkness, almost invisible now as if the night had drawn them away from us. When Dab spoke again, his voice had lost the energy of his story. He sounded almost touched by dread.

"America's a bordertown. All of it, east to west, north to south. Texas and Kansas and Alaska. It's all bordertown. We got the people who were here before us, we took it from. We got the people coming here after, looking to take it from us. And all of us got our stories to make sense of it. Sometimes those fit together. Sometimes they don't. It's a mess. Scares me sometimes, it truly does. But I see how it gives us a a chance, too. Gives us wiggle room where we try to make it all make sense.

"You see what the curandero did, don't you? He couldn't bring back King, but he could change what it was to the Swede. Could trade out sorrow for rage. Black folks in America, even ones like the Swede, they got a particular kind of wound. Indians like that Sahkyo girl? They got one too. Hell, maybe we all do, but not like them. And they can't heal it anymore than we can. All anyone can do is change what the wound means. That's what folks like the curandero and the queer can do. They can change what stories mean. That's why they've got power. You understand what I'm saying to you? You understand why I'm telling you this?"

"Sure," I said.

"You do *not*," he said, stabbing at the air between us. "Look here, I ask you to tell me about meeting the love of your life, and you tell me *one thing led to another*. What the hell is that supposed to mean? This Abby girl, she seems like a fine woman. I like her. But you two don't have a chance in hell, you hear me? Not a single solitary chance in hell.

"If you came here telling me you were getting married, and you had a sixteen-year-old Chinese hooker on your arm seven months in with someone else's baby but you had a good story about it, I'd think you might make it. You come here with this girl, and you love her. I'm not a fool, I can see you love her. But that love doesn't *mean* anything. And if it doesn't, it will wither and it will *die*, and you'll be here three years from now telling me about the divorce and how one fucking thing just led to another. And please Jesus you're not changing a diaper while you do it."

The contempt in his voice was like a slap. He drew one last long pull on his cigar, the ember bright and angry under its darkening ash, then threw the dead butt out onto the lawn. The scent of the smoke was acrid and close. I tried to laugh, to make a joke of it, but the sound was hollow.

"I don't know what to say," I said.

"Think of something," Dab said, and the anger was cut by a sense that he was pleading with me. I opened my mouth, and then closed it. Aunt Mary's voice came out of the gloom, wide as a whale.

"Dab? You didn't just soil my yard with your leavings, did you? After all this time, I did not just see you throw your disgusting old cigar on my grass."

"Now darlin'," Uncle Dab said with a grin, "you know it's good for it. Nicotine's a pesticide. Keeps the chiggers down."

Aunt Mary and the other women of the family came up onto the porch. The old wood creaked under them, and Aunt Mary swatted Dab gently on the back of his head. From inside, we could hear the electronic sounds of the kid cousins at play. Abby detached herself from my mother and sister and came to sit at my side. She looked beautiful. All the small signals of unease that had haunted her—the thinning of her lips, the lines at the corners of her eyes—had vanished. She was among my family now, no longer that northern girl I'd been seeing but my fiancée. The same woman, but her meaning changed. I wondered what it would be like to lose her. I thought I knew, and the fear was like a hand laid gently across my throat.

She tilted her head, a question in her eyes.

"And what have you two been talking about all night?" she asked.

"We've been trading stories is all," Uncle Dab said. "Matter of fact, he was just getting set to tell me about how you two met."

Abby's brows rose. A tiny half smile—amusement, apprehension, pleasure—touched her lips. I was halfway to denying it when she spoke.

"Really?" she said. "I'd like to hear that."

The eyes of the family, all of them including Abby's, turned to me. Uncle Dab folded his hands over his belly, his eyes upon me, daring me, goading me, praying for me. My heart thumped like sneakers in a dryer. My mouth tasted like tin-foil and pennies. I didn't have the first clue what to say. I looked at Abby, then at Dab.

He nodded me on.

"Well," I said, trying to keep my voice from trembling, "actually it's a pretty good story."